With Kisses from Cécile

A Novel

Jan Agnello & Anne Armistead

STORYOLOGY
DESIGN & PUBLICATION

For more information, contact:
Storyology Design and Publication
Storyologydesign.com

First paperback edition June 2019

Book cover design by Jan Agnello
Photography by Kate Kelava, Sitting Pretty
Graphic Art by Andrew Novialdi
Map by Cécile Cosquéric
Layout and Formatting by Jera Publishing
Editing by Mary Beth Bishop

The publishing logo is a trademark of Storyology Design and Publication.

ISBN-13: 978-0578538556

Library of Congress Control Number:2019909117

www.storyologydesign.com
www.annearmisteadauthor.com

With Kisses
Anne Armistead
and
[signature]

To Cécile and Ruth

Il n'y a que les montagnes qui ne se rencontrent pas.
—French proverb

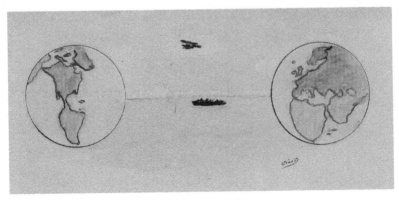

ART WORK BY CÉCILE

…And given with love to a dear
friend. Merry Christmas 2020
Kay
:)

ACKNOWLEDGMENTS

First and foremost, I am grateful for the friendship of my grandmother, Ruth Calderhead Carlock and Cécile Cosquéric that is documented in over 100 letters that they exchanged and served as the inspiration for this novel. I am grateful to my aunt, Judy Carlock Powell, for making sure that the collection of letters came to me after the passing of my grandmother. Much appreciation goes to my daughter Marie Agnello Mancini, who many years ago wrote a short story version of this story that was published in the children's literary magazine, Stone Soup. From that short story, our neighbor and author Lisa Earle McCloud suggested that the story would make a great novel. Thanks to The Atlanta Writer's Club for encouraging me with a contest win for an early YA version of the story, and to fellow writers in my writing group, Jamie Miles and Jennie Helderman. From the bottom of my heart, thank you to my mother Barbara Carlock Wilson for instilling in me a love for books and antiques. And finally, to my kindred spirit Anne Armistead, who like me, never gives up.

With kisses,

Jan Agnello

Writing this book with Jan Agnello has been a labor of love, for I fell in love with Cécile the first time Jan shared her letters with me. Learning about Jan's grandmother Ruth's spiritual endurance in the face of tragedy inspired me to persevere until Jan and I succeeded in bringing this book to you, our reader. Sincere thanks to my writing critique group, who encourage me even when I show up with few words on the page: Ginger Garrett, Sharon Pegram, and Johnna Stein, what would I do without you three kindred souls? Also, thanks to Linda Forte-Spearing and Anna Bragg, dear writer friends with whom I share our creative journey. Special acknowledgments to our beta readers, Jamie Miles and Jennie Helderman, who gave so generously of their time to help us make this story the best it can be. Great appreciation goes to the professionals at Jera Publishing for helping bring this manuscript to published format, and to Mary Beth Bishop, our copyeditor extraordinaire. Most importantly, thanks to my daughters and my brother Chris for their unflagging support, and I especially thank my husband, who unceasingly encourages me to follow my dreams. Lastly, I thank Cécile and Ruth for reminding me of the power of friendship, forgiveness, and love.

With kisses,

Anne Armistead

MATERNAL LINEAGE OF MARGARET "MAGGIE" RUTH ANDERSON MITCHELL

Ruth Jenny Calderhead Carlock
Great-Grandmother

Barbara Ruth Carlock Weatherly
Grandmother

Jennifer Ruth Weatherly Anderson
Mother

**MARGARET RUTH
ANDERSON MITCHELL**

CHAPTER ONE
MAGGIE

Oakland, California
July 2019

The young woman in the passport photo radiated with the contentment of one in love— and loved.

"You're a stranger to me, Margaret Ruth Mitchell." Maggie tossed the passport onto the bed, next to the open suitcase.

Hands on hips, she let out a disgusted sigh at the mess of clothing strewn around the bedroom. She'd made little progress with packing for her trip. Time was running out. Tomorrow she would accompany her grandmother to Paris. The City of Lights.

The City of Love.

That nickname rang hollow. As hollow as her heart.

Maggie had suggested to Cole that they celebrate their upcoming tenth wedding anniversary in Paris. She pictured the two of them taking a romantic stroll along the Avenue des Champs-Élysées. Instead, she'd be taking that stroll with her grams.

The implosion of her marriage stunned their circle of friends. They'd been a couple ever since their "meet-cute" at the UCLA Kerkhoff Coffee shop freshmen year, haggling over the last croissant in the glass case.

Now, they would be haggling over divorce terms, thanks to her husband falling for his gorgeous red-headed co-worker. Maggie had not detected the incoming bomb by the name of Hayley Huntington, who decimated her marriage.

Her throat closed and her chest tightened. Her breathing came in short, shallow pants. Damn it. No way would she give in to another panic-fueled sob fest. How many tears had she cried already? Thousands? Millions?

Maggie forced herself to take deeper and deeper breaths, determined not to give way to the anxiety attack. Exhausted, she fell backward onto the bed, not caring if she wrinkled the clothes spread out beneath her. She stared at the revolving blades of the ceiling fan, remembering how she and Cole had shared this bed with an easy, sexy playfulness. Until it had turned into their battleground over starting a family. He was ready. She was not.

How could they add a child to their already too-busy lives? She had promised herself no child of hers would feel as she did when growing up, in the way of her parents' careers and relationship. Cole's IT job never stopped, even on the weekends. Running her high school's history department and teaching, while working toward her doctorate in education, overwhelmed every minute of her life.

Her reluctance to have a baby drove a hurtful distance between them. They talked less. Laughed less. Touched almost never. He worked longer and longer hours. It was the unexpected news of a co-worker's divorce that prompted Maggie to acknowledge the unraveling of her own marriage.

Cole and she did love each other. She did want his child, for them to be a family. Why let her bad childhood memories prevent that? Her parents had loved her; they just couldn't blend her into their careers and their own relationship. Unlike them, Cole and she could make career, marriage, and parenting work, couldn't they?

Stealing a scene from Lifetime movies, she plotted the perfect seduction for baby-making. She would interrupt his overtime, arriving at his office wearing nothing but a sexy, skimpy teddy under her coat. She'd shift his hard work from job to her.

Maggie discovered him hard at work all right—in a pose with the redhead that left little to the imagination. Before he made it home that night, she had his bags packed and on the front porch. His remorseful pleas to work things out fell on deaf ears.

If only she'd never agreed to see him again.

She'd spurned his every other attempt at reconciliation. Why had she caved in and let him come over that night two months ago? Because she still loved him? She beat clenched fists against the bed, thinking how stupid she'd been.

Her intent that night had been to inform him about the divorce petition. He asked to come over when she said they needed to talk. He arrived with flowers. They had drinks. He put on music, and they danced into bed, reconciliation in the air. The next morning, the redhead's text on Cole's phone exploded all hope of that. *MISSED YOU TONIGHT.*

How stupid, stupid, stupid she had been. Once a cheater, always a cheater. She should have expected that, from supporting her mother through her father's infidelities.

Maggie kept staring at the ceiling fan going around and around, like her life, spinning out of control. She glanced at the clock on her nightstand. In three hours, her parents expected her arrival at their house for the bon voyage party they were giving for her and Grams. She had to conquer her packing demons.

Wearily, she swung to her feet, catching her reflection in the full-length pedestal mirror. She stood sideways in front of it, studying her figure. No one would guess she was eight weeks along, unless they picked up on her being fatigued and appearing at times a little green around the edges.

That one night of reconciliation had given Cole what he had always wanted. What she had also come to want. She'd told no one of the pregnancy, yet. Especially not Cole.

The doorbell startled her. She searched to find her phone. The additional security system she had installed after tossing Cole out included the front-door camera. Every creak and groan in the rambling Victorian house they'd renovated together ratcheted up her anxiety over living alone. Finding her cell, she checked the app.

"No, no, no, no, no." She flung the phone onto the bed.

"Maggie? It's me." Cole rang again. "Please. Let me in."

Grabbing her phone, she stared at him on her screen. He had stepped back enough that she had a good view of him. She couldn't help feeling that familiar tug of attraction. His perfectly tailored stylish suit accentuated his lean physique and broad shoulders. His dark brows framed his greenish-blue eyes, which reminded her of the color of the sea. His tanned face sported a few days' growth of dark stubble, a look that she knew required daily tending or else it gave off a bum-like aura.

He ran his hand through his thick dark hair, something he did when stressed or exasperated, and bit at his lower lip. She hated that she knew the feel of his lips pressed onto hers. She hated that she noticed his damn sexiness. She hated that he *used* to be hers. Before Hayley Huntington stole him. She especially hated that their baby would be born into a broken family. Her hand again rested protectively on her stomach.

"Come on, Maggie." Cole stared directly into the doorbell camera. "Please. We need to talk. About the divorce. Your lawyer contacted me today."

"Anything you have to say, say it him." She paused, complicated feelings about the pregnancy washing over her. She knew she would have to tell him. Not now, though. "Go away, Cole," she said.

"Come on, Maggie." He repeated his entreaty. "Please. I told you that text from Hayley the morning after we—after we were together—didn't mean what you thought. I was supposed to be at a corporate dinner meeting that night. Not with her, not the way you're thinking. I love you, Maggie."

Love. The word scorched through Maggie like a lightning bolt.

Cole stepped close to the camera. "We shared our bed again. Didn't that mean anything to you? It felt so right."

She fumbled with the lock and pulled the door open.

Holding out his arms in an offer of embrace, Cole approached her. Maggie kept her distance from him, shaking her head. "Felt right? Maybe to you. Not to me. If felt *crowded*. You. Me. Hayley. One bed. Three of us."

Cole's arms fell to his side. The hurt in his eyes infuriated Maggie. How dare *he* look hurt.

"Look, Maggie. I don't want a divorce. I want us back together. I want to earn your forgiveness. Please. Let's work this out. Don't let my stupidity ruin our lives."

Vivid memories invaded Maggie. Kerkhoff's. College graduation. Interviews. First jobs. Five years of dating, ten years married. How could he have thrown all that away?

The damn tears she constantly fought threatened once more. Maggie blinked them away, determined not to give him the satisfaction of seeing her cry. She spoke in a low and emphatic voice. "I want a divorce. Go away, Cole. Just . . . go."

She closed the door with a force that said she was done. Through the leaded glass side panel of the door, she watched him linger, his expression a blend of pain and anger, before he finally departed. She sank to the floor, her back against the door, and gave in to an avalanche of sobs.

⌘

The last thing Maggie wanted to do the night before her trip was to make nice at a family dinner party. The dinner had been her father's idea. Giving Grams her trip of a lifetime had been his idea as well.

Maggie couldn't believe how her parents had come full circle; they had reconciled and remarried, ignoring their divorce had happened. It stung that Frank—as she made a point of calling her father—had pretty much disappeared from her life during her high school and college years. His only contact had been attending her graduations and sending birthday and Christmas gifts.

She couldn't deny that his arranging and paying for her to accompany Grams on her bucket-list trip to Paris had been extremely generous.

However, what he expected of her in return was the issue. This trip smacked of an attempt to bring them closer. She also knew that he enjoyed the comments from friends and associates. *That Frank Anderson—what a generous fellow he is.*

Maggie stopped on the way to pick up her mom's favorite pinot noir, assuming she would serve the usual Italian fare. The celebrated Jennifer Anderson, attorney-at-law, rarely cooked, but she did turn out a mean lasagna and served it at every family gathering.

The strong smell of tomato sauce and garlic hit Maggie full force when she entered the kitchen. A momentary wave of first trimester nausea attacked her. She hoped she could make it through the meal.

"Maggie, dear!" Her mom wiped her hands on her apron and leaned toward her for a cheek kiss. Maggie obliged.

"I figured we'd be eating your signature dish," Maggie said with a laugh. She powered through another wave of nausea. "I brought this wine to go with your masterpiece."

"The pinot noir I love! Thanks, Mags." She shot her an appreciative smile. "I'd hoped you would bring red. Your father always buys . . ."

"Sauvignon blanc." Maggie interrupted her with a biting tone. Of course. *His* favorite.

Her mother accepted the bottle with a frown. "Let's sheath the verbal knife tonight, shall we, sweetheart? He means well."

Maggie shrugged. She had a theory why her mother defended Frank. She had grown up without a father, having been born the month after he died in Vietnam. That void in her life resulted in having little patience for a daughter rejecting a father.

However, Maggie had little patience for a dad who had left them for another woman, only to re-enter their lives expecting automatic forgiveness.

Her mother dropped her voice to a dramatic whisper. "Try to be nice for Grams's sake, at least." She put the bottle on the counter next to the bottle of white and called out, "Frank, your daughter's here, and she brought my favorite pinot."

"Coming, Jen."

Maggie was intrigued with her mom opening and shutting drawers in a search for something. "What are you looking for?"

"Those what-do-you-call them. These things." She raised up two oven mitts triumphantly.

Maggie giggled. "Mom, you're a nut."

"I hope your favorite kind of nut?" She slid on the mitts, opened the oven, and checked on her dish. "Almost ready." She pointed a mitt-covered hand in the direction of the family room. "Your dad and Grams have been planning some details of the trip. With the exception of the day you were born, I don't think she's been this excited. I wish I could go with you, but I'm swamped with this huge trial coming up."

"Of course, Mom. When you're on a case, you're laser-focused on only it." Half-listening to her mother's launch into the trial's details, Maggie sat at the kitchen table, its top crowded with piles of folders and open laptops. They served as reminders of how her parents' careers consumed them. She had spent much of her childhood amusing herself in either her mom's law office or her dad's corporate tax attorney office while they worked long hours and weekends.

Thank heaven for her girlfriends. Their homes became hers. Their parents showered her with more attention than her own, who were caught up in their lives and relationship issues. In a way, she should be grateful for her father's affair. It encouraged her to seek counseling to work through her feelings of abandonment.

Or had she? She rested her hand on her slight baby bump no one noticed yet. Could she raise this baby alone? Could she be the type of parent she'd always longed for? Her doubts were keeping her awake at night.

Maggie's gaze wandered to the kitchen desk. The wedding photo of her and Cole with her parents remained in full view. It drew her like a magnet. She picked it up, noticing everyone's happy smiles. Her mother had supported Frank's request to walk her down the aisle and celebrate with the daddy-daughter dance. Little had Maggie known that her wedding would open the door for her dad to slide right back into her mother's life.

"Maggie, hon." Frank's overly-enthusiastic greeting filled the room. "Good to see you."

"Excuse me, dear." Her mom playfully tossed the oven mitts his direction. "You interrupted me telling our daughter about my case."

"I saved you, right?" Frank winked conspiratorially at Maggie. "How's my tiny dancer?" he asked, dropping the oven mitts onto the counter.

She groaned inwardly at the nickname he'd given her when she took ballet as a little girl. "I'm excited about the trip." She placed the photo back on the desk. "Thanks, Frank."

Disappointment registered on his face at her use of his first name. Too bad.

The usual awkward silence descended, mercifully broken by the appearance of her grandmother at the kitchen door.

"I'm excited too," her grandmother announced. "Overwhelmed, actually."

"Grams!" Maggie rushed to hug her. "Are you ready to be my traveling partner?"

"I am, dear. This trip means so much to me. And to share it with you means even more." She linked her arm through Maggie's. "Come. Let's get out from under your mom's feet while she finishes preparing our farewell feast."

Maggie's mom blew Grams a kiss. "Yes, please! You two make yourselves comfortable in the den and chat about your trip. I've put a tray of munchies on the coffee table."

"Let me pour you some wine." Frank held up both bottles. "Red or white?"

"I'll have red with dinner, Frank," Grams answered. "None now."

"None for me now either," Maggie said.

"You sure?" Frank's voice held surprise.

"Uh, yes," Maggie answered, flustered. Normally she accepted any offer of alcohol. It eased her anxiety of being around her dad. She needed to throw out some reasonable excuse for declining tonight.

"I think I'll stick with water. I've read that drinking water helps you stay hydrated for long flights." She started walking with Grams arm-in-arm toward the family room, intent on diverting the conversation—pronto. "I can't wait to hear more about your plans for us in Paris. Mom tells me you have quite a story to tell me about your mother and her French pen pal."

"Oh, Maggie, wait until you read the letters from Cécile," Maggie's mother interjected. "You'll treasure them, as much as you love history. Paris of that time era comes alive through her words. I'm sure your mind will absolutely race with ideas for using them in your lessons."

"I'm sure." Maggie tilted her head toward Grams. "I am curious, though. Why have you both kept all this family stuff from me until now?" A sad look passed between her mom and Grams. "Oh, no. Will I need tissues for this?"

"Families, Maggie," her mother said in a soft voice. "Skeletons in closets. Unspoken secrets. Tragic misdeeds. Through it all, it's love that strengthens us, gives us resilience to face what we must in this life."

Maggie bristled; she suspected her mother's words were aimed at the situation with Cole. "Mom, please."

"Now, sweetheart . . ."

Grams defused the confrontation-in-the-making. "Come, Maggie. Let's make ourselves comfortable in the family room."

Maggie agreed, happy to be removed from a cross-examination about her marital crisis by her attorney mom.

"Have a seat," Grams patted the cushion by her on the sofa. "You look a little tired, dear."

"I am." Maggie perched next to her.

"Let's address the elephant in the room, as they say. Cole and you. Your mom told me she tried to talk you out of filing the divorce petition—second chances and all that."

"I'm not my mother, Grams," Maggie blurted out, frustrated. She should never have confided to her mom about catching Cole with Hayley.

Of course, her mother's Pollyanna view about her own marital fiasco would lead her to encourage second chances.

Grams gently placed her hand on Maggie's knee and leaned toward her. "Your mother's advice comes from her love. We all, including your father, only want your happiness. You were happy with Cole. You and he loved each other deeply for a long time. He still loves you. You've said so yourself."

Maggie's muscles tensed. "Yes, well, that old saying, 'Love conquers all,' is only a saying, Grams." She jumped up, her nerves jittery. Determined to change the subject, she crossed the room to view the family pictures artfully hung in a collection on the wall. She pointed to one of her great-grandmother Ruth. "Mom believes I favor your mother. Do you think so?"

"Oh, yes. She is in the set of your chin and in the way your lips curve into that Mona Lisa half smile when you're deep in thought." Grams's eyes lit with an inner glow. "It's special that we ladies all share the name Ruth, don't you think? Perhaps if you have a little girl, you'll continue the tradition."

Startled, Maggie wondered if Grams suspected her pregnancy. Her grandmother had a sixth sense when it came to her. She prayed their conversation would not steer in that direction, for she'd become an unglued mess.

For once, Maggie welcomed Frank's presence. "Ladies, your bon voyage dinner awaits."

She followed her father and grandmother to the dining room, anxious to eat, leave early, and get home to rest. Tomorrow the adventure in Paris would begin. She prayed she could be the companion her grandmother deserved for this special trip.

Maggie had to admit curiosity about Cécile and her great-grandmother's story. What had her mother said? *Skeletons in closets. Unspoken secrets. Tragic misdeeds. Through it all, it's love that strengthens us, gives us resilience to face what we must in this life.* Perhaps from Ruth and Cécile, she would find the strength to face what she must.

The mad rush to the airport distracted Maggie from Cole's multiple texts, each pleading for them to meet. She reached the limit of her patience while waiting in the security line and blocked his number. She would not let him continue to intrude on this trip.

Once settled into their first-class seats, Maggie half-seriously wondered if having an estranged father intent on buying her affection was too awful. Obviously, he had spared no expense to make sure she and Grams would enjoy themselves.

Once in the air, Maggie's tension melted a bit. They were on their way. She leaned back her window seat, grateful Grams preferred the aisle. The couple across from them, young and obviously in love, reminded Maggie of how she thought her first trip to Paris would be with Cole. She looked out the window to hide her welling tears from her grandmother. No matter how emphatically she told herself she was done crying about the end of her marriage, she obviously wasn't. Damn.

"Maggie, dear. You're deep in thought."

Maggie forced control of her emotions before facing Grams. "Deep in thought about Paris. I can't believe we'll soon be there."

Grams reached into the canvas travel bag stored under the seat in front of her. She'd insisted on carrying it on. She pulled out a decorative wooden box with words in French engraved on its lid.

"Now that we're on our way, it's time I introduce you to Cécile." She patted the top of the box. "The first letter Cécile posted to Ruth was on June 28, 1919, the date of the signing of the Treaty of Versailles, ending the war."

She handed the box to Maggie, adding softly, "The Great War, they called it. They believed it to be the war to end all wars. Unfortunately, many wars have followed, claiming too many lives."

Maggie realized Grams must be thinking of her own husband's death. She'd never remarried, raising her daughter alone on a secretary's salary and military death benefits. Maggie's throat burned. Everything prompted her to cry now, even the death of the grandfather she'd never met.

She pulled down her seat tray and placed the box onto it. Tracing the engraved words with her fingers, she read them out loud in her halting high school French. "Il n'ya que les montagnes qui ne se rencontrent pas." Maggie looked questioningly at Grams.

"Cécile wrote that in one of her letters to my mother. Can you translate it?"

Maggie studied the words once more, translating slowly. "Something about mountains. It is only mountains that never meet?" She furrowed her brow in confusion.

"You translated it literally, but what it means is 'There are none so distant that fate cannot bring them together.' It's an old French proverb."

The saying opened for Maggie the wound of her failed marriage. Nothing could bridge the distance between her and Cole.

Grams added, "Our trip is in tribute to Ruth and Cécile. All the miles between them, along with what fate had in store for each, kept them from meeting. We are thwarting that fate by our trip, though. Their friendship lives on through me, through you. Through your children, Maggie."

That sixth sense of yours, Grams, Maggie thought. She brushed her fingertips across the engraving again. She opened the box. "I can't wait to begin reading the letters."

The scent from the box's interior reminded her of old books, combined with something tangier. Maggie held one of the envelopes to her nose. "It smells faintly of tobacco."

"My mother kept the letters in an old cigar box of her father's until she received this box, a wedding gift from my father — your great-grandfather Clinton. He knew she would enjoy its touch of secrecy." She put her finger on an unnoticeable button on the inside of the box, and a bottom drawer came ajar.

"Oh, look at that!" Maggie pointed. "A secret compartment."

"Yes. That's where my mother kept this lovely necklace my father gave her." Grams dangled the chain with a coin-like medallion hanging from it. Pressed into the medallion were the initials *CC*.

"It's charming," Maggie said.

"Yes. How coincidental that the two most special people in my mother's life shared the same initials: Clinton Carlock and Cécile Cosquéric." Grams returned the necklace to the drawer. "The story behind this gift will keep for now. It's all part of a larger one I will share with you."

"It's one I can't wait to hear, Grams." Maggie studied the envelope she still held. The teacher in her admired the perfect cursive swirls. If only her students could write that legibly! Her mother had been right. Ideas whirled in Maggie's mind about how to integrate Cécile's letters into her World War One lesson plans. She couldn't believe Grams had kept these treasures from her this long!

She read the envelope's address out loud. "Colorado Springs? Hasn't our family always lived in the Oakland area?"

"Not always. My mother's family actually lived in Colorado Springs on a farm when she was a child. She moved to Oakland right after she and Cécile exchanged their first letters." Grams rested her head against her seatback and stared past Maggie, into the darkening sky. "The move was difficult and for difficult reasons."

Maggie's eyes widened. "My curiosity is brimming after what Mom said last night. I'm guessing you've been hiding deep, dark family secrets from me?"

"As a matter of fact, yes." Grams's serious reply heightened Maggie's curiosity.

"Oh, my," Maggie said. "I had no idea."

The idea of family secrets and skeletons in the closet was both intriguing and surprising. Yet she withheld her own secret. How much longer could she keep quiet about her news?

She carefully flipped through the bundle of letters, recognizing different handwriting on a couple of the envelopes. The last envelope, addressed in that different handwriting, showed the postmark of January 1921. What had happened to end the two girls' correspondence?

Maggie angled her body into the corner of the spacious window seat, giving silent thanks once more for traveling first-class. "We have a long flight," she said. "I'm your captive audience."

Grams's expression held the pain of the wisdom that age brings. "I'm glad we'll have this time together, Maggie, for you to become acquainted with Cécile and Ruth. They both confronted unexpected turns in their lives, much like your mother and I have. Much like you are now."

"Oh, Grams." Maggie's voice quivered.

Grams rested her hand on Ruth's arm, her touch gentle. "We share more with my mother than our middle names, Maggie. We also share her traits of courage and fortitude. We Ruths are strong. You will survive whatever pain you must, for you have the strength of all us Ruths inside you."

The idea of these strong Ruths in her family line did help soothe her despair. She placed the letter she'd been holding back into the box with the others, wondering again why Grams had waited so long to share them. Last night, her mother, the tough businesswoman, displayed an uncharacteristically pensive mood about their family's past.

"Your great-grandmother had much joy and sorrow in her life," she'd whispered to Maggie. "Try to be patient and let Grams unfold Ruth's story in her own way."

Patience was not one of Maggie's better qualities. She would try to follow her mother's advice and let Grams spin her recollection in her own way. She returned the box to Grams and stretched her legs out to become more comfortable for the journey.

Grams balanced the box on her lap and folded her hands atop it. "Your mother was expecting you when I shared these letters with her. Impending motherhood frightened her."

"Mom? Frightened?" Maggie's hand again went to her tummy, an instinct now. "I don't think I've ever seen Mom frightened. Angry? Hurt? Of course. Frightened? No. I can't even picture it."

"Oh, yes. She had to be on bed rest the last few weeks before you were born."

"She never told me that!" Her mother and she would have so much to talk about once she confided about the baby.

"Your mother feared something would go wrong with her pregnancy. To help her pass the time waiting for you to arrive, I brought her the box of letters. She met Cécile and heard my mother's story. It gave her strength to endure the bed rest and her worry about delivery. Endure she did. She brought you, a perfect baby girl, into the world. Perhaps my sharing about our family's past will provide you with the strength also, to confront what will come."

Her comment reinforced Maggie's suspicions about her grandmother's "spidey senses." Nothing could be hidden from her. She stared at the box of letters, thankful that Cécile and her great-grandmother's story would provide distraction. She directed the conversation that way, ensuring she projected enthusiasm. "You certainly have built up my expectations, Grams. Tell me all."

"Yes, dear." Grams paused, studying her closely. "Then it will be your turn."

Maggie flicked her eyes downward, avoiding Grams's pointed look.

Grams cleared her throat before speaking. "Ruth, as I'll refer to her, was born in Colorado Springs. She had an older brother named Jesse and three younger sisters, twins Opal and Mable and baby sister, Florabelle. Ruth's parents were farmers." Grams paused, her voice softening while her thoughts went back in time. "However, this story begins with a rooster named Herkimer and a boy named Clinton Carlock. And, of course, with the letters from Cécile."

Over the hum of the airplane engines, Maggie listened while they traveled through the darkness to the City of Lights.

The City of Love.

CHAPTER TWO
RUTH

Oakland, California
August 1919

Ruth knew she should have been listening to Mama, but she wasn't. Her eyes were glued to her pen pal's distinctive cursive swirls in which she had written Ruth's new address: *Miss Ruth Calderhead, 3433 Salisbury Street; Oakland, California; USA.* The mailing date read *1 Août, 1919.* Août was French for August. Her grandfather must have let out a low whistle when he found Cécile's letter in the stack of mail. Dewdad always whistled when something impressed him.

"Ruth Calderhead, did you hear me?"

Mama dangled the egg basket at her, speaking in her do-what-I-say-right-now voice.

"Your grandpa had to rush off to the board meeting at the Chevrolet factory. They won't call it to order until Dewey Addison arrives." Ruth detected the pride in her mama's voice. "He didn't have time for the midmorning egg gathering. You must do it for him."

Ruth's groan escaped. Gathering the eggs meant she'd have to hold her ground against *him*. Herkimer. Her grandpa's prized rooster. Herkimer's nasty spurs would bloody you if he attacked. Ruth's family had kept roosters back home, but none like Herkimer.

Nothing about living with Dewdad in Oakland, California, was like living on her family's farm in Colorado Springs. She couldn't accept that Mama had brought her and her little sisters to live with her grandfather, leaving her pa behind. They had left her big brother, Jesse, behind too—in that lonely cemetery.

Ruth's broken family knotted her up with sadness and left her heart feeling heavy as a stone. A letter from Cécile could chip away at that stone, though. If only she could enjoy the letter and then face the horrid rooster.

Perhaps a sweet-as-can-be approach would convince her mother. "Mama, may I please read Cécile's letter before gathering the eggs?"

Her mother answered with a stern shake of her head.

Ruth's shoulders sagged. She should have known better. She could never cajole Mama to change her mind. Not like Jesse always could. Being her firstborn and only son, he'd always had Mama wrapped around his little finger.

The quiet settled for a moment between them before Mama spoke again, this time in a kinder way. "Ruth, that old rooster is easily provoked." She handed the egg basket to Ruth. "Do be careful not to rile up Herkimer."

"Yes, ma'am." Ruth knew she always managed to do that—upset Herkimer. Whenever she'd go eye to beady little eye with him, he'd come charging at her, pumping his head and squawking his deep-throated threats. She'd end up high-stepping away from the bully of the chicken yard.

And now this stupid rooster—and Mama—stood in her way of reading Cécile's letter. Ruth stomped out of the kitchen, squaring her shoulders for what she knew would be another fight with her feathered enemy.

Mama's warning trailed after her. "Don't slam that screen door, young lady."

Ruth let it slam.

∞∞

Nearing the coop, Ruth stopped to gather her courage. Herkimer stopped in mid-peck to stare at her.

She had to admit that he was a beauty. His reddish-orange breast feathers were the color of flames. The large scalloped red comb on his head and the red wattle hanging long from his yellow beak reminded Ruth of the helmets that Greek warriors wore. She knew about Greek heroes because her favorite teacher, Mrs. Castleberry, had read the *Iliad* and the *Odyssey* to her seventh-grade class last year.

The chicken-yard stink turned her eyes watery like they got when Mama mixed ammonia with vinegar to wash windows. Thinking about how much she missed Mrs. Castleberry, Pa, and Jesse made her eyes water more.

Herkimer's beady eyes warned Ruth not to cross into his territory. She used her arm to wipe her tears and concentrated. Any sudden moves she'd make would rile up his hens, and he'd take off after her. He'd fly toward her and flap his wings, aiming to dig into whatever part of her he could with his sharp spurs.

She held her breath while she inched tortoise-like toward the coop. Ducking her head to enter, she cooed, "Nice chickees, nice chickees, let's don't upset you-know-who. Nice chickees, nice chickees."

The loose feathers in the coop smelled like old, musty feather pillows. They floated around in the air while she made her way from nest to nest. One feather brushed against her nose, making it itch. She rubbed it hard, almost flattening it. She knew what was coming.

A sneeze.

And not just any sneeze.

A Ruth Calderhead sneeze.

Her sneezes were legendary. She remembered how Jesse always said they reminded him of a pitcher throwing a baseball. Her *ah* was the windup. Her *choo* was the fastball whizzing across home plate. Her sneezes were the kind that teachers frowned at, other kids tried to imitate, and Mama gave lectures on.

"Ruth, ladies don't yell *ah-choo*," Mama always corrected her. "They turn their heads to the side, cover their mouths with their hankies, and muffle their sneezes."

Now Ruth wished she'd practiced Mama's ladies-don't-sneeze rule. With one *ah-choo* from her, the hens would squawk, bringing Herkimer to their rescue. Twisting her mouth in circles, she tried to twitch the awful itch away. No luck. She sniffed like a bunny, swallowing hard, hoping to hold the sneeze in.

Ruth gathered the last of the eggs into the basket lickety-split and exited the coop. The inside of her nose was burning as if on fire. The impending sneeze tickled like crazy, ready to explode. Herkimer stared at her, standing at attention. Warily, she tiptoed across the yard, taking things slow and steady.

No rooster war yet. And no sneeze—not yet.

Only ten more steps to clear his turf. Then, nine, eight, seven, six . . .

Uh-oh. It came out of her like a monster who'd invaded her body. It closed her eyes and raised her head back. It pried her mouth open. *Ah–Choo!* It was the loudest Ruth Calderhead sneeze ever, a real kablooey. Mama would have been horrified. Jesse would have loved it.

She glanced back. Herkimer was taking off in midair, heading straight at her.

Five more steps to safety. Five. Four. Three... Ruth sprinted faster, hearing the swish of the rooster's wings closing in on her.

Thump.

He hit against her back. She stumbled forward, her long legs going rubbery, but she held her balance.

Two, one.

She crossed out of the dirt yard and stood on the path next to it. The eggs somehow were all accounted for in the basket. Herkimer blinked his beady eyes at her.

"You pestered me again, you stupid old thing." Ruth gasped. "You wait. One day I'll be the one pestering you."

She shook her finger at him. "One day!"

⌒⌒

With the eggs gathered and another battle lost to Herkimer, Ruth headed for the kitchen with only one thing on her mind: Cécile's letter.

It had been the early spring of the 7th grade school year when Mrs. Castleberry had found out about the pen pal program between American and French students. Ruth had immediately signed up when her teacher offered her the opportunity. She had forgotten about it after all that happened to Jesse.

However, when she received Cécile's first letter in June, she found relief in writing to someone far away who had no knowledge about her family's tragedy. Cécile was sixteen and Ruth thirteen, but their age difference didn't matter. Cécile had a way of making Ruth feel special.

Like Jesse always had.

Ruth had exchanged only one letter with her pen pal before the move to Oakland. She'd sent Cécile her new address, but each day no answer came. The sight of the letter on the kitchen table had flooded her with happiness. She hadn't lost her pen pal after all.

Mama met her at kitchen door. "I see that you survived Herkimer." She held her hand out for the basket. "Your grandpa should be back soon. He'll be glad that you had no trouble with his old rooster."

"Yes, we got along fine," Ruth answered, her fib stinging her conscience. Something inside her wouldn't let her admit she'd let that stupid bird upset her again.

Mama pulled from her apron pocket a thick envelope. Cécile's letter! She handed it to Ruth. The dark smudges under Mama's eyes made her look sterner than usual. They also indicated she hadn't been sleeping well. Maybe because she missed Pa so much?

Ruth knew better than to ask. Whenever the twins or Florabelle asked for Pa, Mama explained he had to stay behind to finish the fall harvesting. Mama didn't know that the night before they were to catch the train for Oakland, Ruth had heard her arguing with Pa. She had seen Mama lean against Pa's chest and sob, "Charles, how could you have let this happen to our son?" Ruth realized at that moment Pa wasn't moving with them because Mama didn't *want* him to come.

Taking Cécile's letter from Mama, Ruth ran to get the cigar box Pa had given her in which to keep the special pen pal correspondence. She placed the newly received letter inside. Her mother gave permission for her to sit by the creek and read it. She promised to return when Mama rang the "come home" bell.

Ruth scurried to the garage. Leaning against the wall, an adventure on wheels beckoned. Her bicycle. She had discovered it a couple of weeks after Mama moved them to Oakland. Dewdad said he had bought it for a boy named Clinton, who had done some chores around the house. Clinton's mama believed keeping the bike would be taking charity, and she made him refuse it.

"Fine by me if you procure it," Dewdad had told Ruth.

Dewdad always said things like "procure" when all he meant was that you could have it. That was his way. He helped Ruth pump up the tires and give the bike a new coat of shiny red paint.

Her long legs fit the height of the seat, making her glad for once about being tall at her age. She always suspected her mother wished for a daintily-built daughter, not one big-boned and sturdy-built like Pa.

Mama had words with Dewdad about Ruth and the bike. "Papa, she could fall and get hurt. I moved my children back home from Colorado Springs to keep them safe after . . ." She had choked up, going silent.

Ruth finished in her mind the end of her mother's sentence. *After Jesse died.* No matter how hard Ruth tried, the memory of his death sneaked up on her when she least expected it, tightening that awful knot in the pit of her being.

She placed the cigar box in the bike's basket and wheeled it from the garage. She knew Jesse would have loved her riding it. He always believed she could do anything he could do, no matter being a girl. He never told on her when she'd chase behind him to explore the woods.

One time he let her tag along with him when he hopped a train. They rode from Colorado Springs to the next station and back, riding the rails like hobos. Jesse daydreamed about traveling to every continent. Mama told him had been touched by the wanderlust.

Each time Ruth heard a train whistle, she'd remember the scary freedom of riding the rail with Jesse. Would she ever have the courage to do something like that again, alone? Or did you have to be a boy to have real adventures?

Riding a bike wasn't like hopping trains, but it did offer a little bit of an adventure. She pushed off, pedaling against the wind toward her special place on the banks of the creek. There, she'd travel to Paris through Cécile's letter. At least for a while, she'd think about happier things. Not about moving here and leaving Pa behind. Not about facing a room full of strangers on the first day at a new school. Not about the dreadful secret.

Ruth hadn't gone far when she heard the familiar noise of Dewdad's automobile's horn announcing his arrival. She made a U-turn. He was steering the black, shiny Chevrolet toward the garage. Its gleaming tires with their red spokes resembled whirring fireballs.

Next to Herkimer, Dewdad was most proud of having one of the first Chevrolet coupes that had come off the new factory's assembly line. He had invested his own money and time to get the factory built in Oakland, and Mama said it had brought jobs to the city.

Ruth wondered what it would feel like, being in command of something magical as a car. She figured driving one would make you like Houdini, the great magician. *Abracadabra* and *poof,* the car transported you here and there. Being in control of an automobile that could take you anywhere in no time flat had to be the best adventure in the world.

Better than hopping trains. Definitely better than riding a bike.

Ruth pedaled back into the garage, wanting to show off her greatly improved riding skills. Dewdad hung his keys and tweed driving cap on the wall pegs. When he greeted her, his bushy handlebar mustache wriggled like it always did when he grinned.

"Looks like you have mastered the operation of the velocipede," he said

"The what?" Ruth asked.

He hooted with laughter. Ruth giggled. Her sneezes were definitely loud, but no one's laugh sounded as thunderous or strange as Dewdad's. It erupted like a pig's snort and a donkey's heehaw put together. Whenever he laughed, Mama would say, "Papa, please."

Dewdad repeated the strange word. "Velocipede. Your bicycle."

"Oh." Ruth could impress Mrs. Castleberry with the vocabulary words she was learning, if she ever saw her again.

Dewdad began polishing the car's hood with a cloth. "Heading out for a ride?" he asked.

"Yes, sir."

"Be careful you don't get your dress tangled into the chain."

"I'll be careful." Ruth pedaled in a circle around the empty space next to the car to show off again and headed out.

Pedaling in a dress was tricky. Once she cleared the bridge spanning the creek, she hiked it up and tucked it into her sash, letting her shorter muslin petticoat show. Mama would be horrified.

Wearing a pair of Jesse's overalls would certainly be more practical for bicycling. Ruth thought about sneaking a pair from the trunk that held his belongings but never dared. After he died, Mama had packed his belongings away. She kept his things sealed up tight, the same way she kept her grief sealed up tight inside.

When they moved in with Dewdad, Mama placed the trunk in the nook beneath the attic stairs that led to the room Dewdad had prepared for Ruth. When she climbed to her bedroom, she'd glimpse the trunk, and sorrow would overtake her. She wished she could talk to Mama about Jesse, but her mother couldn't bear to hear his name.

The front bike tire hit a rut in the dirt, and the wheel jerked in Ruth's grasp. She held on tight and kept control, glad that the rough patch hadn't jostled the box of letters from her basket. She pedaled the path more carefully, wondering if Cécile rode a bicycle too. If so, did *she* get to wear overalls?

Reaching her favorite willow tree, Ruth braked and hopped off, laying the bike on the ground. Her fingers ripped through her boot-laces. She yanked off her stockings and wriggled her bare toes into the damp dirt.

"Ahhh." Her voice rang out against the chirps of birds and rustling water.

With the box under her arm, she parted the tree's curved branches and settled behind the willow's lacy leaves. When she opened the box, the nutty, woodsy scent took her back to the warm nights sitting on their porch in Colorado Springs, with Pa puffing his cigar while searching the night sky to point out a falling star heading toward Pike's Peak. She'd make a wish, and he would ask her, "What did you wish for, daughter?" The answer would be easy: "For nothing to ever change."

Everything had changed.

Except she still had Cécile as a pen pal. "Merci, bonne amie," she whispered, settling back for her visit with her friend. Although she practically had Cécile's first letter memorized, she decided to re-read that one to let her excitement over this newly arrived one keep building.

Ruth opened that first letter from Cécile, who wrote it in June at the time of the Paris peace talks. Her friend had lived through much real history. Reading her letters transported Ruth to Paris. She settled back against the trunk of the tree and met Cécile for the first time, once more.

CHAPTER THREE
MAGGIE

"This is the first letter Ruth received?" Maggie took the envelope her grandmother handed her.

"It is. Now, you'll meet Cécile, as Ruth did long ago." Grams's glowing face conveyed delight at the introduction.

Maggie pulled the thin paper from the envelope, along with a post-card and a strip of paper with neatly printed English words. She read the letter out loud before examining the other items.

>   *18, bis Avenue d 'Italie*
>   *Paris 75013*
>   *France*
>   *Paris the 28 of June 1919*

I put my letter in the
Letterbox the day
of the peace.

Dear Miss Ruth,

I have known today your address. Since a long while I was looking for an American friend to correspond with me in French or in English. If you want to correspond with me I shall be very glad. I'm 16 years old, My name is Cécile Cosquéric, I live in Paris with my parents. I have a brother, Lucien. We call him Lulu. He is soon twenty years old. His birthday is 21ˢᵗ of September.

I was not born in Paris, I was born in Bretagne, at Quimper, a small town near the Atlantic Ocean. I have come in Paris at eight years old. Last month I have passed my brevet elementaire and I have been received, then I have leaved school and now I'm learning stenography and dactilograph. There are many American soldiers in Paris. Near my house bombs are dropped in a house which have been demolished, many persons have been killed.

My hair is dark, and I have a white complexion. By your name I see you are of English race. I am 1 metre, 58 high, 4 ft 8 in your manner to count. As I am thin I seem tall.

Do you speak French? I do, naturally. I write English sentences, just like I speak French. Some of my school fellows say always, "English is too difficult." As I am very fond of English conversations and reading, I was the first in English and my teacher was interest with me. I send you my first lesson of English. You can see how I was well up. During the war sometimes there was no school so I would practice with English at home.

Do you know other countries than Colorado? Is it a large town? Are there many inhabitants in your town? At cinema I have seen many views of the mountains of Colorado. Have you seen the films "Hands Up" with Miss Ruth Roland? The French people admire your Hollywood stars Charlie Chaplin, Mary Pickford, and Douglas Fairbanks.

Have you seen the President Wilson? I have seen him, with his wife, his daughter, and the General Pershing.

Is there many Indians in your country? Are they pretty?

With hopes for our friendship, I send you a postcard of pretty flower Edelweiss which grows on the alps. Do you know the flower, Edelweiss? It smells very good.

The postcard says Bonne Année, which means Good Year. We shall have a good year, writing, will we not? I kiss the Edelweiss picture I enclose. Kiss it too and like that, we shall kiss the both. Do you understand?

By waiting news from you, I kiss you and say au revoir.

With kisses, Cécile

Maggie studied Cécile's English lessons and the Bonne Année postcard. Impulsively, she placed it against her lips. "I kiss it too." With that, Cécile became her own pen pal.

"It's clear why your mother loved these letters," she commented. "Cécile transports you to Paris. Imagine having seen President Wilson and General Pershing. The history teacher in me is quite impressed." Maggie carefully folded the letter. She inserted it and the other contents back into the envelope. "This letter marked 'the beginning of a beautiful friendship,' to quote *Casablanca*."

"Oh, I adore that movie too, sweetie." Grams stroke an oratory pose, one hand reached out. "We'll always have Paris."

"And, we will, Grams." Maggie gave a playful grin.

"Just as Ruth and Cécile. Cécile's first letter started it all. In her reply back, my mother sent a leather wallet with a painting of an Indian and also a clipping of a fern that grew wild by her Colorado farmhouse. Her father gave her the cigar box in which to keep the letters. Later, my father gifted her with this engraved box for a wedding gift."

Maggie tilted her head, a realization dawning. "I've never heard about Jesse before. When I made my family tree way back in kindergarten, Mom never told me to make a leaf for a Great-Uncle Jesse."

"She and I agreed that you were too young to hear about his story," Grams replied.

"Death is a hard concept for a child," Maggie observed.

"Yes." Grams dabbed at tears. "For the longest time, Ruth didn't speak of Jesse's loss, not even to her mother."

"What a terrible burden for a young girl to carry!" Maggie returned the letter to Grams, who replaced it into the box and removed a bundle of three letters tied together with a ribbon. "These three letters were in that thick envelope that Ruth's mother handed her." She untied the letters and handed Maggie one. "Read the first one now."

18, bis Avenue d 'Italie
Paris 75013
France

1 August 1919

My dear little friend,

I have received your first letter from Oakland. Some letters were returned to me and I thought I had lost my American friend. The envelopes were nearly destroyed and it made me sad to know that you had not read them. I will enclose with this letter my two returned letters for you to finally read.

Do you like sports? In France there are only men who make sports. Do you like Dempsey in USA? Today in newspaper I see some wounded men have written to him to ask why he stayed in a ship-yard during the war while others American boys were felling down the boches. I see too, some stars of Los Angeles were very pleased to see Dempsey; so I don't know very well what is your opinion about your boxing champion?

I go on bicycle. I learn to skate and perhaps I shall learn how to swim in a piscine. Do you like to paint? I do. Do you like music? I am very fond. I teached the Star-Spangled Banner to my cousin. Do you like the Marseillaise, our national hymn?

I live in such an old city where each monument is a remembrance, rather than in new cities like you in U.S.A. In Paris, we have still arenas, catacombs, palaces of Emperors, aqueducts constructed by the Roman people. Old churches, old palaces date from Francois the

First. Houses where ancient great men were born, etc…we have in Paris, so much monuments that many person doesn't know all them.

At what distance is Oakland from Colorado Springs? Then now you have crossed all the U.S. do you see the Pacific Ocean? I know only the Atlantic. I will be pleased to cross the channel and probably when I shall be older I shall go in London, to learn English better, because I cannot speak English well. Sometime we speak English, my brother Lulu and me. If you were hearing us, sure you would laugh.

What do you prefer: The mountains of Colorado or the coast of California?

Can you tell me why you leave Colorado for California?

With kisses from your 'loving farther from you still' friend,
Cécile

"What are the answers?" Maggie asked. "Did Ruth prefer the mountains of Colorado or the coast of California? I gather that her mama moved her and her sisters to Oakland because of her brother's death?"

The flight attendant interrupted them before Grams could answer. Before Maggie could object, he reached past Grams to place a glass of wine Grams had ordered for her and snack of cheese and crackers on Maggie's tray. Grams let her tray table down and placed the box of letters to one side to make room for her glass. The attendant placed a glass of wine and snack on Grams's tray.

Grams held up her glass to Maggie. "Cheers." She clicked her glass against Maggie's and continued her story.

CHAPTER FOUR
RUTH

Ruth had delayed the joy of reading Cécile's new letter long enough. She opened the thick envelope and unfolded it, dated August 1, 1919. She leaned back once again against the tree, letting the leafy curtain hide her.

My dear little friend, it began. After a moment, Ruth gasped. The thick envelope contained two older dated letters from July that Cécile had mailed to Colorado Springs but had been returned to "the sender." Ruth had three to read, not one! She tucked the July letters back into the envelope to read later.

Ruth read through the current letter slowly, pausing to consider Cécile's question: *What do you prefer: The mountains of Colorado or the coast of California?* The answer was clear. She preferred her *home*, Colorado, not Dewdad's rambling stucco house on the outskirts of Oakland's city limits. Not that she didn't love her grandfather. However, she wanted her family together again, living back on their farm in Colorado Springs, the way it used to be.

Do you see the Pacific? Ruth had to laugh at that question. In the month they'd been in Oakland, Ruth hadn't laid eyes yet on the Pacific, and unlike Cécile, she hadn't ever seen the Atlantic either. Her life had been landlocked when she lived in the middle of the

USA. Now it didn't matter where she lived. Jesse's death kept her locked up tight inside.

Except when she read Cécile's letters. They unlocked a whole new world for her. Cécile's Paris was filled with ancient ruins, cathedrals, palaces, monuments. Thank heavens the city hadn't been destroyed—and that Cécile hadn't been killed in the bombings of Paris during the war.

A clanging bell sent the message: *Ruth, come home.* Time to leave Cécile and Paris behind.

Ruth kissed the Bonne Année postcard. *Like that, we shall kiss the both. Do you understand?* "Yes," she whispered. "I understand."

She slid the letters and enclosures into their envelopes and placed them in her box. Pulling her bicycle upright, she put the box in the basket with her stockings and ankle boots. Being barefoot felt too delicious. She would put her shoes and stockings back on once she reached the garage.

Ruth pumped the bike's pedals slowly at first and then faster and faster until she flew across the bridge. She wondered if she'd find Dewdad polishing up his Chevrolet. He'd called her friendship with Cécile divine providence. Ruth liked that description. How else to explain two girls finding each other when they lived far apart on separate continents? Maybe divine providence would reunite her family. They had to be together again with Pa. They just had to.

Ruth pumped the bike pedals harder and faster, hurtling past the chicken coop. When Herkimer strutted across the pathway right in front of her, she couldn't stop her motion in time. "Move! Out of the way!" She stomped on the brakes.

Herkimer didn't obey.

She stomped again, hard. The pedal broke off, and the rear tires spun sideways on the rocky driveway. She flew over the bike's handlebars like a stone spit out of a slingshot. The bike flipped past where she landed. It skidded, raining gravel on her like stone confetti. With loud squawks, Herkimer took off toward her and gained altitude, his spurs scraping against her scalp.

"Ow! Get off me, you awful old . . ."

"Herkimer!" Dewdad came to her rescue, scooping Herkimer up and heading toward the coop with the rooster underneath his arm.

Struggling to her feet, Ruth winced at the blood trickling from her knees. She checked out her aching hands. Her scraped-up palms were dotted with dirt, specks of pebbles, and blood.

She moved her mouth back and forth, checking for damage to her throbbing jaw. Was this like being walloped by Jack Dempsey, the famous boxer?

Pressing her fingers gently to her scalp, she checked for cuts. Luckily, there were none. Herkimer's spurs hadn't penetrated through her hair. She'd never complain again about it being too thick and wavy. When she bent to pick up her shoes, stockings, and cigar box, her whole body screamed, *ouch*.

"What a spill!" Dewdad hurried toward her. "Maybe your mama is right, and you riding that bike is dangerous."

Ruth glared at him. At that moment, she wasn't sure if her anger raged most against herself for wrecking the bike, Herkimer for attacking, or Dewdad for having the stupid rooster in the first place.

"Let's get you cleaned up before your mama gets a look at you." Dewdad wrapped his arm around her shoulders.

She brushed tears away with the back of her hand. "Think the bicycle can be fixed?"

"Let's worry about you first, then the velocipede." Dewdad walked her to the back of the garage to the well. While pumping a bucket of water, he asked, "Where did you ride?"

"I went across the bridge to sit by the creek and read my letter from Cécile that came in the mail today."

"I knew you'd be excited to receive it." Dewdad finished pumping and sat the bucket next to where she was perched. "I'm glad you two are remaining in touch. Soak your hands and I'll get the first aid kit to take care of those scrapes on your legs."

Ruth doused her sore hands in the cool water, thinking how Dewdad understood the importance of Cécile's letters to her. Jesse would too, if he were alive. Mama surely didn't.

Dewdad returned with the kit, a green metal box with a red cross painted on its lid. He selected from it a bottle filled with nasty-looking liquid—iodine. Ruth knew the doctoring up would not be pleasant.

"This will sting, Ruffis," Dewdad warned.

She managed a slight grin at the nickname. When they were fixing up the bicycle, Dewdad had started calling her Ruffis, a silly play on her name that made sense only to him. Mama bristled at it. "Nicknames are not proper. Please use her given name of Ruth." She added, "What would Mrs. Grundy say?"

Mama loved Mrs. Grundy, a character in some favorite play of hers, who always pointed out what was and wasn't proper behavior. In Ruth's opinion, Mama referred to Mrs. Grundy way too often.

Funny how Mama didn't like nicknames. It had been her idea to call her papa Dewdad, not Grandfather or Grandpa. He preferred it too. Ruth had never met anyone quite like Dewey Addison. Long and lanky, he wore gray flannel trousers that Mama called "grayers," held up by suspenders. He sure dressed differently than Ruth's pa, who favored deerskin jackets.

At the first dab of the iodine on her cuts, Ruth held a fist to her mouth to stifle her cry. If she'd let herself, she could scream loud enough for Pa to hear from across the Rocky Mountains, but Jesse had taught her not to be a sissy. She'd take her lickings.

Finishing up the bandaging, Dewdad gave a complimentary nod. "You kept your chin up."

Ruth's cheeks grew warm at his praise. "I'm not a little girl anymore. I'm a month away from turning fourteen."

"You're becoming a lady." He echoed Mama's words, but winked. "Gather your belongings. I'll put away the first aid kit, and we'll check out the damage to the bicycle."

Ruth hobbled toward the mangled mess. When Dewdad joined her, she asked, "It's pretty torn up, isn't it?"

He pulled the frame upright and frowned.

"My stars in heaven, Ruth Calderhead. What has happened to you?" Mama viewed her from the porch, where she stood with Florabelle hoisted on her hip and Opal and Mable on either side.

Ruth imagined how disastrous she appeared. She prepared herself for a tongue-lashing, one that would surely make her ears ring.

Dewdad laid the bent-up bike back on the ground and wiped his hands on his trousers. "Let me handle this one, Ruffis." His mustache twitched.

Ruth had little hope. No one could handle Mama when she became angry except for Jesse. Once, Jesse rescued Ruth from one of Mama's switchings when their mother had caught Ruth playing marbles with him.

"Ruth Calderhead, a lady does not sprawl on the ground in her nice dress and shoot marbles," she had said, pointing a hickory stick at her.

"Now, Mama," Jesse said, "she's admiring this green glass shooter marble, as green as your eyes." He put his arm around her shoulder and held the marble up to the sunshine. "What a beaut—like my mama."

Mama had pretended not to like Jesse's malarkey, but she blushed all the same. "Ruth, get up out of the dirt and act like a lady." She tossed the stick aside and walked away smiling.

Not even Pa could sweet-talk Mama like Jesse could. No way Dewdad could do it either.

Ruth focused on pulling her stockings on, easing them over her bandaged legs while Dewdad addressed Mama. "Ruth's fine, Dolly. We have her all fixed up. No need for you to get upset. You must keep calm like your mama always did when you and your brothers got into your little scrapes. Remember?"

Mama hadn't always acted ladylike? Ruth's eyes darted to her mother, who had turned a slight shade of pink.

"Never mind that," Mama answered.

Ruth took note of her mother's matter-of-fact, brisk mannerism she used whenever she didn't want to discuss something. Or someone.

"Lunch is ready." Mama added in an annoyed voice, "Put that bicycle away." She swept Mable and Opal with her through the kitchen door, with Florabelle riding her hip.

With her stockings and boots back on, Ruth tucked the box of Cécile's letters under her arm and let Dewdad help her stand.

"Strong grip for a gal," Dewdad said.

She shrugged, trying to hide the embarrassment his compliment brought.

"You remind me of your mama at your age." Dewdad lifted the bicycle. "She was quite adventurous too."

Ruth followed him to the garage, amazed at the thought. Mama adventurous? Taking a dunk in the swimming hole back in Colorado Springs without wearing her swimming stockings and hat marked the only adventurous thing Ruth had ever seen her Mama do. She tried to picture her prim-and-proper mother in "scrapes" with her brothers.

As if he could read her mind, Dewdad said, "Yes, your mama did have a sense of adventure about her at your age, as well as now. It was adventurous of her to resettle back here in Oakland." He glanced at Ruth. "After all, a move is hard on a family."

Ruth locked in her gaze straight ahead.

Maybe he would call what Mama did adventurous, moving the family away from Pa and the only home they'd ever known. Ruth didn't call it that. Mama was running away from the sadness, running away from Pa and giving Ruth no choice but to run with her.

Every day they lived apart caused Ruth to doubt they'd ever be a family again.

∞◦∞

They ate lunch in silence, and Mama served butterscotch pie for dessert. Ruth's came with two aspirin on the plate. "Your body must be aching," she said. "Take these pills."

Ruth wondered if Mama's offer of medicine meant she felt more sorry than angry for her.

The pills reminded her of when Jesse and she had gone treasure hunting at Cragmor Sanatorium. Most patients never left after checking in there; they died of their illnesses. If their families did not claim their belongings, their stuff would be boxed up and placed in the back of the property until a worker carted them to the local dump.

"I dare you to go poke around Cragmor with me," Jesse said.

"I double-dog dare you," Ruth answered, not letting on that her insides went scrambling at the idea.

The two of them sneaked out late on a sunny Saturday afternoon after chores were through. Mama, her belly big with the baby she'd name Florabelle, lay resting with the twins while Pa sharpened tools in the shed.

Like they had heard, boxes were stacked behind Cragmor. In one, Jesse found a glass bottle of little yellow pills. He wet his finger, rubbed it on one of them, and tasted. "Yum. It's like sugar."

The two split the candy and ate it all. On their walk back, Ruth's stomach began aching. By the time they reached home, they both were groaning in pain. They couldn't eat a bite of dinner. Mama and Pa peppered them with questions until Ruth finally confessed what they had done. Jesse pulled out the empty bottle from his pocket. He had grown pale as the mashed potatoes on his plate.

"Charles, we must get them to Cragmor to have a doctor check them out." Mama choked up, her hands resting on her baby bulge.

Pa hitched the wagon to their mule, and Ruth lay in it under quilts with Jesse and the twins. Over the clacking of the wheels, she could hear Pa comforting her mother. "Shush. Dolly, stop your crying. They'll be fine."

At the sanatorium, Pa handed the bottle to the doctor. "What kind of medicine was in this?" he demanded.

The doctor examined it. "Mr. and Mrs. Calderhead, do not worry. What your children ingested will not harm them. Give them hot tea until the cramps subside."

"What do you mean? Exactly what did they ingest?" Pa asked.

"We call them placebos. It's a medicine we prescribe to make our patients feel better—mentally, that is." The doctor shrugged. "It's only sugar."

Over the click-clack of the wheels on their trip back home, Ruth heard Pa say, "Those poor sick people. They are being given false hope."

False hope.

Was that what she was holding onto, false hope that Pa would join them soon?

Mama's tap of her fingers on the table drew Ruth from her remembrances. "The aspirin."

Ruth washed the pills down with chugs of her milk. Their bitter taste matched Ruth's bitterness at her Mama's refusal to share memories, especially the ones they had of Jesse. Ruth wanted to remember. Didn't Mama?

When the younger ones settled in for their afternoon rest, Dewdad escaped to his garage to "do this and that."

"Ruth, let's mend your clothes," Mama said. "Set up the ironing board."

Ruth wished Mama would've let Dewdad purchase her at least one new dress for school. He had offered, but Mama had turned him down, saying she couldn't let him spoil his grandchildren. To ready Ruth for school meant letting out her old dresses, skirts, and blouses.

Ruth tried on each piece of clothing, and Mama marked the measurements. Each time, Mama repeated, "You've grown like a dandelion weed," until Ruth wondered if she should let out a "fee-fie-foe-fum" like the giant in the fairy tale.

Over the summer, Ruth *had* shot up—just shy of Mama's five foot five, a good size for a woman but not for a girl of thirteen who had more growing to do. She was certain that her tall, gawky figure and huge feet would give others something to snicker about on the first day of school. She wished she could be struck with some mysterious disease—not a painful or deadly one, of course. Maybe a sleeping sickness? Anything to avoid starting school.

By the time she tried on the last skirt, Ruth had convinced herself she had come down with something. "Mama, I'm feeling flushed. I'll probably be too sick to go to school on Monday." She held her hand to her forehead and put on her pitiful look.

"Stuff and nonsense, Ruth." Mama didn't even look up. "It's the heat from the ironing. I'm sure you will do well in your new school. You're a sharp one with your lessons, always making your pa and me proud."

"Oh, Mama . . ."

Mama kept her head bent over the sewing. Her fingers deftly wove small, tight stitches in and out. Since Jesse died, Mama's heart had become like those stitches: small and tight.

Ruth longed to tell her mother how much she missed Colorado Springs and Mrs. Castleberry. How much a new teacher and new classmates frightened her. How much she feared she'd never quit growing. Most of all, she longed to tell her mother what happened that day Jesse died.

She remained silent, pressing the hot iron against the new hemlines.

CHAPTER FIVE
MAGGIE

Taking a break from her story, Grams sipped the last of her wine and nibbled the last bite of her cheese and crackers. Maggie played with the still-full glass resting on her tray. Refusing the wine last night and not drinking any now would further spark her grandmother's suspicions. She was finding it emotionally difficult to keep her baby news secret. Maggie had no doubt by the end of the flight she would confide in Grams about the pregnancy.

She and Ruth had keeping a secret in common. How alone her great-grams Ruth must have felt, grieving for Jesse and for their divided family, keeping something tragic to herself that was tearing her apart. In the momentary silence between her and Grams, Maggie recognized that her heart was aching for someone other than herself for the first time in months. Worrying about someone other than herself felt good.

"Would you prefer something other than the wine?" The flight attendant's question drew Maggie's attention.

She reached over Grams's tray to hand the glass to the attendant. "Some water, please?"

Grams intercepted the glass of wine. "If you don't mind, I'll finish that."

"Of course." The attendant flashed them an amused smile.

"Grams!" Maggie laughed. "Don't drink too much. You've only begun telling me Ruth's story!"

"Pshaw, girl. Two glasses of wine won't faze me." Grams straightened the box of letters on her tray. "Now, where was I?"

"Letting out the hems on Ruth's clothes. Remember? Poor Ruth. It must have been tough to be the new girl. I'm glad I didn't have to go through that. Although I definitely empathize with being a tall girl." Maggie stretched her legs. "I know now from whom I inherited my height."

"Both you and Cole are tall," Grams commented. "You'll most likely have tall children, don't you think?"

Maggie blushed. Grams kept opening up opportunities for her to confide about the mess her life had turned into. She had to wrap her head around becoming a mother before talking about it with anyone, even one as understanding as Grams. How much longer could she stall telling Cole?

Her mind drifted to good times the two of them had shared. The lazy Sunday afternoons, sprawled on the sofa watching old movies, his arms wrapped around her and her head resting on his chest. The Christmas holidays, play-arguing over which tree on the lot to purchase and sipping hot chocolate while unwrapping the ornaments they'd collected from their travels. The Valentine Day bubble baths ending with long, sensual lovemaking on a rose petal covered bed, amidst a candle-filled room.

She had let herself believe his contrite apology, his claim of loving only her, his tears of shame over straying from their vows. She'd opened her love once more to him, believing they could move forward, willing to share in the blame of their faltering relationship.

How stupid she had been.

When she'd discovered his continued betrayal—the text from *that* woman—she'd excised him from her heart, but she could never excise him from her life. Their child would forever connect them. The greatest wound of all would be sharing a child but not a family.

With a deliberate breath, she directed her attention from herself to Cécile's second letter of the three that had been bundled together. "Am I to read this one next? It's dated July 5, 1919."

"Yes." Grams's voice vibrated. "I've planned for us to visit Quimper and Penmarch. This letter will explain why."

18, bis Avenue d 'Italie

Paris 75013

France

5 July 1919

Dear Ruth,

I spend my holiday on the coast of Bretagne, called Brittany, with an auntie who live in Quimper. You pronounce kem-pair. From my window where I write you, I see the sea and large island called Ile de Groix. The country is beautiful and very wild. The sea is quite dangerous at Penmarch where I have been. There is a large stone where five persons have been taken by one of that dangerous waves. My parents have found me changed by the sea air. I am not so pale than before.

I send you little things that grow in the sea. I don't know English word. I make the card for you.

The weather is still stormy. Last night I awake by the storm's noise. I dislike nighttime storms. They make me think of the bombings during the war. Have you never heard of Berthas and Gothas which bombarded Paris from 31ˢᵗ of January 1918 to the Armistice?

Have you animals? I have a pretty cat, five years old. Its hairs are long. We call it Bidart. I enclose a pattern of my cat's hair. Don't you think he is nice? I shall be so glad if you could know him as I do, cause, you surely will like him he is a lovely darling. My cat Bidart; he is just like me, fearful, when it is stormy.

You ask how to say my name? You say mine Saysell…Gab ree ella, like Estella = Gabree-ella…Koss-kay-ric. I don't know how to pronounce your Christian name. Is it Root-Rooth-Rut-or Russ?

Yesterday was warm and I was a barefoot girl. When I am on the seaside I never wear stockings and so when I come back Paris my legs are tanned. In Paris when I go in the street I put on stockings and shoes. It is more correct!

Many kisses thro the ocean from your friend, Cécile

Maggie's grip on the letter tightened when she read the description of Cécile being haunted by the terrifying sounds of war. "Oh, Grams. A firsthand account of surviving the bombings of Paris! Poor Cécile. How terrifying."

"Yes. My mother often said how grateful she was that Cécile's family survived. She always wanted to visit Quimper and Penmarch, to stand at the place Cécile describes, looking out onto the rough sea." Grams's eyes grew misty. "Now I'll fulfill her dream for her."

"Thank you for letting me experience all of this with you, Grams." Maggie leaned her head onto her grandmother's frail shoulder. "Perhaps we'll walk by the sea, two barefoot gals."

"Barefoot gals." Grams echoed her words. "My mother described Jesse as a barefoot boy."

"What do you mean?" Maggie leaned back again into the corner of her window seat. She pulled a soft throw from her carry-on and snuggled into it. "Explain."

CHAPTER SIX
RUTH

The afternoon slid into evening. The sewing had been completed, dinner eaten, and the kitchen cleaned up. Prayers had been said with Florabelle adding an extra "God bleth Pa and Jesse" at the end.

Ruth sneaked a look at Mama, whose jaw had tightened at the mention of their names.

While Mama rocked Florabelle, Ruth settled the twins into their bed. Dewdad perched on the edge of it, reading them a nighttime story like Pa always did. Saying her goodnights, Ruth headed off to climb the stairs to her bedroom. Passing Jesse's trunk, she sent up a prayer for her brother. The bandages on her legs pulled when she took the stairs two at a time.

"Ruth, slow your pace," Mama called from her bedroom where she was tucking Florabelle into the trundle bed. She added, "Ladies don't run up the stairs. They walk slowly and with grace."

"Sorry, Mama." Ruth slowed her pace, doubting she'd ever turn into this lady Mama kept describing. After all, what kind of adventures did ladies have? Probably not many.

She plopped onto her bed, pulled off her shoes, stockings, and dress, and slipped into her long cotton nightgown. The gravel burns on her legs and scrapes on her palms stung. She remembered the freedom and adventure of speeding against the wind on her shiny bike. With freedom and adventure came pain, she figured.

She cranked open the two long, narrow attic windows to let in the cool night air. A sliver of moon shone in a sea of blinking stars. She caught her breath in awe over the idea that she and Cécile shared the same night sky.

Sitting at her vanity, Ruth avoided catching her likeness in its trifold mirror. Ever since Jesse died, she disliked her sad reflection. She opened the cigar box placed on top of the dressing table and breathed in the scent of Pa's cigars. She pulled out the letters dated from July that Cécile had enclosed with the new one.

One of the letters was dated the same day Ruth had arrived at Dewdad's: July fifth. Somehow, Cécile must have perceived that Ruth's life was being turned upside down. She and her pen pal shared that special connection, similar to what Ruth observed between the twins.

Dear Ruth, I spend my holiday on the coast of Bretagne, called Brittany, with an auntie who live in Quimper. She read the letter out loud, her pulse pounding at Cécile's description of the waves of Penmarch, the bombings of Paris, the storminess of the weather. She enjoyed the description of Bidart the cat. She slowed at the part where Cécile explain how to pronounce her name. *Say-seel Gabree-ella Koss-kay-ric.* Ruth practiced again and again until she could say her friend's name as she imagined a French girl would.

Her tired body, aching from its tumble, told her to go to sleep. She would definitely save Cécile's other July letter for the morning. She returned the letters into the box and stored it in her vanity drawer next to Jesse's compass. He'd received it from Mama and Pa on his twelfth birthday. At the funeral, Pa had pressed it into her hands, saying, "Your brother would want you to have it, Ruth."

What a coincidence that Cécile called herself a barefoot girl. The inscription of the back of the compass read *"To our barefoot boy, Love, Mama and Pa. 2/28/1915."* Mama had loved a poem called "The Barefoot Boy." She said the poet could have been writing about Jesse. He'd turn red whenever Mama would recite the poem. Ruth loved the words, especially the lines "Outward sunshine, inward joy: Blessings on thee, barefoot boy!" Jesse was that: all sunshine and joy.

One day he was whole and strong and alive. Then, gone.

Like the people at Penmarch.

Cécile described how they had been enjoying the sea before their sudden deaths. They had been like Jesse: enjoying life one minute and swept away the next. Did they struggle to stay above the water, gasp for air? Did they scream when the currents claimed them forever?

The night breeze rustled the curtains in her attic window. Thunder rumbled in the distance. Rain would be falling soon. Until Jesse died, Ruth used to love storms, hiding beneath the covers and listening to the boom and rattle. Now she feared them like Cécile, for whom storms brought back frightening memories of bombings.

To Ruth, storms now sounded like Hell.

The thunder rolled again, getting closer this time. Lightning streaked through the darkness. Ruth closed the vanity drawer. She caught her reflection in its trifold mirror. Three versions of herself stared back. She glimpsed the back of another Ruth, reflected in the pedestal mirror across the room.

The longer she stared, the more the reflections stretched on and on, until she splintered into more pieces than she could count. The mirrors sucked her in, and from inside the glass, she peered out on a girl who stared, wide-eyed, into a vanity. She could see through that girl's skin and past her bones—into her darkest self.

Thunder cracked, breaking the strange spell. She slumped in exhaustion, her mouth dry and her breath coming raw in her throat.

The rain started falling, at first gently before slapping hard against the roof. Ruth crawled into bed underneath the patchwork quilt she had helped her mother sew. Its softness comforted her while the rain lulled her to sleep.

CHAPTER SEVEN
MAGGIE

G rams's voice, full of sadness, trailed off.

Maggie tugged her throw closer around her, comforted by its softness like Ruth had been by her patchwork quilt. Her great-grandmother's situation had bruised Maggie's heart. Perhaps her emotions were heightened because of . . . she gently moved her hand to her belly. Telling others about the baby would be exciting, she hoped, despite the sadness it brought regarding Cole.

She retrieved her cell from her purse and read through his pleading texts. Her anger surged, spurring her to select and delete each one. Closing the message app, she stared at her screensaver, last summer's photograph of her and Cole with three other couples, her best girlfriends and their husbands, against the backdrop of the ocean. They'd been in each other's weddings, and the four couples had a tradition of beach vacations together and a group photograph commemorating each.

These trips would continue, she assumed, but obviously without her and Cole. She hoped she'd be able to remain close to her girlfriends, no matter the divorce. They would flip out over her baby news when she'd tell them.

Thank heaven Grams was keeping her preoccupied with Ruth and Cécile. Maggie had to admit her curiosity was piqued about what exactly happened to Jesse. Why did Ruth suffer such guilt? Maggie knew she'd find out in good time. She couldn't rush Grams to get to that part of the story.

She could definitely connect with Ruth's pain that came with a broken family. When her parents split, Maggie had her close-as-sisters girlfriends there to support her. Not even they could keep her from feeling alone while her family fell apart.

Maggie shifted from dwelling in her own pain to worrying about her grandmother. A faraway expression had settled upon her face. She touched Grams's arm, concerned all the storytelling had exhausted her. "How about a little nap. We'll continue the story later."

Grams shook her head. "Oh, no. I'm not tired at all. At times I get lost back in the years, dear. It's fine. Sometimes a trip backward helps us move forward."

That observation struck a nerve with Maggie. If only her unhappy childhood memories had not been at the root of her hesitation about starting the family Cole had wanted. Her scars ran deeper than either of her parents realized, which made her worry more intensely about becoming a parent. What if she were as clueless about her child's feelings as her parents had been about hers? Why couldn't Cole understand her apprehensions rather than accuse her of being ungrateful for her privileged upbringing, so different from his financially unstable one?

Right now, moving forward overwhelmed her, period. She could, however, handle the present, as long as she focused on Grams's story.

"May I read another letter?" Maggie asked.

"Of course." Grams handed her Cécile's second letter dated from July. "As a history teacher, you'll love these details. Remember, when Cécile wrote it, she did not know yet of Ruth's move to Oakland."

Maggie slid her cell phone back in her bag before unfolding the letter and reading it out loud.

18, bis Avenue d 'Italie
Paris 75013
France

18 July 1919

My dear little Yankee,

I have no letter yet from you but I write you any-
way. I hope your letter arrives to me soon. It is so
long for letters to come from Colorado til Paris. I
am impatient to have news from you. Why do they not make a daily
service of aeroplanes? I don't despair to see that one day. Because I
have much to say and love to use my English I will write you always
and not wait for your letters to reach to me. You do the same and
our letters they will crisscross sometime, but not a problem?

Monday was a fine day, the 14 July. First, Joffre and Foch
have passed under the arc de triomphe, then the American troops
with their flags, the sailors and Pershing; English soldiers, Belgians,
Italians, etc…and last French troops composed by several men of each
regiment. Four millions of persons have seen the soldiers pass. We call
this day Bastille Day and it was the first since the end of the war.

I speak English now for two years and I have spoken to an
American soldier in the train coming back to Paris. He was under-
standing me, but I could not understand what he said. I am sure
that I make mistakes in my English. Please correct the important
mistakes and note them on sheet of paper you will enclose in your
letter. Did you know French people call the Americans Yankees,
and the soldiers Sammies, the English people fils d'Albion (Albion's
son) or John Bull.

I like very much to walk along the banks of the Seine: this nice
green water resembles the water of the Ocean. Last Tuesday we went,

Ninette and me along the banks, we bought some old books at an old bookseller who stay on the quarys. I have bought a little book of English, not adventure book, only a book of reading for children; but I like it, since I understand nearly all the contents.

To thank you for your using French words in your letter writing and because I understand English children book I make paper dolls of a sweet boy and girl.

You will begin again school soon. For me school is ended. Next month I shall work and earn. What do you prefer in school? I prefer geography, then history, and at last Arithmetic.

From your affectionate friend, with kisses,
Cécile

Maggie pressed the letter between her two hands. "What treasures. History, alive on these pages! Cécile is full of joy. No wonder Ruth couldn't wait to receive letters from her."

"Yes." Grams chuckled. "In this day of instantaneous global communication, it's difficult to imagine having to wait until a letter reached your mailbox. My mother told me about going to the mercantile to mail hers and do some shopping."

The glint in her Grams's eye signaled more storytelling to come. Maggie settled back to listen.

CHAPTER EIGHT
RUTH

The sweet smell of the hotcakes and salty, smoky bacon roused Ruth from her sleep. She jumped out of bed and immediately groaned. Her sore body ached from the tumble yesterday. Ignoring her pains, she reached for her box holding Cécile's letters. She had one more to read before writing a reply.

July 18, 1919. My dear little Yankee, I have no letter yet from you but I write you anyway. I hope your letter arrives to me soon. It is so long for letters to come from Colorado til Paris.

Ruth read the letter quickly, fascinated by the interesting detail. The history her French friend witnessed first-hand amazed her, Viewing victory parades. Meeting soldiers. How could anything she wrote back be of interest?

She did realize she had quite a bit to tell her pal, especially about bike riding and that darn old Herkimer. Reviewing what she'd written, she admired her use of *Bonjour* and *Au revoir*, wishing she knew more French words. She added in some corrections to Cécile's English, as her friend requested.

Folding her letter for mailing, Ruth wished like Cécile for aeroplane deliveries to speed their correspondence to each other. However, she could only ask her grandfather for a speedy automobile ride to the post office. She ran lightly down the stairs, the breakfast smells encouraging rumbles in her stomach.

"Good morning, Ruth." Dewdad raised his coffee cup in greeting. "What have you there, an epistle for Cécile?"

Hah! Ruth knew *epistle* meant letter. "Yes. Could we go into town to mail it today? Tomorrow's Sunday, and Monday I have to," she switched to a dramatic whisper, *"start school."*

"I'll drive us after breakfast." Dewdad placed the letter in his shirt pocket. He brushed the back of his hand against his mustache and added, "School won't be that abominable."

Abominable. That word met her expectations.

Mama set the platter of hotcakes in the center of the table. "Ruth, get the blueberry syrup for us, please."

It was Pa's favorite. Ruth wished he were here eating breakfast with them, teasing the twins and complimenting Mama's cooking. Did Mama wish the same thing? Ruth had no idea. She fetched the syrup from the cupboard and put it on the table.

"Thank you, Ruth," Mama said in a brisk voice. "Your grandfather's right. You'll enjoy school. You've been lonely since we've been here. Making friends with a nice girl will help."

A nice girlfriend to make her more ladylike, Mama meant.

"By the way," her mother continued, "there will be a Cotillion class offered through school. It will meet once a month through the fall. I've enrolled you. I've already purchased the pattern and white fabric to make you a new dress."

"A new dress!" Ruth exclaimed.

Mama beamed. "I'm glad you agree that you should attend. From what I understand, the young boys your age are also attending. You'll learn how to dance properly and improve your manners and social graces."

Ruth dreaded what Mama described. Manners and social graces were more ladies-don't rules. And dancing? There were never any boys her height or taller. She had to talk her mother out of this terrible Cotillion.

"Mama . . ."

A knock at the door interrupted Ruth's please-don't-make-me-go, it-will-ruin-my-life speech.

"Whoever could that be, visiting this early?" Mama's bluntness indicated her irritation. "Ruth, go see."

From the glass side panels framing the front door, Ruth glimpsed a petite woman and a girl about her age. The woman's pinched face signaled she meant business. She held a leash attached to the tiniest terrier Ruth had ever seen.

The girl had blonde hair that fell in ringlets. Her stylish store-bought dress fit her perfectly. However, even with her porcelain complexion and china blue eyes, something about the way she held her nose tilted in the air kept Ruth from thinking her beautiful.

Ruth greeted them in her most polite and ladylike voice. "Good morning. May I help you?"

The little terrier yapped and growled and lunged for her feet.

"Hey!" Ruth jumped back.

"Stay calm, Teacup," the woman said, stooping to pick up the vicious ball of fur, which kept yapping and baring its teeth. "I'm here for Mr. Addison."

Dewdad appeared at the door, untucking his napkin from his shirt collar. "Mrs. Givens. Phoebe. Good morning." He spoke sharply.

Ruth's body tightened at Phoebe's sizing her up. With a toss of her ringlets and a curl of her lip, Phoebe informed Ruth that she definitely didn't measure up. Teacup growled again, agreeing.

"Have you any idea what that rooster of yours has been up to this morning, Mr. Addison?" Mrs. Givens asked.

"Papa, please ask the ladies in." Mama joined them, patting her hair into place. She held her hand out. "I'm Dolly Calderhead, Dewey's daughter. This is my daughter Ruth."

The dog growled and snipped at Mama's open hand.

Mama pulled her hand back. "Oh, my," she said. "Feisty little one."

Anger flicked inside Ruth. Mrs. Givens ignored Mama's obvious fear of the dog and offered no apology for its rotten behavior. What a bully!

"I'm Mrs. Roberta Givens," the woman announced. "This is my daughter, Phoebe. I believe our daughters will be in class together when school begins."

Ruth swallowed her groan.

Mrs. Givens nuzzled her dog to her chin. "And this is Teacup, who is lucky to be alive."

"Your stupid old rooster came out of nowhere and pecked at Teacup," Phoebe chimed in. "It's a horrid old thing and you should . . ."

"I should what, young lady?" Dewdad interrupted.

"You should get rid of it. That's what," Mrs. Givens said. "We're part of the city limits, not the country. City ordinances forbid roosters, hens, and other livestock. After all, this is 1919, and we are a citified community, not some backwoods."

"And he *is* a mean and nasty rooster," Phoebe added, stamping her foot.

Teacup growled.

Quiet descended, thick as a snow blizzard back home.

Dewdad finally broke the silence. "If you have a problem with Herkimer, file a complaint with the city council." He jutted his chin toward Teacup. "In the meantime, I'd keep a closer eye on that mongrel of yours."

Mrs. Givens and Phoebe both gasped.

From the kitchen, the twins and Florabelle let out deafening shrieks.

"Ladies." Dewdad closed the door.

"Papa!" Mama gasped, horrified. "How dare you shut the door on them!"

"That woman is a busybody, and her daughter is a little gossip. The fruit doesn't fall far from the tree." Dewdad gave an *harrumph*. "Anyway, we have more important matters to which we should attend. What's the ruckus happening in the kitchen?"

Mama swept past him. Ruth followed, with her grandfather on her heels.

A loud Herkimer *brawk* greeted them.

"Oh no!" Ruth pointed at the kitchen door, standing agape. "He came in the house!"

The rooster bobbed and weaved through the room. Opal and Mable shouted in duet, "Cock-a-doodle-doo!" Florabelle knocked her dish, sending the last few bites of sticky hotcakes flying to the floor. Herkimer strutted toward the mess, ready to peck at it.

"Shoo, shoo!" Mama snapped her dishcloth at the rooster. He dodged each snap, feathers flying, and escaped back out onto the porch.

Over the confusion, Dewdad barked orders. "Ruth, get your other chores done. When you're finished, we'll proceed to town to get that letter mailed. Dolly, make me a list of what to collect for you at Swan's Mercantile."

Mama's attention was riveted on calming the reining chaos. Ruth stepped in to help. She moved through her chores lickety-split. She might have been in one of those Charlie Chaplin movies that Cécile loved, where everybody moved at such a high speed.

Dewdad pulled up to Swan's Mercantile at the stroke of ten on the town square clock.

When they entered the store, its scent, musty yet clean, reminded Ruth of the mercantile in Colorado Springs. This one offered similar items: fresh produce in baskets on the sidewalk by the entrance, colorful fabric lined up on bolts, pots, pans, and hardware stacked on display, jars of candy lined on the counter.

Ruth remembered how she'd go with Jesse and Pa to shop back home. Jesse and she would look through the adventure books displayed in the back of the store and choose the one with the most exciting cover. They'd sit on the floor, sucking on candy Pa would have bought them and reading until the shopkeeper's wife saw them. "You can't read it if you don't buy it!" she'd exclaim and return the book to the shelf. When she'd left them alone, Jesse would whisper, "All clear," and grab the book again. They'd continue reading, their heads almost touching.

"Morning, Addison. Adjusting to a house full of grandchildren?" The clerk let out a laugh.

"Well, let me tell you one thing." Dewdad tipped his tweed cap, and his mustache twitched. "It *is* an adjustment, Clarence—an adjustment."

Ruth was acquainted with her grandfather well enough to detect the humor in his reply. His answer held no true complaint.

Dewdad handed Mama's shopping list to Clarence. He began filling the order, placing items in a cardboard box.

Ruth wandered around. A rack of girls' dresses drew her attention, especially one similar to Phoebe's. How many store-bought ones did that girl own? She bet Phoebe's Cotillion dress would be the fanciest one of all.

Swan's had books in the back of the store, too. Ruth couldn't bear to look through them without Jesse. She checked out a display of stationery that could be ordered with your initials or even your name. Cécile drew her own monogram on each of her letters, a *C* with a line crossed through it. Ruth would love to have her own personalized stationery.

Next to the stationery were a few short stacks of postcards. Ruth picked up one that had a picture of the Oakland City Hall and joined Dewdad at the store's counter.

"Ruth, don't you have some business to attend to with Clarence?" He held out Cécile's letter.

"Yes, sir." Ruth took the letter. "May I send this postcard to Pa too?"

"Sure thing. Use my pen to address it." Dewdad pulled out a heavy dark blue and gold ballpoint pen.

She had never written with a pen like it before. At the post office counter, she addressed the card to Pa and wrote, *Hope you are well. We all miss you very much, me especially. The twins have grown taller and I have too! School starts Monday. Oakland is nice, but I miss Pike's Peak. All the love in the world, Your "same old Ruth."* She added a row of Xs and

*O*s, hoping when Pa got the card, he'd hop the next train there. She gave Dewdad back his pen and held the card up. Her irregular handwriting style fell short of Cécile's neat and perfect cursive.

Clarence peered at her from over the counter. "Young lady, may I help you?"

"May I please mail this postcard to Colorado Springs and this letter to Paris, France?"

"Would that letter be an answer to the one that came all the way here the other day from Paree?" Clarence asked.

"Yes. I have a French pen pal, Cécile Cosquéric." Ruth handed the letter to him. "We write to each other often, but it takes so long for our letters to reach each other."

"Well, it is around fifty-five hundred miles straight as the crow flies from here to Paris—and even more miles considering the route this letter has to go." Clarence weighed and stamped the envelope. "Maybe someday mail between continents will go on airplanes, and presto—you'll mail your letter here today and it will arrive in Paris in only a couple of days."

"Cécile and I dream of that." What if she could fly on one and personally deliver her letter, Ruth thought.

"You aren't joshing about writing each other all the time." Clarence chuckled. "Another letter came for you today."

Another so soon!

"Read it to me on our drive back, Ruth," Dewdad suggested.

"I'd like that!" she agreed, excitement fanning through her.

CHAPTER NINE
MAGGIE

"I'm sorry to interrupt your story." The same flight attendant who had been serving them stood at Grams's seat, ready to serve dinner salads. "I hope you don't mind my eavesdropping? I'm fascinated!"

Grams smiled broadly. "Not at all. I'm happy you appreciate family mementoes."

"Thanks. I'm Brian by the way."

Maggie accepted her salad from him. "Nice to meet you, Brian. This is my grandmother, Mrs. Weatherly, and I'm her granddaughter Maggie—" she caught herself before adding her married name. Would she keep it for the baby's sake? That dilemma could be solved another day, she decided.

"Pleased to meet you." He waited for Grams to relocate her box of letters to her side in her roomy seat before placing her salad on her tray. "Is this your first trip to Paris?"

"Yes, it is," Maggie answered. She glanced at the couple across from them. They were cuddled against each other, their world shrunk to each other. If only that were Cole and her. A cold fist closed over Maggie's heart.

"I confess," Brian said, handing them bottles of water, "that I can't stop listening about Ruth and Cécile." He reddened. "Obviously. I'm on a first-name basis with them both."

Grams laughed. "You're a sucker for a good story!"

"Absolutely." Moving to the passengers behind them, he winked. "I'll catch back up with you later."

The two munched on their salads, their conversation turning to inconsequential chitchat about Grams's close friends from her assisted-living residence. Her banter reinforced to Maggie that it had been a good decision for Grams to sell her home and move. Maggie's mom had worried that the change would be difficult, but Grams had adapted to her new lifestyle with zest.

"We have season tickets to the community theater in the neighborhood. Guess what the next production will be?" asked Grams. "*Les Misérables*. You'll have to attend with me to extend sharing this exciting adventure in Paris together."

"I would love to," Maggie answered, handing her empty plate to Brian when he passed by to collect from Grams.

After a sip of her water, Maggie held her hand out, fanning her fingers in a come-here way. "My excited anticipation matches Ruth's when she awaited another letter. Which one should we read now?"

Grams opened the box and flipped to locate the next letter in date order. She slipped it from its envelope, along with an enclosed hand-drawn map. Grams pointed on the map where Cécile had indicated the location of "our house."

"This stop will be one of our first in retracing Cécile's life," said Grams. "She wrote that she lived near the Jardin des Plantes." Grams's eyes shone.

Maggie closely studied the map before reading the letter aloud.

18, bis Avenue d 'Italie
Paris 75013
France

15 August 1919

Dearest Ruth, my American friend,

Do you think your new city Oakland to be a great city? Paris I think is a great city. The city has 8 miles from North to South and 9 miles from West to East. I live in the south near the gateway near the Jardin des Plantes on Avenue d'Italie. Paris don't you think is a great city?

Before I live in Avenue d' Italie, I have lived sometime in an island of the Seine, Ile St. Louis. Now I live near the Jardin des plantes. There are nearly twenty bears, white and browns, some were born in the Jardin. There are too, lions, tigers, panthers, eagles, and elephants. Tortoises, very large giraffes, drome darries, camels, and many many other wild animals. I can't say, serpents too and buffalos, bisons etc…it is very interesting to visit that park.

Before to live in Avenue d' Italie, I have lived sometime in an island of the Seine, Ile St. Louis. I draw you a picture of Italie Square near my house on Avenue d'Italie, which was ancient Roman crossroad.

I have marked my house and where father works at the 13th city hall. During the war the Germans drop Gotha bombs and shell Paris with Berthas. A bomb fall in house near Italie Square and close to my house killing our neighbors.

Since yesterday I begin work. I have leaved school, but I shall go on my lessons of steno and of English. My typewriter is called Smith Premier. It is made in the U.S.

The house where I work stands on a great boulevard in the heart of the city, called Boulevard Monmartre. I stay ¾ an hour to work on the metro, and I change train in a great station. To take the metro, the tram or the bus is so difficult. In the metro you are so compressed you can't move your little finger. We are so numerous in the city! I send you ticket and map of Nord-sud.

Well I stop here. I am talkative today. I am chatterbox for me and you!

Much kisses from your affectionate friend, Cécile

Maggie examined the map of the Nord-Sud, which was the Paris north-south underground, and the stamped ticket Cécile she'd enclosed. The underground had been a new mode of transportation at that time. Maggie could picture Cécile hurrying to work amidst the bustling crowd of Parisians, relieved the war had ended and their lives could return to normal.

Insight into the past from Cécile's letters reinforced her fascination with history. Maggie shuddered in her description of the Gothas and Berthas intruding on the lives of innocent Parisians. She wondered about Cécile's neighbors who had been killed in the bombing. The way Cécile wrote about their fate projected a matter-of-fact attitude. Maggie imagined that those who lived through war's atrocities must become practical in their outlook and in accepting loss.

Maggie returned the letter to Grams. Delicious goosebumps crawled over her when she glimpsed the other letters, anticipating more glorious historical detail. "I cannot wait to walk the streets Cécile walked and see her Paris. I wonder how different her neighborhood is today compared to then."

"I Google-Mapped the address when I planned our trip." Grams's voice held a hint of pride. Maggie marveled at her grandmother's technological know-how. "The neighborhood is more commercial now, but I want to visit the address to help me envision what it might have been like in Cécile's day."

"You haven't mentioned anything about Cécile marrying or having children." Maggie finished the last of her water, realizing the salad had whetted her appetite. She hoped the dinner would be tasty. "With all your googling, were you able to find any of her family we could visit?"

"Disappointingly, I couldn't find any family to contact. Regarding Cécile's love life, you will find her quite a flirt." Grams patted the box. "You'll learn the details."

"I can't wait!" Maggie leaned her head back against the seat. "Just think. If anyone in Cécile's family were to look for any of Great-grams's family, they would find us."

Maggie cherished her families' collection of old photos showing their lineage. She had displayed family wedding pictures at her reception when she married Cole. The one of Ruth and Clinton Carlock in a heavy silver ornate frame showed them in profile, their eyes locked in love.

Cole and she had a similar picture from their own wedding. It had been Maggie's favorite. She'd packed it away with her wedding album and anything else from that day. At her child's wedding, it wouldn't be displayed. How could it be, since her child would never have both parents together, loving and raising her? Or him. What if she bore a son, a spitting image of Cole?

Maggie stared out the window. The plane was hurtling, like her, through darkness. At least the plane had a destination. She had no idea what was on the other side of her journey into single parenthood.

"Maggie, dear. Brian is handing you the menu."

"Oh, sorry." She accepted the pencil and menu from him, glad for the disruption of her pity party.

"Please check your choice, and I'll come back to collect," he said.

Maggie gave the choices a quick glance, no longer ravenous. Her impending divorce had a way of ruining her appetite. Yet she checked off a choice, grudgingly accepting she must eat.

Grams stared absentmindedly at her menu. Maggie tapped her pencil on it. "I'm getting the chicken dish. What about you?"

"Oh, that will be fine." Grams checked off that choice. "How wonderful it would have been if Ruth and Cécile had actually met in person.

I'm sure Cécile would have loved your great-grandfather. Have I ever told you how my parents met?"

"No. Please, do tell!"

"I think we left off with Ruth at the mercantile. Little did she foresee how meeting a certain paperboy that day would change her life."

CHAPTER TEN
RUTH

Dewdad backed the Chevrolet from the parking spot while Ruth read aloud from Cécile's letter: *Dearest Ruth, my American friend.*

"Excuse me for interrupting, Ruffis," Dewdad said. "I think I'll offer that young'un a lift. He doesn't live far from our house." He called out his window to the boy standing on the sidewalk on the opposite side of the street. "Clinton Carlock. How'd you like to ride in this Chevrolet your daddy helped build?"

Ruth recognized the name. Clinton was the boy who couldn't accept the bicycle from Dewdad. He wore a newspaper satchel strapped across his chest. His pants were a tad too short for his long legs. His leather boots were scuffed. A thatch of sandy-brown hair hung over his forehead, and his long straight locks brushed the collar of his faded work shirt. Everything about him provoked Ruth's interest.

Clinton hurried across the street toward them. He leaned in Dewdad's open window, glancing at her in the passenger seat. His cornflower-blue eyes crinkled up at the sides when he flashed her a broad smile. Her shyness begged her to look away, but she couldn't.

He was the most handsome boy she'd ever seen.

Except, of course, for Jesse.

Dewdad nodded to the back seat. "If you want to hitch a ride, hop on in."

Ruth's stomach flipped.

"Thanks, Mr. Addison." He folded his tall frame into the back seat. "I sure appreciate the lift."

Dewdad resumed driving. "How's the paper route, son?"

"Not bad. Kind of tough making the deliveries on foot."

Dewdad tugged on his driver's cap. "That bike would've come in handy, but I understand your mama's position on it." Ruth's heart squeezed tight at the mention of the bike, a wrecked mess. "Your dad would be proud of you. Pete's missed around here, that's for certain." Ruth's heart squeezed even tighter. She knew what it was like to grieve.

"By the way," Dewdad nodded her way. "I forgot to introduce you to my granddaughter Ruth Calderhead. Ruth, meet Clinton Carlock. You two will be in school together come Monday."

Ruth sent up heavenly thanks that Dewdad hadn't slipped up and called her Ruffis. Her cheeks flamed. She always got tongue-tied talking with boys other than Jesse.

To her relief, Clinton spoke first. "Pleased to meet you, Ruth."

"It's nice to meet you," she managed to say.

Dewdad stopped at the curve before reaching his driveway. Ruth observed an unpainted wooden house set off an overgrown dirt road cut through the woods lining the road. Dewdad shifted in the seat to address Clinton. "Tell your mama I said hello. If you two need anything, the factory will provide it."

"Thanks. I'll tell Mama." He climbed out of the car on passenger side. He paused at Ruth's window, shaking his long hair out of his eyes. They held the same sadness she detected in her own. "If you want, I can wait for you here Monday morning, and we can walk together to school."

The blush returned to her cheeks. "Yes, thanks."

With a wave out the window, Dewdad drove them away. In less time than it took to pluck a daisy, they'd reached home and were parked in the garage. Ruth hadn't had a chance to read her letter from Cécile. Or to find out anything more about Clinton.

Mama met them in the kitchen. "Thanks, Papa, for shopping. Were you able to get all the items on the list?"

"Yes," Dewdad answered, "and Ruth got her letter to Cécile mailed."

He didn't mention her postcard to Pa.

"I received another letter from Cécile," Ruth added.

"You must be excited to read it," Mama said. "First, help me put these groceries away."

Mama had spread the fabric for her Cotillion dress across the kitchen table. Ruth studied the picture on the pattern's packaging. This dress would be a match for any of Phoebe's store-bought-fancy ones.

She wondered if Clinton would attend Cotillion. At his tall height, she'd definitely not loom over him. In fact, he'd loom over her! Cotillion wouldn't be too awful if he could be her dance partner.

Mama held out a bag of potatoes. "Ruth, put these in the bin, please."

"Yes, Mama."

She helped put away the rest of the groceries, her mind on Clinton and his cornflower-blue eyes. Would he really be waiting Monday for them to walk to school together?

Finished helping with the groceries, she galloped up the stairs to her room. Mama's reprimand followed her. "Ruth, remember. Ladies walk!"

Ruth ignored her mother and galloped even faster. She had a new letter from Cécile to read and news to write to her. She'd already written in her mind the first paragraph of her letter. It would be all about a certain paperboy.

Monday morning, Ruth waited for Clinton. He didn't show. The walk to school stretched twice longer without him.

When she reached the schoolyard, the younger kids were playing tag. A ring of girls were circling Phoebe, who glanced Ruth's way and whispered to the other girls, who giggled. When Ruth passed them, she caught snatches of Phoebe's comments: "She's all feet... Her clothes are *so* out of style."

With no place to hide, Ruth perched on the steps of the school entrance, waiting for the bell to ring and trying to pretend she wasn't absolutely miserable. When Clinton entered the schoolyard, he gave her a wave. Her heart lifted at the sight of his friendly face.

Phoebe waved to him. "Hey, Clinton!" He ignored her.

By the time the start-of-school bell rang, Ruth had figured out two things: Phoebe had branded Ruth an outcast, and Phoebe liked Clinton.

Phoebe and her girlfriends crushed against Ruth when running up the stairs, tossing their various shades of curls. Ruth followed behind them, feeling like prey in a sea of sharks.

"Ruth, wait up." Clinton, his long legs moving quickly, took two stairs at a time. "Sorry I missed you this morning. Delivering my papers took me longer than I expected."

"I understand." He hadn't forgotten her!

"Don't let those girls bother you," he said, flipping his hair from his eyes.

"What you're talking about?" Ruth purposefully acted dumb, not wanting to give away her hurt feelings.

"Phoebe and her group. She tells them what to do. If she wants them to be mean to you, they will be. They were all mean to last year's new girl, Winnie Smith. This year, Winnie's part of the group." He shrugged. "I guess she figures it's better to be Phoebe's friend than her enemy."

"I don't care." Ruth's voice quivered.

She didn't *want* to care about fitting in. It made her angry to care. It made her feel sorry for herself to care. She wished that she didn't care one little bit. But she did.

No way would she admit that to Clinton. She'd admit it to no one— except Cécile. In her next letter to her, Ruth had an answer to her pen pal's question: *No, I don't think Oakland is a great city.*

When they filed into the classroom, students headed toward their seats without hesitation. Ruth froze on the spot, uncertain of where to sit. She approached the teacher's desk.

"You're the new girl?" Miss Newton peered at Ruth over the half glasses perched on her nose. She examined Ruth from tip to toe. "The names are taped on the desks. Find your seat."

Ruth flushed with embarrassment. Why hadn't she realized that? She walked down the first row, reading the names on either side of her. They were seated alphabetically. *Calderhead* would sit in front of *Carlock*! Her excitement dimmed at the presence of the name *Givens* taped on the desk across the aisle.

When Ruth took her seat, Phoebe tossed her curls and whispered to another girl. The girls both giggled and stared at Ruth. She could feel the heat coming off her blush.

To Ruth's dread, Miss Newton proved to be nothing like Mrs. Castleberry. Miss Newton wore her hair swept up in a tight bun with a couple of pencils stuck into it. Her penetrating gaze swept the classroom like a hawk ready to pounce on any student who dared to break her classroom rules. She warned that she'd swat a ruler against any misbehaving student's open palms. Ruth tightened her hands into protective fists.

With morning session over, Ruth joined the others walking in a single-file line to the lunchroom. She sat far from Phoebe and the other girls. To her shock, Clinton slid into the seat next to her. He had an extra carton of milk on his tray.

"Here." He placed the carton by her.

"Thanks."

He opened his bag and took out a sandwich and an apple. Ruth spread out her cheese, crackers, and slice of walnut cake.

"How about my apple for your cake?" he asked.

"Deal."

It was the best apple Ruth had ever tasted.

After lunch, Ruth dreaded returning to class. When she found out the afternoon would be arithmetic lessons, her dread lessened. She loved the precision of numbers.

Miss Newton paired them with another student to quiz each other on multiplication and division tables. Ruth's pulse quickened when she was partnered with Clinton. She couldn't help but be secretly happy that Phoebe, her countenance dark as a thundercloud, was partnered with Horace Hastings, a short squirt of a boy. Ruth wondered if he hated his lack of height as much as she hated her abundance of it.

Tinkling her class bell, Miss Newton announced, "Review time is over. Open your arithmetic book to exercise one for a timed practice." She perched on her stool with a stopwatch in her hand. "Phoebe, you won the arithmetic contest last year for your class. Congratulations. Perhaps you'll win again when the contest is held next month."

Phoebe beamed.

Ruth beamed also, confident in her ability to win.

Miss Newton held the stopwatch up. "Ready, set . . ." She clicked the timer. "Go."

In no time flat, Ruth wrote her last answer on the sheet and placed her pencil on her desk. Phoebe finished a split second later. Clinton's pencil kept scratching all the way up to the time Miss Newton clicked the stopwatch and said, "Stop. Exchange across the aisle to grade."

Swapping papers, Phoebe glared at Ruth. To Ruth's delight, after they swapped back, Phoebe had not marked any of Ruth's answers incorrect. Phoebe had missed two. Ruth's pride set her aglow, as if she had ingested a ray of sunshine.

The rest of the day dragged. The end-of-day bell couldn't come quick enough for Ruth.

She gathered her belongings and made a beeline out of the building.

"Ruth."

Clinton! She slowed until he reached her side.

"Want to walk home together?"

Her tongue tied, Ruth managed to answer, "Yes."

Clinton did all the talking on the walk home, and that suited Ruth fine.

She learned about his pa being in the war. "The army needed him because he was an expert with homing pigeons, which were used during the war to send important messages in the battlefield," he said. "After the war, he worked at the Chevrolet factory until he got sick with the Spanish flu. He died a year ago." His voice thickened. Ruth worried he might cry. He swallowed hard and added, his chin held up proudly, "Now I care for Pa's pigeons."

He talked about his paper route and about his mama taking in mending and laundering. "Every little bit helps to make ends meet." He sounded very grown-up.

Ruth learned that he was about to turn fifteen to her about-to-turn-fourteen. "I didn't go to school last year after Pa died. Ma needed me to be around. That's why I'm in your grade."

Ruth understood. She hadn't returned to school after Jesse died. She finished her 7th grade year only because Mrs. Castleberry had come to her home to teach her.

For all she learned about Clinton, he didn't learn much about her. She didn't tell Clinton that her pa's part in the war had been to stay in the USA and grow vegetables for the war effort. She didn't tell him about how Jesse's death had split up her family. She didn't tell him about seeing all those reflections of herself in the mirror, about how sometimes her pulse raced and her mouth got too dry for her to speak. She didn't tell him that she sometimes fell into a pitch-black nothingness.

She did tell him about Cécile.

"I'd like to read some of her letters sometime," Clinton said.

Before she could answer that she'd love to show him, Ruth heard loud giggling, announcing that Phoebe and her girlfriends were walking close behind.

"Ignore them," Clinton said. "Like I told you, Phoebe is a trouble-maker, like her ma."

"They're causing trouble for Dewdad," Ruth confided. "Mrs. Givens is on the warpath because of Dewdad's noisy rooster."

When they reached the road leading to his house, Ruth stood by his side while the girls walked past them. Their giggling stopped, and Phoebe fanned her fingers in a flirty wave toward Clinton. After they walked on, the giggling started up again, this time even louder.

Clinton frowned.

"What's wrong?" Ruth asked.

"She's out to make trouble for you. She's always afraid new girls will steal her thunder."

Ruth held in her laughter. She couldn't imagine how her big feet and let-out clothes could in any way threaten Phoebe. "Thanks for the warning. I'll be careful."

"Good. Meet you tomorrow morning?"

Her answer jumped out. "Okay."

Rounding the curve to Dewdad's, Ruth groaned. Mrs. Givens and Phoebe were engaged in conversation. Phoebe's eyes didn't leave Ruth while she talked to her mom. Ruth predicted trouble was brewing.

Thinking of Clinton, Ruth skipped down the driveway. She passed Herkimer strutting around in the fenced-in chicken yard, his flapping wings expressing his unhappiness at his confinement. Obviously, Dewdad didn't want to chance another episode with Mrs. Givens.

"Too bad you're penned in, Herk," Ruth called out. "You could have attacked the mom, daughter, and dog all at one time."

⋘⋙

Cécile wrote about bombs called "Gothas."

Ruth's bombs were called "Phoebes."

Mama's temper had exploded the minute Ruth arrived home from school.

"Mrs. Givens gave me an earful at Swan's Mercantile this morning. She asked about my allowing you to walk back and forth with Clinton

Carlock to school." Mama's stare scorched through Ruth like a hot iron through cotton. "She said you had been walking with him for the past three weeks, ever since school started. Did you assume I would not find out? Do you perceive how this makes you appear?"

"Yes, Mama." Ruth answered respectfully, but inside she fumed. She had heard all the gossipy whispering about her and Clinton that Phoebe spread during recess. *Did you know they hold hands? Did you see how close together they walk? Did you see he carried her books?* Phoebe had filled Mrs. Givens's ears with her gossip too. Mrs. Givens had two strikes against the family: Herkimer and that "fast" girl Ruth.

Her mother's fury spent, she ordered Ruth to change into her Cotillion dress for a fitting. She stepped up onto a kitchen chair for Mama to mark the hem.

"Quite fidgeting, Ruth. I can't pin evenly if you're moving." Mama's irritated mumble told Ruth that she was getting on her mother's last nerve.

Mama tugged on the last part of the hem. "There. All done." She returned the measuring tape and tailor's chalk to her sewing basket. "I'll have this ready for your first session tomorrow. Be sure to thank Dewdad for the bows and lace he bought for me to trim it."

"I will." Ruth stepped off the kitchen chair, adding, "Thank you, Mama, for making me such a pretty dress."

Mama's demeanor softened a bit. "Go change. I'll press the dress for tomorrow." She opened up the ironing board and heated the iron. Ruth headed for the attic stairs.

"Ruth?" Her mother called her back.

"Yes, Mama?"

"We are clear? No more unchaperoned walks with boys." She stated her rule in a flat, no-point-in-arguing-with-me way.

Ruth's breath quickened. If she answered, "Yes, Mama," it would be a falsehood. Clinton and she walked the same direction at the same time. They were not to walk together because of a ladies-don't rule? How ridiculous! She wouldn't let stupid gossip stop her.

She didn't answer her mama at all.

The next morning at breakfast, Dewdad said, "Ruth, your mama and I need to have a word with you." His seriousness spooked her. Mama must have shared Mrs. Givens's gossip with him.

He motioned for her to sit at the table. He joined her. Mama stood

Brushing his mustache with one hand and tapping his fingers of his other on the table, Dewdad announced, "We need to straighten out a thing or two."

The room was quiet except for Herkimer's crowing outside the window. Facing Herkimer would be easier than facing them.

"Your mama told me what Mrs. Givens said about you walking with Clinton to and from school." Ruth braced herself for Dewdad's support of her mother's rule: no more walking with Clinton.

He leaned back in his chair and gave her a wink. "Let me go on record. Clinton Carlock is a fine young man. Anyone should be pleased to have him walk their daughter or granddaughter anywhere, anytime."

Relieved, Ruth sneaked a look at Mama, whose jaw had tightened.

Dewdad continued. "You needn't worry one whit about his company during your walk to school. Your mama agrees."

She didn't look like it.

Dewdad had won this battle. Maybe not the war but definitely this battle.

"And if anyone says anything about it or accuses my granddaughter of not being a lady"—Dewdad made a fist and thumped his chest with his thumb—"then you tell them they have Dewey Addison to reckon with."

"Thanks, Dewdad," Ruth whispered. She leapt up from the table to give Mama a tight hug. "We're not in the dark ages, Mama. It's a walk to and from school. Out in broad daylight. Gee whiz."

Mama frowned. "Don't use such expressions, young lady."

Another ladies-don't rule: ladies don't speak in slang.

Ruth didn't care how *ladies* spoke. She enjoyed saying "gee whiz" and "spill the beans" and other popular, fun sayings. She was young, wasn't she? Did Mama expect her to speak like an old fuddy-duddy?

Dewdad put his finger to his mouth, warning Ruth not to irk her mother.

"Yes, Mama," she said, respectfully.

"Let me go check what the rooster is up to," Dewdad said. "Ruth, you need to leave for school."

"Don't forget. I expect you to act like a lady at all times," Mama reminded her.

"Yes, Mama."

Ruth followed Dewdad out of the kitchen. He slipped something in her hand. Another letter from Cécile. This day had started out beautifully. She hoped no more Phoebe bombs were aimed her way.

"Well, were there?" Maggie asked when Grams paused for a sip of coffee she'd requested from Brian.

"Were there what?" Grams asked.

"More Gothas aimed at Ruth from Phoebe?"

Grams eyebrows arched. "You can be assured Phoebe was not finished with tormenting my mother."

Maggie frowned. "I had a Phoebe when I was a little older than Great-grams. Beth Ann. She made my life miserable. In ninth grade, we were sweet on the same boy. Anthony Drennan. Beth Ann would go out of her way to make sure he paid attention to her, like Phoebe tried to do with Clinton." Maggie's frown deepened. "Girls can be petty and mean."

"Yes," Grams agreed. "You can't leave me hanging, Maggie. Who won Anthony's attention? You or Beth Ann?"

Maggie laughed. "Neither of us. We found out much later, when we all gathered back for our five-year high school reunion, that we weren't his type. He brought Jake."

"Oh my!" Grams joined in Maggie's laughter.

"I'm happy for him," Maggie said. "He and Jake are a great couple." She fell silent for a moment. At the reunion, Anthony had shared how he knew Jake was the one for him the minute they'd met. Hopefully they would have the happily-ever-after she'd expected with Cole. The happily-ever-after her great-grandparents enjoyed. "It's sweet to hear about how Ruth and Clinton met. What a charming love-at-first-sight story."

"Yes. My mother described it as such." Grams nodded knowingly toward Maggie. "Like you and Cole if I remember correctly?"

Maggie stared at her left hand, where her wedding ring used to reside, remembering. They were riding the crowded campus bus on a rainy fall day. She was damp, aggravated, and hungry. Grabbing hold of the overhead handles dangling from the bus's ceiling, she'd lost her footing and lurched backward into the person standing behind her. She regained her balance, turned to apologize, and found herself staring into the most gorgeous blue-green eyes. The electricity ramped up between them, matching the lightning streaking through the darkened sky. "Hi. I'm Cole," he'd said. "Hi. I'm Maggie," she'd replied. Later the same day, fate found them both at Kerkhoff's, each trying to claim that last croissant. They agreed to share it—and dinner—that evening. When she'd told her girlfriends, they'd declared she'd experienced her own rom-com "meet cute."

She and Cole had been together ever since. Until . . .

"Clinton and Ruth's love-at-first-sight lasted." Maggie couldn't keep the bitterness from creeping into her voice. "They were together until, according to the vows, death do us part."

"Death sometimes doesn't end the vow." Grams stared at her left hand, on which her plain gold wedding ring gleamed.

Maggie throat thickened. "Oh, Grams."

"Menus?" Brian asked.

Maggie welcomed the interruption of the emotional moment.

"I hope you're catching a little bit more of the story?" Grams asked.

Brian grinned. "Something about unchaperoned walks with a boy?"

"Old-fashioned and sweet, don't you think?" Maggie asked.

"Gee whiz, I do," Brian answered with a teasing manner.

Maggie giggled. "Yes, Grams is spilling the beans about her mama, isn't she?"

"You two are clever," Grams commented in a lilting voice.

"Your dinner will be served in a few minutes." Brian said.

"Thanks." Maggie outstretched her hand. "We have time for another letter."

Grams handed one to her. Maggie could feel it had more heft to it. "What's enclosed in this one?"

"Something special."

The enclosed photograph of Cécile drew an "oooh" of admiration from Maggie. "Grams, she is darling!" After admiring Cécile for a few more seconds, Maggie focused her attention on the letter.

> *18, bis Avenue d 'Italie*
> *Paris 75013*
> *France*
>
> *3 September 1919*

My Sweet Ruffis, (for that is what your dear Dewdad call you, no?)

I have received your letter and still I laugh. Your Herkimer must be the sight. You remind me of when living as a young child in Quimper, a farmer ask me to find a lost rooster. Chickens are nice but roosters can chase you. Like you I am afraid of the pecking of the rooster to hurt me. But I didn't want to let the farmer know that I feared them so I help him but not really. Don't you think chickens look silly? Don't they? They walk funny. You are brave to battle Herkimer. Bonne chance!

Maggie laughed. "That Herkimer. I love how both Cécile and Ruth have rooster stories to share!"

"Yes. My mama grew to love Herkimer. They shared quite a bit together."

Something in the way Grams's voice broke a tiny bit made Maggie worry. "This won't be another story in which the dog—in this case, the rooster—dies?"

Grams waved her hand. "You will learn all in good time, dear."

Maggie tried to push away her concern. She returned her attention to Cécile's letter.

At what age, you, American girls do you go alone without parents? It is not the custom here for a girl to walk alone. She must stay with her parents till she marries. That custom is felling down! Many girls who work far from home start on the morning and come back home in the evening. When I go out, Maman is certain that I always go with Lulu.

Do you like to dance? In Paris the Parisians are very fond of fox trot, one step, and boston too. I go to my ex-school to learn how to dance and to sing. I dance with my friend Ninette, we are only girls, and we should learn new dances, fox trot, on step, boston. Now we learn polka, skating steps and an American dance we call the Quadrille American which is danced by eight persons composed by 4 couples. I don't frequent the dancing hall, because Maman says I am too young. When I shall be 18 years old she has promised to let me dance.

Brown are your eyes I believe? Mine are dark green blue near the eyeball and green and yellow all around. Like this, I draw here for you. Maman says they are not so green as I picture. Imagine a round made of gray-blue-green-yellow. My brother Lulu's eyes are same as mine. I long to in your next letter to see your face for the first time. Me, my dear, when I was young, I was a big fleshy girl and now I seem long because I have become so thin.

But I send a picture for you and so you must send me yours now with no delay. Au revoir, mon petite amie.

With kisses, Cécile

Maggie studied the illustration Cécile had drawn of her eye. "She obviously had artistic talent."

"Yes," Grams agreed. "You'll find many of Cécile's letters have sketches in them. She enjoyed art."

"Did she become an artist?" Maggie impatience burned. She wanted to learn more about Cécile's life. "What career did she have? Did she find her own Clinton to marry and raise a family with?"

Grams's guise clouded over. "We'll get to that."

A foreboding chill chased over Maggie. Did Grams expression bode a tragic outcome?

She dismissed the portentous feeling "It's funny how Cécile and Ruth are experiencing many of the same things in their lives. Roosters." She laughed. "And, boys and dancing. I guess coming of age is the same no matter what your culture is—or what era you might live in."

"That's why Cécile's letters are timeless, I think."

"I agree." Maggie leaned back. "Tell me more, Grams."

"Gee whiz. I'd love to."

They both laughed.

CHAPTER TWELVE
RUTH

Ruth found Clinton waiting for her around the curve for their walk to school. He reached for her books. "Let me carry these."

"Thanks." Why not? According to Phoebe's gossip, he carried them for her each day, didn't he?

"What's that?" Clinton asked, pointing at the envelope in Ruth's hand.

"It's my latest letter from Cécile."

"Would you read it to me?" Clinton said.

Ruth thought how nice it would be to share Cécile with her only friend in Oakland. She opened the envelope and gasped. "Oh my! It's a picture of her. I've never seen one before. She's beautiful." She held it out for Clinton to see.

"She's a looker," Clinton agreed. "I wouldn't say she's got anything over you."

Her pulse roared in her ears. How could he even think she matched Cécile's looks? Her family had been the only ones who had ever complimented her appearance, and they didn't count. To distract from her blushing over his compliment, Ruth turned her attention to the letter. "I wonder what news Cécile has for me."

She skipped over the salutation addressing her as *My Sweet Ruffis*. Cécile's comments about requiring chaperones when with boys served as another coincidence in their lives. *At what age, you, American girls do you go alone without parents? It is not the custom here for a girl to walk alone.*

Clinton interrupted her reading. "That's interesting. How does your mama feel about us walking together, alone?"

Ruth suspected he asked because he'd heard the gossip about them. She doubted his mama cared as did hers. How unfair that boys didn't have to worry about *their* reputations. A boy could kiss a girl right in public yet only the girl would be talked about.

"She and Dewdad gave me permission. They're not *that* old-fashioned." At least Dewdad wasn't.

"I'm glad."

"Me too."

Ruth finished reading Cecile's letter by the time they arrived at the schoolyard. She survived the dragging school day by replaying Clinton's compliment and daydreaming about dancing with him at Cotillion.

On the walk home from school, Phoebe and her friends Winnie and Margaret followed behind Ruth and Clinton.

"Clinton," Phoebe called.

To Ruth's aggravation, he stopped for the girls to catch up.

"Are you going to be at Cotillion?" Phoebe asked. "I hope so."

Winnie and Margaret giggled.

"Nope, I won't." He glanced at Ruth.

She tried to keep her disappointment from showing.

"I hope you change your mind." Phoebe eyes danced with flirting. "We'll miss you." She dropped back to walk with Winnie and Margaret, and all three of them giggled.

"Come on." Clinton took off, and Ruth stretched her legs to keep pace. By the time they reached the cutoff to his house, the three girls were far behind.

"About Cotillion." Clinton avoided Ruth's gaze. "I didn't want to say my real reasons in front of Phoebe. I don't have a suit or the money. Otherwise," he looked straight at her, "I would be there."

His honesty touched Ruth. "I'll miss you." She meant it more than Clinton could know.

∞∞

Standing in front of her pedestal mirror, Ruth slipped out of her school dress and into her Cotillion one. The reflection could not possibly be Ruth Calderhead, all grown-up and wearing such a beautiful dress.

What would Jesse's opinion be, seeing her gussied-up? He would have teased her, for sure, yet in an admiring way, she bet. A complicated flood of happiness and sadness rushed through her. She had a future ahead, but Jesse lay in that cemetery back home without one. All because . . .

"Well, what do you think?" Mama stared admiringly at her in the mirror.

Ruth turned and wrapped her arms around her mama. "Thank you! It's gorgeous."

"It is! You are!" Mama gave her a slight hug before disengaging. "Let's not wrinkle it."

Ruth sat patiently while her mama braided her hair and pinned it on top of her head. Dewdad had polished her Sunday shoes, and when she slipped them on, she felt transformed into a princess on her way to a ball. Opal and Mable oohed and aahed. Florabelle clapped.

"I wish Papa could see you," Mama said.

"Me too," Ruth agreed.

If only Clinton could, too. Remembering he wouldn't be there robbed a little of the glow.

Dewdad spun her around, whistling. "You're quite the beauty, Ruth Calderhead. If your mama will allow, I would love to arrange a photography session for you. We could send pictures to your papa and to Cécile."

"Could we, Mama? Cécile has been begging me for a picture. She sent me one in her last letter. I haven't even had a chance to show you!" Ruth ran to get the letter and pulled out the picture. Everyone repeated their oohing and aahing, this time for Cécile.

Mama agreed to the photography appointment. "Ruth, you'll wear your Cotillion dress for it."

Ruth rushed to give her mother a grateful hug. Mama laughed and held her at arm's length. "Be careful, daughter. Don't wrinkle your frock."

With goodbyes from Mama and her sisters ringing in her ears, Ruth left with Dewdad, who drove her to the school in his shiny Chevrolet. She couldn't wait to write Cécile all about Cotillion, her dress, and the dancing. Cécile would love to hear about the dancing!

"Knock 'em dead, Ruffis," Dewdad said, pulling into the school driveway.

"Thanks." Ruth exited the car, careful not to trip in all her finery. Her feet hardly touched the school steps. Maybe Cotillion without Clinton wouldn't be so terrible.

Her optimism quickly evaporated.

The students were gathering in the large lunchroom. Ruth stood alone against the wall, wishing that she could turn invisible. She had heard the term wallflower before, and now she was living it.

Phoebe and her friends stared at her, whispering. Ruth glanced at Phoebe's dress and at her own, confident hers matched Phoebe's fancy one. They could snicker and stare all they wanted.

Miss Newton rang a bell officially starting Cotillion. "Attention, attention, ladies and gentlemen." She introduced the leaders, Mr. and Mrs. Preston Emerson.

"Form two lines. Boys on the right, girls on the left," Mr. Emerson directed.

After their shuffling, Ruth's heart leapt. Clinton stood across the room, lined up with the boys. He *had* come. He had slicked back his hair and wore a vaguely familiar-looking black suit. He gave a slight wave and she nodded back.

Mr. Emerson instructed the boys on the proper way to request a dance. Mrs. Emerson instructed the girls on the proper way to accept the request.

"Boys, invite the girl across from you," Mr. Emerson called out.

Ruth's hopefulness of being Clinton's partner immediately drained away. Directly across from her stood pipsqueak Horace! He didn't hide his disappointment about being her partner, either. With a slight scowl, he bowed and asked for a dance. Ruth curtsied and accepted.

A sickening wave of jealousy coursed through her when she realized Clinton was bowing in front of her rotten enemy. Phoebe accepted with a curtsy, shooting a triumphant glance at Ruth. Clinton straightened back up, smiling. Ruth's stomach lurched. He was *smiling*. At *Phoebe*.

After Mr. and Mrs. Emerson instructed them on the box step, Miss Newton cranked the Victrola again and again to replay "The Merry Widow." Horace kept his head down, focused on his feet's movements, making Ruth hover even taller over him. Ruth smelled a mix of pickles and peanut butter on his breath when he counted the beat aloud: one and two and three and four. Their feet became tangled. Her huge right foot came down on top of his left one.

"Ouch!" His head jerked up, and he gave her a dirty look.

"Sorry." Tears collected in Ruth's eyes. She wished she were anywhere but this dumb Cotillion.

When the music ended, Mr. Emerson announced, "Time to switch partners to the right."

Ruth backed away from Horace, hoping to exit this misery before catching anyone's attention. A tap on her shoulder stopped her. She expected to find Miss Newton glaring at her. To her surprise, Clinton stood before her. "Miss Calderhead, may I have this dance?"

A million butterflies burst loose inside her. "Yes, Mr. Carlock," she replied, tipping her head up.

Clinton bowed slightly. Ruth curtsied. He held out his hand, and she took it, trembling at his touch. While they waited for the next instruction, it was Ruth's time to gloat. Phoebe was now partnered with Horace.

Mr. and Mrs. Emerson demonstrated the waltz, dancing to "The Blue Danube." Ruth's breath caught at the strains of the melody. It brought the memory of Mama and Pa waltzing to this tune in their kitchen back in Colorado Springs. Pa had saved up money for months to buy a phonograph for their anniversary gift. Mama had been surprised. Pa had only enough money to buy one record, and he had chosen "The Blue Danube." After a special anniversary dinner and waltz between them, Mama waltzed with Jesse while Pa danced with Ruth.

Miss Newton began the music for the students to dance. Clinton whispered, "Are you ready?"

"Yes." She closed away her old memory to create a new one of swaying in Clinton's arms.

His hand rested lightly on Ruth's back. They glided across the floor. Clinton counted "one, two, three, one, two, three" to keep them in time. His breath smelled minty, another improvement over horrible Horace. When the music ended, Clinton bowed and Ruth curtsied. She wondered if the butterflies would ever calm in her stomach.

Miss Newton announced, "Our next dance will be a folk reel to 'Bonnie Lassie,' a Scottish song."

The group started off slowly while they learned the movements, and soon they were whirling around, passing each other in a zigzag and changing partners when their hands touched. According to legend, at the end of the reel, the boy's partner became his "bonnie lassie"—his girl. Ruth sent up a quick prayer to be Clinton's bonnie lassie.

At the end of the reel, she was breathing hard and not only from the fast dancing. Her prayer had been answered: she stood side by side with Clinton. Phoebe again had ended up with Horace. Ruth couldn't have planned a better revenge.

Mr. and Mrs. Emerson guided them through different scenarios in which they followed the dictates of good manners: the boy walking on the right of the girl, pulling out the seat for her, and opening the door for her to pass through first. By the end of her first Cotillion lesson, Ruth believed her accomplishments would make Mama proud.

Mr. Emerson dismissed them. "Ladies and gentleman, we are concluded for this month. Next month we shall continue molding you into proper ladies and gentlemen. Young men, please escort your ladies from the room."

Ruth filed out of the lunchroom with Clinton walking on her right. Phoebe and Horace were in front of them. Phoebe tossed her head back to glare. The girl's catlike squint made Ruth feel as if she were a mouse being stalked.

Ruth straightened up and stood tall. She would be no one's mouse, especially Phoebe. More trouble might be coming from that girl. Ruth didn't care. She, not Phoebe, was Clinton's Bonnie Lassie. It was divine providence.

Dewdad was parked in front of the school. Clinton opened the front passenger door for Ruth.

"How about a ride home, son?" Dewdad offered.

"That would be swell, Mr. Addison," he said, relieved. "I'd hate to get something on this fine suit. It took some slick talking to get Mama to accept it from you."

Ruth stared at Dewdad, whose mustache was twitching. He had made sure Clinton had a suit. She would have bet a kiss on Herkimer's beak that it had been Dewdad who'd paid Clinton's registration too. Pa would have done the same if he'd been here.

Ruth remained quiet during the ride. Her mood flip-flopped between the enjoyment over dancing with Clinton and sadness over not having Pa and Jesse here to share her special night. Her secret robbed her happiness, always. Of course, it should, shouldn't it?

Dewdad braked at the road leading to Clinton's house. Clinton hopped out and leaned into the front passenger window. "Bye, Ruth."

"Bye." Ruth tried to put all she felt toward him into that one little word.

The sway of the car around the curve reminded her of swaying in Clinton's arms. While his reflection in the passenger mirror grew smaller and smaller, he grew larger and larger in Ruth's heart.

CHAPTER THIRTEEN
MAGGIE

"She knew right then, didn't she? That Clinton was the one for her." Maggie's moment of instant attraction to Cole flashed into her mind again. A pang of sadness chased it from her thoughts.

"Remember, the course of true love never runs smoothly."

Grams's quoting of that old saying aggravated Maggie. "Happily ever after is a fairy tale for some people, Grams." She felt an immediate twinge of remorse at her sharp retort. She craned her neck to check for Brian. Where was that flight attendant when she needed him?

He appeared in a few minutes with their dinners. Grams requested another cup of coffee while Maggie stuck to water, aware again her beverage choice did not go unnoticed. She would be in the throes of cross-examination if her mother were sitting beside her. At least her grandmother showed patience.

They ate in quiet. Maggie moved the food around on her place, feelings of discontent about the state of her life teeming within her. At least she did truly love history and her job. That provided some consolation. Yet it also provided trepidation she'd turn out like her parents, with her career being everything and her child suffering. She rested her hand on her tiny baby bump, promising she would not let that happen.

Brian appeared to collect the dinner trays, and Maggie was happy once again for the interruption. Eyeing her full plate, Brian offered to server her alternatives. "Could I get you crackers? A sandwich perhaps?"

She shrugged. "I don't eat much when I fly. Thanks, anyway."

"You're welcome." Taking Grams's plate, Brian added, "I guess you're anxious to get back to your story. Notice I didn't ask if you needed ear-buds or help with the media system. You two are providing your own entertainment."

"We are," Grams agreed.

While Grams thumbed through the box to select the next letter, Maggie thought how her great-grandmother and she shared the experience of parents living apart. Her parents' reconciliation hadn't brought her much peace of mind. She hoped Ruth would find peace, if her parents reunited the family. Her impatience was getting the best of her in wanting to know how the events played out. "Grams, did Ruth's parents—your grandparents—reconcile?"

Grams paused in looking through the box's content. "You'd learn in good time, my dear. Charles and Dolly did experience much sad-ness, and they went through emotionally tough times. They longed for understanding of why they lost Jesse." Grams pulled out another letter and scanned it. "Yes, this is the one in which Cécile talked about the game she called 'weejee,' spelled differently than how we are used to seeing it. She drew an illustration of the board, and it looks similar. Have you played Ouija?"

"When younger, at sleepovers. We played Ouija and Magic Eightball to look into our futures." Maggie laughed. "Remember that crush of mine, Anthony? I asked the Ouija Board if he would like me. The board spelled out *N—O*. How right it was! I didn't realize that game existed back in Great-grams's time."

Grams gave Maggie the letter. "You will find Cécile's description of playing it interesting. And, look at this old postcard of the Louvre she sent, lighted in celebration of the end of the War."

Intrigued, Maggie first studied the drawing of the "weejee" and then the postcard. The thrill of touching the past through Cécile again sent a flush of excitement through her history teacher self. Settling back, she read the letter.

18, bis Avenue d 'Italie
Paris 75013
France

12 September 1919

Dearest little Ruthie,

I write you to-day because I wish my letter will arrive as soon possible to present you with my better wishes of health and many others for your birthday. I may write another before your big day arrives!

When Gothas and Berthas were bombarding our city, we were not numerous at school and my friend Ninette and I we enjoyed ourselves very much with the weejee game. When you play, you must be scrupulous and patient! And people say the box will advance and the match will indicate the letter or the letters, if you desire to words or sentences, numbers, yes and no. Ninette and I tried to get an answer, but the box stayed at the same place after an half hour waiting. I forget to tell; "Don't put your hands heavily on the box." When we finish playing, we would prepare our packages that we sent to the soldiers on the battle line during the bombardment of the city. We sent rintintin, a protection from bombs, shrapnel, etc.

Yesterday, the town-hall was lighted, because our city has received the War Cross. To-day the king of Spain is arrived. From the window of the class we have seen a French regiment pass, coming from the station he where he has landed. I send you a view of a great shop of Paris, the "Louvre" lighted up for the day of peace, no, the night of peace. Do you see the entrance of the Metro, that is

an underground railway, the tube of London, and the metro and
Nord-sud of Paris that is what I will use when I begin work. From
your loving friend, who sends you in her letter as many kisses as
you have years in your life.

Cécile

P.S. Do you like chewing gum? I like very much the flavor of
California fruit.

"Oh, her postscript is adorable." Maggie reached in her bag for a pack of
Juicy Fruit. "Makes me want to enjoy a piece of gum." She offered Grams
a piece, who declined. "I wrote a report in fourth grade on the history of
chewing gum. The best part about that project was Mom allowing me
to sample quite a bit of the product I was researching." Maggie popped a
stick in her mouth. "Gum became popular during Ruth and Cécile's era,"
she mumbled through her efforts to soften up the Juicy Fruit.

"When a child, receiving chewing gum in my stocking at Christmas
was considered a treat." Grams chuckled. "Such small items meant a
great deal then."

"What can you share with me about the *rintintin* she mentioned?"
Maggie referred back to the letter. "She writes that she and her friend
sent it in the packages to soldiers protecting Paris from the bombings."

"Ah. Rintintin. That's quite a story. The tiny yarn dolls were considered good-luck charms in Paris at that time. They were called Nenette
and Rintintin. They had to be given, not bought, for the protection to
work. Also, the yarn connecting the two dolls must never be broken or
their power to protect would be lost."

"Isn't Rin Tin Tin the name of a famous dog?" Maggie asked.

"Yes, spelled a little differently. An American soldier rescued two
German shepherd pups during World War One in Paris and named
them Nenette and Rin Tin Tin, three words, after the dolls. Rin Tin
Tin became quite the famous dog in America. His descendant became
a mascot during World War Two when the K9 Corps got started."

"How fascinating. These letters paint such a vivid picture of the time."
Maggie folded the letter carefully. "Cécile writes that she sends 'better
wishes' for Ruth's health. You've described how Ruth's secret—whatever
that may be—caused her much turmoil."

"Jesse's death proved difficult for Ruth to accept, for many reasons."
Grams's eyes were full of pain. "We will get to that later."

Maggie knew not to hurry a storyteller. "Cécile also wished Ruth
happy birthday. Was this a happy birthday for her?"

"It had its ups and downs. They visited Idora Park, their era's version
of a Six Flags amusement park. My mother told me all about that day."

"Now tell me." Maggie relaxed in her seat, enjoying her gum and
listening.

CHAPTER FOURTEEN
RUTH

The day would be just another day, Ruth told herself.

She entered the kitchen to find oatmeal simmering on the stove and cinnamon French toast frying on the griddle. Where was Mama? Dewdad? Anyone?

She stirred the oatmeal, flipped the toast, and checked what else needed to be set out for breakfast. Two letters and a wrapped flat box were at her place. She recognized Pa's cursive handwriting, large and bold, on one envelope. The other piece of mail was from Cécile.

They had remembered what Ruth was trying to forget.

Today, October 4th, was her birthday.

Her first birthday after Jesse's death.

Jesse would forever be her sixteen-year-old brother who loved to go barefoot, recited poetry, rode the rails like a hobo, and cried when he hunted and killed a deer. Ruth's birthdays were pushing her closer to his age. One day she would be older than her older brother.

It was never supposed to be that way.

"Happy birthday to you," Dewdad sang in his deep baritone. "Happy birthday to you. Happy birthday, dear Ruffis. Happy birthday to you."

"Thanks, Dewdad." She turned her attention to the stove to hide the tears pooling. She gave the oatmeal another stir and took up the toast.

Mama rushed into the kitchen, Florabelle on her hip. "Thanks, Ruth, for saving your birthday breakfast from burning! I didn't mean for you to cook it yourself. It took me longer than I expected to help the younger ones get dressed." She gave Ruth a quick hug and whispered in her ear, "Happy birthday from both your pa and me."

The twins ran in, yelling, "Happy birthday, Ruth!" They handed her a card illustrated with a big brown triangle and a bright yellow sun hanging in a cloudless blue sky. Pike's Peak. Ruth recognized it easily, even drawn by her five-year-old sisters. Inside they had printed their names, a few of the letters slanting in the wrong direction.

"Thanks, Opal. Thanks, Mable. I'll keep your card always." Ruth picked each up and swirled her around.

Florabelle begged, "Me too! Me too!" Ruth swung her around as well.

"How about me?" Dewdad asked.

Ruth giggled. "Hmm. I don't think I could manage that."

Dewdad tapped on his china coffee cup with the edge of his knife. "Hear ye, hear ye. In celebration of Ruth's birthday, I've planned an outing for the entire family. We're going to catch the trolley and head to Idora Park."

Ruth gasped. "Thank you! How much fun!"

Her mama echoed thanks, over Mable and Opal's excited squeals. Florabelle shouted, "Ithdora Park! Yeah!"

"Today will be a lovely day of smiling faces. Dolly, pack up a picnic lunch." Dewdad reached into his shirt pocket, pulled out bright red trolley tickets, and waved them in the air. "We are to catch the trolley at exactly eleven o'clock."

As if on cue, Herkimer crowed at the screen door.

"Sorry, Herkimer," Dewdad said. "You're not invited."

Everyone laughed.

Dewdad clanged on his china cup again. "Before anything else happens, Ruth needs to open her note from her pa."

She opened the envelope and read his note out loud.

Dear Ruth,

I hope you enjoy your 14ᵗʰ birthday. Have a wonderful day.
I wish I could be there with you all. I enjoyed the postcard
you sent. Oakland looks like a place of adventure.
Although you are growing up fast, you'll always be
my "same old Ruth."

Love, Pa

Pa hadn't said a thing about joining them in Oakland. Her tears trickled out before she could withhold them. Sniffling, Ruth picked up Cécile's letter. It would help lessen the sting of disappointment.

"Read it out loud. Read it out loud," the twins shouted.

"Maybe later," Mama said.

They would get back late from the park, and Ruth knew she couldn't wait that long. "May I read it now, Mama?"

"Read it," the twins shouted again.

"Of course. We'd love to hear it," Mama said.

When Ruth got to the part about the Gothas and Berthas, the twins asked, "Who are Gotha and Bertha?"

Her sisters were too young to hear about bombs and destruction. Ruth diverted the conversation by telling them other facts about life in Paris during the War, amazing them all at how much she'd learned from Cécile. When she got to the part about the War Cross and about the Louvre shining bright with lights, she passed around the postcard Cécile had sent.

"How interesting," Mama remarked, examining it closely.

Mama was impressed! Having Cécile be her pen pal filled Ruth with pride.

After Mama passed the postcard to Dewdad, she pointed to the gift on the table. "It's time for you to open your gift from pa and me. We hope you'll like it. Dewdad suggested it."

Ruth's insides tingled. She tugged on the ribbon and carefully unfolded the wrapping to find the set of white linen stationery with her name printed in script on each sheet. "Mama, thank you so much!" She couldn't wait to fill up the clean, fresh pages with her news. "I have so much to write to Cécile and Pa."

Mama's smile faded at the mention of writing Pa, convincing Ruth she must. She'd tell Pa how much Mama missed him. He'd come if she told him that, and he and Mama would work everything out. They would all be a family like they used to be. Except without Jesse. Her heart ached at that truth.

When Dewdad clanged his knife on his cup for the third time, Ruth chased her grief away, although she knew it would eventually return.

Dewdad winked at her. "Ruth, help your mama pack us a picnic. I'll collect midmorning eggs. I don't want the birthday girl to get pecked by an ornery rooster on her special day."

Ruth called out to him. "Make sure Herkimer is locked behind that fence to stay safe while we're gone."

"You're right about that." Dewdad stroked his mustache, his forehead wrinkled. "The last thing we need is another run-in with the Givenses."

Mama became a whirling dervish while she prepared for the outing. Ruth knew Pa would have loved to come. If only he could be there. If only. . .

So many if-only longings.

Ruth's stomach soon became a whirling dervish too.

⌀⌀

Ruth helped the twins and Florabelle board the crowded trolley. Dewdad gave Ruth a quarter to buy five tickets for five rides and an extra nickel for carnival games. When the loud clacking of the trolley's wheels slowed to a stop, Ruth jumped off. Dewdad helped Mama step off while Ruth helped the twins and Florabelle.

Ruth's eyes widened at the sight she beheld. Cupolas topped the entrance to Idora Park, complete with waving flags. Her pulse quickened at the beat of the music from the bandstand, and she could almost taste the cotton candy and caramel corn, whose sweet aromas filled the air. How Jesse would have loved this craziness!

Dewdad pointed toward the sign that listed all the shows for the day. Ruth's jaw dropped. Standing next to it was Clinton! She had been making mental notes on what to include in her letter to Cécile about this special day. Clinton's surprise appearance would definitely be a headline!

He approached them, flicking his hair off his forehead. "Hey, fancy running into you here on your birthday." He winked.

"Fancy that," Ruth replied with a grin. She glanced at Mama, whose jaw had tightened in that tell-tale way it always did when displeased.

"We're going to stake out a good spot for our picnic. Once we get settled, you two may go ride some rides," Dewdad said.

Mama's jaw tightened even more.

Ruth helped select a picnic table next to the carousel and across from the bandstand. When Dewdad took the girls to the carousel, Ruth begged her mama to let her go with Clinton to the rides. She thought she'd faint from holding her breath, waiting for an answer.

Her mother nodded. "You must be back here no later than an hour. Remember, being at an amusement park does not excuse you from acting like a lady."

"Yes, Mama." Ruth's respectful reply projected no indication of the fireworks exploding inside her.

"And, Ruth, I expect you to use one of your tickets on something of cultural value."

"Yes, Mama."

Ruth waved at Dewdad and her sisters when she and Clinton passed the carousel. They stopped at a racetrack-themed miniature car ride inside an arched pavilion. She hopped into a miniature car, and Clinton climbed into the one next to her. She hung on while steering her car on an exhilarating ride of quick turns, ups and downs, and long stretches of high speed. By the end, her throat burned from screaming.

On the way to the Helter-Skelter, Ruth kept talking about the cars. "I want to learn how to drive a real one."

"That I would love to see." Clinton winked. "I've never seen a girl drive."

Anger rose in her. "Then I'll be the first one."

He laughed.

She shrugged off his reaction. Her mind was set. She *was* going to learn to drive, and when she passed him on the road, she'd blow the horn and whiz on by.

"Come on. There's the Helter-Skelter." She walked away, leaving him to catch up with her. They climbed up inside the high tower. When her turn came, she slid down the outside slide, hands up and screams erupting. Clinton landed behind her.

"What's happening over there?" Ruth dragged Clinton with her toward the crowd gathering at a tent. A large woman was singing in a high soprano voice. Ruth was intrigued with her thick makeup, her cheeks highlighted by round splotches of rouge on each. She wore a long evening gown, and her white gloves stretched past her elbows. A silver tiara sparkled in her pinned-up, obviously dyed red hair.

"She must be an opera singer," Ruth whispered to Clinton.

"She's some singer, that's for sure," he whispered back. "But, what in the world is she saying?"

"I think it's Italian," Ruth replied. "My teacher last year played a record of the famous opera singer Enrico Caruso singing 'O Sole Mio,' and he sang in Italian. Mrs. Castleberry said a lot of opera is sung in Italian."

Ruth covered her ears when the singer held a high pitch to end the song. She mouthed, "Ouch" to Clinton, who grimaced back. With the last note reverberating in the air, Ruth tugged Clinton's arm. "I've something cultural to report to Mama. Let's have some more *real* fun."

"Wait a minute." Ruth waited while Clinton shoved his right hand into the corresponding pocket of his pants. "I have a birthday gift for you."

Ruth's stomach fluttered. "For me?"

"It's not much. Before you got here, I had it made at a jewelry pressing booth." He pulled out a chain with a flat metal medallion hanging from it. "I had them press into it *C C*. It's your pen pal's initials, and . . ."

"Yours too." Ruth took the necklace from Clinton and ran a fingertip over the pressed initials before placing it around her neck. "Thank you. It's the most perfect gift. I'll wear it always, Clinton."

He flushed beet red, and not from the heat or the amusement-park fun, Ruth knew. She leaned in and gave him a quick peck on the cheek before turning away quickly to hide her own blushing. "Come on. Let's explore," she said.

They walked past rows of entertaining acts, each stranger than the next. Ruth laughed at Clinton's amazement over Mademoiselle Marzella and her cockatoos. An array of multicolored birds perched on the woman's outstretched arms. One kept asking, "Where's my cracker?" Another burped and said, "Excuse me. Sorry. Excuse me."

"I like my homing pigeons better," Clinton said.

"Maybe I'll get to meet your birds?" Ruth pressed her lips together, stunned she'd practically invited herself to Clinton's home.

"Come anytime." He acted as if he meant it.

"I'd like that." Had they made a date? Her hand touched the medallion. Was he now her boyfriend?

They continued walking through the park, coming eventually to a black velvet tent with a sign that read "Ouija Board Readings: Let the mysterious talking board answer your questions and predict your future."

"Look! That's what Cécile wrote about in my birthday letter!" Ruth stopped to read the placard that said, "Ouija answers all questions. One ticket per question." She pointed to the word *Ouija*. "Cécile spelled it *w-e-e-j-e-e*, though. She and her friend played it when they had to stay inside while bombs were being dropping on Paris. Imagine that! She said to keep your fingers lightly on the box and not to force it to move. You want to do it?"

"I'm not sure,"

Ruth didn't hesitate. "I'm going." She gave the woman a ticket and went inside the tent. A second later, Clinton joined her, his clenched hands expressing his uncertainty.

The gypsy waved her hands across the board, overacting like a silent film star. In what Ruth assessed to be a fake accent, the woman explained, "To obtain the best results, it is important that you concentrate your minds upon the matter in question. If you ask ridiculous questions and laugh at the Ouija, you will call disruptive influences into the process." She waved her arms again.

Ruth half expected the woman to say "abracadabra."

The woman continued, "The Ouija is a great mystery. It's important to mention that the success of your Ouija séance hinges on your total belief in the process. Now, place your hand lightly on this part of the all-knowing, all-seeing instrument of divinity, like so."

After she demonstrated the proper hand placement, Ruth placed hers where the lady indicated.

"Now, ask the talking board your question," said the woman. "It will move to spell out your answer."

"Must I say my question out loud?" Ruth asked.

The gypsy woman shrugged. "No, you may ask it silently."

Even though she suspected the game to be fake, Ruth posed the question that weighed heavily on her mind. *Will my family ever be together again?* She maintained a light touch on the instrument, and it began moving.

As it did, the gypsy woman called out the letters. "*G-O-B-A-C-K.*" Ruth's mouth went dry.

The instrument stopped moving. The gypsy woman quickly scrawled the message on a slip of paper and handed it to Ruth.

"What does it mean?" Ruth asked.

"Only you can interpret based on your question." The woman shrugged. "Secret, secret, secret. You kept your question secret."

Secret, secret, secret. The tent started to close in on Ruth. *Go back.* Was that the answer? Should she go back and get Pa? Go back to Jesse's grave?

Her breathing grew shallow, leaving her dizzy. What was wrong with her? She jumped up and fumbled with the tent's curtain to escape the darkness.

"Ruth, wait up!"

Ignoring Clinton's call, she kept on walking. The world around her smeared into a blur. *Go back, go back.* She shook her head, trying to clear the words from her brain.

The glint of the sun bounced off a row of mirrors in a variety of shapes and sizes. People crowded in front of them, laughing at their distorted images. Ruth caught her reflection in one of the mirrors. It made her look short and squatty. She caught her reflection in the next mirror, which stretched her neck like a giraffe's and her legs like basketball poles.

The crowd's laughter echoed loudly in her ears. Were the people laughing and leering at her? Were they seeing her as the liar that she was? Multiple images of herself stared back at her from the left to the right, as they had done that night when she sat at her vanity and got lost inside the mirrors. Left, right, left, right. *Go back. Go back.*

"Ruth!" Clinton roughly spun her around. "Are you all right?"

She stepped back from him. "Yes, yes. I'm fine."

"You scared me there for a minute." He frowned. "What's going on?"

It's a secret, a secret, a secret.

"Nothing. Let's go back to the picnic. I'm starving. Last one there's a rotten egg!" Ruth took off, snaking her way through the noisy, laughing crowd. She checked if Clinton followed and slowed for him to catch up. On their return to the picnic, he didn't say anything else. Neither did she.

CHAPTER FIFTEEN
MAGGIE

Grams opened the box and pushed the button to make the drawer come ajar. She pulled out the medallion necklace. "Ruth cherished this necklace."

Maggie held it and rubbed her fingertips against the initials. "Poor Ruth." Maggie's throat constricted. "Her panic attacks she suffered must have frightened her. Will she return to Colorado Springs? You have to tell me now, Grams!"

Grams shook her head. "I can't skip ahead, Maggie. You must hear it all."

"I have something in common with your mother," Maggie admitted. "Panic attacks." She had never told anyone except her doctor. Until now.

Ever since she had found out about Cole, she had suffered from such intense anxiety that at times couldn't breathe or even speak. She'd experienced the same anxiety when her dad cheated on her mom and disappeared from her life.

"Maggie, dear. I am sorry. I hope you are taking care of yourself through all this stress."

Grams's gentleness encouraged Maggie to announce her pregnancy, but she didn't trust she was ready to speak the words out loud. Like Ruth, she carried her secret locked deep inside. For now.

She changed the subject. "Ruth did seem to enjoy most of the day at Idora Park. I wonder where Cécile visited on holidays and special occasions."

Grams's eyes lit up. "Remember, she went to Quimper."

"Oh, right. We're visiting there."

"Yes. Cécile's hometown was in Brittany. She wrote a letter to Ruth about the traditions of the town and the native costumes. Let me find it." Grams thumbed through the letters. "She even drew a picture of a costume, which Ruth later copied to make a Halloween costume for herself."

"They celebrated Halloween in 1919? Trick-or-treating like we do now?" Maggie asked.

"Not exactly. Mostly they went to parties and had costume parades. Not trick-or-treating door to door in a neighborhood. However, Cécile hadn't heard of such a holiday. In France, Halloween is not celebrated like it is in America."

"Yes. A friend of mine who lived in Paris for a while told me that her French friends didn't exactly comprehend our traditions." The colors in the sketch of the letter Grams shared were vivid despite the age. "Cécile was such a good artist." She read the first lines and laughed. "She is scolding Ruth for telling the truth. Cécile *is* a pretty girl!"

She read on.

18, bis Avenue d 'Italie
Paris 75013
France

20 September 1919

Ma chere petite Ruth,

By your receipt of my letter you will be fourteen! I hope you received my other letter and this one before your big day! I want to scold you, darling. You write you think that I am a very pretty girl: you mistake! My face on the paper is always prettier than in life. In French who have a word "photogenque" which means: who is prettier on a picture than really. So, why don't you send me your photograph? I love you very, very much, but, when I shall see your face, I shall love you more than now!

Do you like my caricature of girl of Quimper, you pronounce kem-pair? In Brittany there are many native costumes. I draw you the one from my town Quimper, the small tranquil town where the Odet and Steir rivers come together. I would like you to see it one day I know you will like it. We would have crepes and cider at my auntie's house on the Odet river. My auntie has pretty faience pottery to serve which is made in Quimper.

The costume of Quimper is very pretty and is usually a gift to a girl when she marries. My maman's is very nice. The shoes are call sabots and the bonnets are called coiffes. The Quimper head-dress is smaller than in other parts of Brittany where they are great "monuments" on a woman's head. I like the embroidered aprons they are nice too. Men wear felt hats with ribbons and embroidered waistcoats. The costume is worn for pardons, when good Catholics seek forgiveness of their sins and for fetes.

Brittany is old Celtic land and has much independent thoughts of France. Many people still speak Briton language, not French, I understand it but I don't speak it. The railroad change Brittany because now people travel from Brittany to Paris and back is easy. I like because I like visiting my cousins and Aunties. Brittany is very beautiful, full of wild moorlands, wild and rocky coasts, and pretty bathing resorts and little ports.

Good-bye, dearly; I send you by this letter 1000 kisses.
Cécile

Maggie lay the letter on her tray, the closing words touching her heart. "*I send you by this letter one thousand kisses.* How quaint and lovely."

"Ruth always referred to these letters as *Kisses from Cécile.*"

"What a perfect description, Grams. If only we had Ruth's letters to Cécile. I would love to read them."

Her grandmother shrugged, a defeated look crossing her face. "As I said, I searched for Cécile's family, hoping if I located any members, perhaps one might have kept my mother's letters. Unfortunately, I didn't find any."

"That's disappointing. We do get a glimpse of what Ruth wrote through Cécile's replies. Did Ruth send Cécile a photograph?"

"Oh, yes." Grams reached for her purse and pulled from her wallet photograph of Ruth as a young girl. "Your great-grandmother told me about the day this was taken. She not only sat for her portrait, but she also had quite another run-in with her favorite pal, Herkimer."

Maggie couldn't wait to hear. "Do tell, Grams!"

CHAPTER SIXTEEN
RUTH

Ruth used eight pages of her new stationery to catch Cécile up on her life: the outing to Idora Park, her idea for the Quimper outfit for Halloween, and, of course, news about Clinton—especially about the necklace.

She wore the medallion always, making sure to tuck it under her clothing for fear Mama would make her return it. She could hear her now: "Ladies don't accept gifts from men."

After the photography session, Ruth would be ready include her photograph and send the letter on its way. She would make sure Mama sent a photograph to Pa.

Outfitted in her Cotillion dress and her hair pinned up to appear bobbed like Cécile's, Ruth patiently waited for Dewdad to finish his last sip of coffee before driving into town. A surprise awaited them in the Chevrolet. "Dewdad! Look!" She pointed at Herkimer, settled in the back seat.

"Skedaddle!" Dewdad shooed Herkimer out.

Ruth held her nose at the stench of the rooster droppings. "Why do you keep this silly old thing anyway?" she asked in a nasal voice, waving at the smell in the air.

Dewdad paused from wiping the back seat and gave Ruth a wink. "He's got spunk, Ruffis. You have to admire him for the way he struts around protecting what's his. Fencing him in all the time would strip his spirit."

"If having spirit and spunk means pecking at people, I'd rather have a rooster without either." Ruth took a rag from Dewdad and gave the front seat a vigorous wipe, careful to keep her dress clean.

"Maybe the two of you are too much alike. You and your mama argue about her dislike of the newfangled ways of girls your age. Something tells me you don't want to be penned in either."

The fact that he overheard her squabbles with her mama shamed Ruth. She handed Dewdad the cloth. "I don't mean to argue with Mama all the time. You are right, though. I don't like being penned up inside all of Mama's dos and don'ts."

"You want to be who you are, Ruth, not who someone else wants you to be." He patted her shoulder and added, "That requires time to figure out. Remember, your mama and pa love you and want what's best for you."

Ruth shrugged. What was best about Pa staying behind in Colorado Springs? What was best about Pa and her keeping their dreadful secret about Jesse's last day from Mama? Grownups didn't always do what was best. They did what they believed was easier, when it wasn't.

"Let's go, Ruffis." Dewdad removed his keys and hat from the pegs. He tugged on his driver's cap and prepared for departure. Ruth scooted into the front passenger seat and smoothed the front of her dress.

A quick check in the car door mirror assured her that her hair remained in place, all pinned up. Mama had agreed to the bobbed style after Ruth pointed out that Phoebe wore hers that way to school. Ruth hadn't shared with Mama that Phoebe arrived at school with her hair down and quickly pinned it up in the restroom before the bell rang. She wasn't exactly lying to Mama. She'd kind of left out some facts.

While Dewdad drove the automobile, whistling away to "Alexander's Ragtime Band," Ruth studied how he swiveled the steering wheel to guide the car in the direction he wanted, how he pressed his foot on the accelerator and shifted gears, and how he slowly pushed on the brake to bring the car to a stop.

She concluded driving a car was manageable. If given the opportunity, she could drive this machine. After all, she had driven the miniature cars at Idora Park without a problem! She dismissed the fact that they were affixed to a track and she couldn't lose control of them.

When Dewdad braked at the traffic light in the city square, Ruth broached the subject. "I would love to learn how to drive. Would you teach me?"

"Well, Ruffis, I guess you probably could learn." He swung the car into the parking spot in front of the photography studio. "Your mama sure wouldn't like it." He chuckled. "I've offered to teach her to drive. She flat-out rejected the idea. It's too rakish and dangerous for a woman to be behind the wheel, according to her."

"Why? Both Mama and I rode horses when we lived in Colorado Springs. Driving a car is easier and safer. It doesn't rear or buck like a horse." Ruth recognized her whininess wouldn't win Dewdad over. She shifted to a more grown-up approach. "It's the future of the country, Dewdad. You've said so yourself. That's why you're involved with the Chevrolet factory. I'm sure everyone will soon own a car. Many already do!"

Dewdad uttered his low whistle. "You do listen to my opinions. Maybe I'll let you drive us down the driveway when we get back home."

Disbelief buzzed through Ruth. "Do you mean it?"

"We'll see."

He guided the Chevrolet into the angled parking space in front of the photography studio. Ruth followed him into the studio. His keys jingled like music to her ears. This day would be one to remember always. Both a photography sitting and driving for the first time! What a day for sure.

∽∾

"Say cheese," Mr. Higginbotham called out. He stood on a wooden crate to work the camera perched high atop a tripod.

Ruth addressed the camera seriously.

"A smile, Ruth?" Mr. Higginbotham requested.

She allowed a small one. At the flash of the camera, she blinked, hoping she didn't look goofy. She'd been determined to appear grown-up, matching Cécile's demeanor in her photograph.

"I'll have these photographs ready for you in two hours," Mr. Higginbotham said.

Exiting the studio, Dewdad nodded toward Swan's. "While we're waiting let's pick out that fabric you need."

"Yes, sir!"

Ruth matched Dewdad's long stride and followed the jingle of his keys into Swan's, with the list in hand of what she needed to purchase. A costume in the traditional style of Quimper like the outfit Cécile had drawn would be perfect for the school Halloween party. Such a unique costume would spark Phoebe's jealousy. Ruth also believed it would win her first place: five dollars! She would use the money to repair the bike and get Dewdad to convince Clinton's mother to let him have it.

Clarence was measuring pink crinoline off a bolt. Creamy white satin fabric sat folded on the cutting table. "Be with you in a minute, Dewey, as soon as I finish with Mrs. Givens," he called.

Mrs. Givens glanced at Ruth. Phoebe acted as if she were invisible, which suited Ruth fine. Ruth's curiosity ate at her. What was Mrs. Givens making Phoebe out of the pink crinoline and white satin? Maybe her Halloween costume?

Phoebe and Ruth competed in arithmetic and for Clinton's attention. Ruth had the winning edge in both. Competing for the best Halloween costume could be trickier. After all, Phoebe had her licked in the looks department.

The cash register started ringing. Mrs. Givens paid Clarence for the fabrics and other items, including white satin shoes. "Size four," Phoebe said loudly when Clarence rang up the sale.

Ruth glanced at her feet, their enormity embarrassing.

Mrs. Givens handed Phoebe one of their parcels, and the two made their way toward the door. "Mr. Addison," Mrs. Givens sniffed at Dewdad.

Dewdad tipped his driving cap. "Mrs. Givens."

Phoebe said, "See you at school, Ruth."

Ruth could decipher fake from real friendliness, especially when it came to Phoebe. "See you," she answered with matching phoniness.

Clarence helped Ruth find the material she needed for her costume. After the purchase, they returned to collect the photographs.

Mr. Higginbotham handed them to Ruth. "You're pretty as a picture."

Both she and Dewdad groaned at his pun. She studied the pictures while Dewdad paid. How much she favored her brother took her breath away, though she was nowhere near as pretty as Jesse had been handsome. Still, with her hair pinned up in the bob and with how tall she'd grown, if Jesse were alive, they could have been mistaken for twins. If he could see his tomboy sister all dressed up, ladylike, he'd laugh his head off.

She missed him. She missed Pa. She missed how things used to be. She hoped Pa would be impressed with her photograph. Would he think she looked like the same old Ruth? Or more grown?

She and Dewdad returned to Swan's. At the postal counter, Ruth inserted one of her photographs into the envelope containing Cécile's letter, along with maps and gum they'd bought at Idora Park.

"All these letters back and forth from France make my job more interesting," Clarence joked.

"They make my life more interesting," Ruth replied.

"Clarence, I have another letter for you to post." Dewdad pulled an envelope from his vest pocket, inserted a photograph of Ruth into it, and sealed it. When he turned it over, Ruth recognized it was addressed in Mama's handwriting to Pa.

Her imagination ran wild. What had Mama written? Was she asking Pa to move here to be with them? Would he answer by appearing at the front door, shouting, "Where are my girls?"

The anticipation set her spirits flying.

The ride home was a quiet one, with Ruth deep in thought about Mama's letter to Pa. When Dewdad turned off the road into the driveway, he braked. "Ruffis, are you ready to give it a try?"

"I'm ready!" Ruth leapt from the car and ran to the driver's side. She stretched her posture straight and positioned her hands on the steering wheel like she'd seen Dewdad hold it. The hum of the engine vibrated, giving her a feeling of power.

Dewdad took off his cap and stuck it on her head. "For good luck."

Ruth tugged on its brim. "What do I do first?"

"Push in the clutch with your left foot," Dewdad instructed, "and slowly give it some gas with your right foot while letting the clutch out."

Ruth held her breath, following his instructions. The automobile lurched forward, and she let out a little yelp of panic. "It's moving! What do I do?"

"Give it a little gas while you're easing up on the clutch."

The automobile jerked forward again, and Ruth's stomach lurched with it. They sped down the driveway toward where the chicken coop stood.

"I need to stop! How do I brake?" Ruth asked, her body taut with trepidation.

"Remove your foot from the gas and stomp on the brake."

Ruth stomped the brake, her leg muscle straining.

"Brake harder!" Dewdad yelled.

She did. The tires burned against the gravel, and dust and chips of rocks flew. Herkimer squawked and flew up in a rage against the windshield. Dewdad covered his face with his hands.

With Ruth's screams filling the air, the automobile collided with the henhouse. The sudden stop propelled Ruth to within an inch of the windshield. Dewdad's cap had slid down her forehead. Peering from under its brim, she was eye to beady eye with Herkimer, who had landed on top of the car's hood.

"Oh, my," Ruth whispered breathlessly.

Dewdad viewed the damage.

"Oh my," he echoed.

Ruth removed the cap and surveyed the scene in front of her, her breathing accelerating. The side of the henhouse where the automobile was lodged had collapsed. Hens and eggs were scattered, and feathers floated through the air.

"Maybe learning to drive wasn't such a great idea?" Ruth offered in a trembly voice. "I hope your car isn't ruined?"

Without a word, Dewdad exited the car. With his handkerchief, he wiped the egg yolk from the hood. Herkimer strutted around brawking as if he were counting the hens in his harem and making sure none of them were lost. Ruth hoped so too. She scrambled from the car to the sight of her mother standing on the porch, hand to mouth and eyes blazing.

Mama's look at Dewdad said, "How could you?" She didn't look Ruth's way at all before re-entering the house. Ruth could tell from the square of Mama's shoulders that a severe tongue-lashing was in store.

Ruth also knew somehow, sometime, she would drive again—and again and again, no matter how much trouble it brought her. Mama would enjoy driving a car too, if she'd forget those stupid ladies-don't rules. Ruth refused to believe their adventurous spirits were that different from each other.

Were they?

CHAPTER SEVENTEEN
MAGGIE

"She and her mama were quite different, though," Maggie commented, thinking of how that observation fit her mother and her. Especially when it came to forgiving straying husbands.

How could her mother forget the hurt her father had caused both of them?

How could Maggie forget the hurt her husband had caused her?

Holding in anger against both her father and her husband exhausted her, but she couldn't find a way through it.

"Maggie?" Grams's touch on her arm wrestled her from her confusing questions. "Would you like to talk about what's on your mind?"

Brian appeared with coffee and cookies. He served Grams another cup of coffee and offered Maggie one.

"No, thanks. I would love a glass of orange juice."

He handed her a package of cookies. "I'll get that for you."

Maggie sensed that ever-observant glance from Grams.

The flight attendant returned with Maggie's orange juice. "In case you were wondering how much storytelling time remains, we're halfway to Paris."

Grams opened the airplane magazine and flipped to the back, where the flight maps were located. She pointed out to Maggie the route from Oakland to Paris, comparing the map to a sketch from one of Cécile's letters. "Look at how she drew their distance from each other, yet through their letters they remained close."

Maggie studied Cécile's sketch of two globes with a plane and ship traveling in between. "The idea of ordinary people being able to arrive at other's side in less than a day would have been quite unimaginable at that time. It would have been fun, though, to travel on an ocean liner."

"That would have given me much more time to tell the stories of my mother and Cécile." Grams laughed. She read the first paragraph of the letter in which the sketch was drawn.

18, bis Avenue d 'Italie
Paris 75013
France

1 October 1919

Dear Ruth,

I am just like you and think like you; France is so far from California! I look for your letters to bring you closer to me. Yes, I think as you, our characters are the same. I think so. You are perhaps more vivacious than me, but we have surely the same ideas and heart. You ask me in one of your letters about your heart. Oh! I know where it is. I see it in your many letters.

"Oh, how sweet." Tears quickly gathered in Maggie's eyes, and she brushed them away. "Ruth must have written about feeling alone and questioning herself. Cécile embraced the goodness in her. What a precious friend."

"Remember the French proverb? There are none so distant that fate cannot bring together."

Maggie nodded, the words bringing that pang in her heart as before.

"Cécile believed that despite their distance, fate had brought them together." She handed Maggie the letter. "Read the rest to us."

"My cat Bidart sleeps while I write," Maggie read. *"He is a sweet lazy cat!"*

A picture of the cat was enclosed. "He was adorable," Maggie commented before continuing.

Last night I dreamed you came to Paris and I was so happy! After dinner we sat on terrace of Musee de l'Orangerie. The terrace is near the Seine, in the garden called the "Tuileries." From that terrace I show you the Museum "Le Louvre", "The Concord Place", the two arcs of triumph, "The great, and the arc of Carousel" built by Napoleon to celebrate military victories. I show you the parliament "Chambre des Deputes", the Eiffel Tower, the "Great Wheel", and "The Invalides." It is a nice view and you liked it very much. We go to top of Eiffel Tower and ride the Great Wheel and you love it!

Do you like birds? I like them very much. On the quays of the Seine in Paris center there are many shops where they sell birds, cats, dogs, mice, rabbits etc…I like to look at the nice birds but I don't know the names of the birds in English. Oh! I have a dictionary and I look at merles, blackbird, nightingales, goldfinches, wrens. The birthday of the Armistice will be soon, in November. I remember how I have shouted. On the grands boulevards there was thousand and thousands of people crying, running, dancing, singing, pushing, selling guns taken on the front. I have seen an English nurse on the top of a gas lamp in a street, singing the Marseillaise and the God Save The King. Round her there was 500 or more perhaps singing with her. Farther in the Avenue de l'Opera an American soldiers was making noise with the motor of their motor cars. What a jazz band!!!

Au revoir for now, with much kisses,
Cécile

Once more, Maggie felt the thrill of stepping through a portal in time, into Paris of 1919, through Cécile's words.

"You notice that Cécile loves birds?"

Grams's question pulled Maggie back to the present. She reread that section of Cécile's letter. "Yes. We must explore the quays of the Seine she writes about."

"It will be interesting to compare her description with what we see," Grams remarked. "My father inspired my mother's love of birds—and mine—with his homing pigeons."

"How they find their way home is incredible," Maggie commented. "It's like people, I guess, who feel that tug of home. Like your mother's connection to Colorado Springs."

Like her own connection to the home she and Cole had created. Until he ruined everything. She swallowed hard, trying to control her swirl of emotions.

While engaged, she and Cole had purchased a vintage Victorian in historic Alameda, south of Oakland. Her love of history and his handyman skills combined nicely in undertaking the house's preservation in order to turn it into their home. They'd scrimped on everything else to afford the purchase and devoted their hard-earned dollars to its renovation.

Every room brought back too many memories. They'd made love in each one, sometimes covered in sawdust, other times with paint-speckled skin. They'd suffered electric shocks from re-wiring, falls through caved in floors, an almost-sliced-off finger from bungled sawing, and smushed fingers from mislaid hammering. The local ER knew them on a first name basis. Through it all, they laughed. Loved.

Every memory, every accomplishment now felt meaningless. The house, no longer a home, echoed with emptiness. She'd had realtors visit to guide her on the listing of it. Cole would be devastated at that idea, but she couldn't remain and raise their child in the house that had once meant so much.

She pressed her miserable thoughts out of her mind and tuned back into her Grams's stories.

"My mother loved telling me about the first time she held one of my father's homing pigeons, not long after she met him. She must have written Cécile all about it, not to mention telling her about Clinton."

"I feel the story about to continue, Grams." Maggie welcomed the intrusion of the past into the heartbreak of her present. "Especially since we left off with a destroyed henhouse!"

CHAPTER EIGHTEEN
RUTH

Dewdad announced at Sunday morning breakfast that he'd hired Clinton to help him repair the henhouse and the car that afternoon. Clinton's impending arrival distracted Ruth's attention from the preacher's sermon.

Not long after they returned from church and finished dinner, the crunch of gravel in the driveway announced Clinton's approach. He was behind the wheel of an old Model T truck filled with wood planks. Ruth had no idea he could drive!

She followed Dewdad to the porch.

"Whose truck is that?" she asked.

"It belonged to his pa." Dewdad paused, his attention focused on Clinton parking his truck. "Clinton's mama lets him drive it sometimes, especially to take the pigeons out and release them. They need exercise."

Cécile had written about her love of birds in the letter Ruth had received. Again, she marveled at the connections in their lives. Their friendship certainly had been fated.

"Clinton told me that he cares for homing pigeons." Ruth wiped her hands, wet from washing dishes, on her gingham apron. "Remember the story from the newsreels at the movies about that famous one, Cher Ami? I'm going to ask Cécile in my next letter if the bird is as famous in France as here."

Dewdad brushed his mustache before speaking. "I remember that story. Cher Ami carried a message that saved two hundred lives at the Battle of the Argonne. She was shot through the breast, and the bullets blinded her in one eye and destroyed one of her legs. They made a wooden leg for her. She returned here and lived long enough to receive medals for her bravery."

The bullets hitting Cher Ami and her bleeding body reminded Ruth of Jesse. If only her brother could have survived, even if for a few minutes. They could have said their goodbyes. The memory of that day, of Pa's shock, of her screams—it all made her shiver.

"Are you chilly?" Dewdad hugged her. "It is a cool afternoon."

Ruth leaned against him for a minute. "No, I'm fine."

"Hey, Ruth." Clinton waved to her. He stood next to the pile of lumber.

She waved back, thinking how if she'd not moved to Oakland, she would have never met this boy. If only such sadness had not brought her to Dewdad's.

∞∙∞

While Mama accompanied the twins and Florabelle on a walk, Ruth finished pressing the last piece of her Quimper pattern. She walked out to the porch to snatch a glimpse of Clinton. Dewdad was mopping perspiration from his forehead with a handkerchief. Clinton had pulled off his work shirt to wipe his face. Ruth couldn't keep from staring at his taut, flexed muscles. Flustered, Ruth returned to the kitchen, unable to shake that image of Clinton from her thoughts—not that she tried very hard to do so.

A few minutes later, Dewdad joined her. "Repairs are done. We replaced the busted headlight, buffed out all the scratches on the car, and rebuilt the henhouse. Clinton's packing up to leave."

"Dewdad, I'm sorry I caused so much trouble. I could've helped with the repairs, if you'd let me." Ruth poured them each a glass of lemonade.

"Thanks for your apology, Ruffis. Your mama probably would not approve of you swinging a hammer, though. Don't think I'm letting you off light. You'll help me wash and wax the car later today."

"Absolutely," Ruth answered.

He tipped the glass toward her. "Here's to your first driving lesson."

She tipped hers back. "My first! Do you mean that you'll let me drive again?"

"Well now, at some point. I'm not in a rush." He winked.

Ruth sipped her lemonade, her spirits lifted at the thought.

Dewdad finished his drink. "Why don't you offer Clinton some lemonade? He's worked up a thirst."

"That's a nice idea." Ruth filled a glass and took it to Clinton, who was piling the lumber scraps into the bed of the truck. "Lemonade?" she offered.

"Thanks." He drained it with one swallow. "Hey, do you wear the necklace I gave you?"

Ruth pulled it from where it hung beneath her blouse. "Just because you don't see something doesn't mean it's not there." She tucked it back.

Clinton cocked his head to one side. "Would you like to come to my house and visit my homing pigeons? I'll drive us there and bring you back."

"I'll have to ask permission from Mama." Ruth dared to believe her mother would say yes. "Come with me. She's back from her walk."

She and Clinton approached her mother, who was sitting with Florabelle on the porch swing. The twins sat on a blanket playing with their dolls. At Ruth's request, Mama's jaw went tight, her signal of disapproval Ruth knew well.

"How long have you been driving your truck?" Mama asked Clinton.

He gave Mama a serious, mature look. "More than a year. We aren't going far. I live around the curve." He added, "I'm a careful driver. Ask Mr. Addison."

"Can we go too, Mama? Can we go too?" Mable begged, with Opal chiming in.

"Shush, you two." Ruth shot them her be-quiet-or-else look.

Mama stood from the swing. "I think since the distance is short, I'll allow it. Clinton, I will hold you to your promise that you are a responsible and safe driver. Ruth, the twins must accompany you."

Ruth opened her mouth to exclaim "gee whiz," but she bit her words back. She would at least get to go, even if the twins had to come also.

They arrived at Clinton's house about ten minutes later. The twins and Ruth followed him inside.

"Ma, I'd like you to meet Ruth and her sisters, Mable and Opal," he said.

"Hello Ruth. My goodness, your two sisters are spitting images of each other." Mrs. Carlock's eyes shifted back and forth with an exaggerated look of confusion. "I imagine you two girls are used to people mixing you up."

Ruth pulled Opal to her right. "This one's Opal, with the pink bow in her hair." She pulled Mable to her left. "This one's Mable, with the white bow in her hair. Without that trick, we'd have a tough time telling them apart."

Mrs. Carlock laughed. "That's a clever way, I must admit."

Clinton opened the kitchen door that led to the backyard. "Ma, we're going to visit the homing pigeons."

Mrs. Carlock's loving gaze at Clinton reminded Ruth of how Mama had always looked at Jesse, delighted and amazed to have created her strapping, perfect son.

"Your pa sure loved those pigeons," Clinton's mother said softly.

"Let's go! Let's go!" Mable and Opal shouted together.

"Follow me," Clinton directed.

He led them to a clearing in the far part of the property. There on short stilts stood a wooden hut with a shingled roof. On both sides were double-screened cages. Clinton took out one of the pigeons. He cradled it into the palm of one hand, holding its feet between his fingers. With his other hand, he held the pigeon's wings. The twins and Ruth took turns stroking it.

"It's silky," Ruth whispered.

He returned that one and brought out another.

"How do you tell them apart?" Ruth asked.

Clinton pointed out the different shades of the birds' feathers. "They're like members of your family. Each one is unique." He held the bird up and showed Ruth the band on its leg. "Each one has a banded number that identifies it. A few times a month, I drive to the lake and let them out to fly back home for exercise. If one doesn't make it back and someone finds it, the band identifies it as mine, and the finder gets in touch with me. That's never happened though. They all always make it back, safe and sound."

Ruth wished she were like Clinton's pigeons, who knew where they belonged, where to call home. She didn't anymore. Part of her belonged back in Colorado and part of her belonged here.

Clinton placed the bird inside its cage. "Maybe you could come with me sometime when I release them. It's a beautiful sight to see."

"I'd love to go." She wondered if Mama would allow her, if the twins came.

Clinton knelt in front of the girls. "Mable and Opal, I have a couple of peppermint sticks, if you want them."

"Yes! Yes!" the twins chimed, jumping up and down.

"You have to promise me you'll stay in the house to eat them. Promise?"

"Yes! We promise!"

Clinton waved them toward the house. "Run on and tell my mama I said to give them to you."

The twins disappeared in a blink of an eye, leaving Ruth quite happy yet feeling awkward to be alone with Clinton. Neither spoke until Ruth commented, "They're nice pigeons."

What a dumb thing to say, but she couldn't think of anything else.

Clinton shrugged. "They keep me close to my pa."

Ruth's pulse quickened. She understood missing someone who had died, realizing you'd never be with him again, in this world.

"Come on." Clinton broke the silence between them. He tugged at her arm, leading her to his truck. "Want to drive her?"

"Me?" She stared at him with disbelief. "After what I did to Dewdad's henhouse and car? What if I wreck into your pigeon hutch? Or your truck?"

"I'm willing to risk it." Clinton's eyes sparked mischievously. "I'll drive us to an open field behind my house. There's nothing you can hit there."

"Very funny." Ruth hesitated for a split second. What was she waiting for? She couldn't refuse such a glorious opportunity. "Let's go." She jumped into the passenger seat.

The rocky road they traveled dead-ended into an open field. Ruth and Clinton switched places. He talked her through each step, and before she could believe it, she was driving around the field with only a few sputters and lurches.

After her third lap, she stomped on the brakes. "I'm exhausted!"

Clinton laughed. "It's time for me to drive you home anyway. We'll do this again. If you want to, that is?"

"You bet!" This time she didn't hesitate with her answer.

They collected the twins, whose sticky fingers and mouths had to be washed before they departed. On the ride back, Ruth began composing in her head her letter to Cécile. She had so much to share, and writing about everything would let her re-live it.

Clinton sped up when they reached the curve. Ruth spied Mrs. Givens and Phoebe out for a Sunday afternoon walk with their yappy Teacup.

"Slow down, Clinton!" Ruth begged.

With a devil-may-care expression, he pressed the accelerator and steered closer to them, beeping his horn. Startled, they jumped aside. Mrs. Givens grabbed Teacup up into her arms. Ruth had to admit she enjoyed Phoebe's look of shock. Was it caused by the car getting close or by the sight of Ruth riding with Clinton?

Clinton brought the truck to a stop in her driveway, and Ruth helped the twins out. The little girls scampered up to the porch, where Dewdad sat. Each twin talked over the other while describing the pigeons.

"Thanks, Clinton." Shyness overcame Ruth. She added, "I had a great time."

"Me too." Clinton shoved his hands into his overalls. "I'll wait for you like usual in the morning to walk to school."

"See you then."

Mama came to the kitchen door. "Ruth, come inside." Her no-nonsense tone held a warning: "Ladies don't flirt."

Under her mama's observant eye, Ruth didn't linger to talk with Clinton. That didn't mean Clinton wouldn't linger in her dreams. Even *ladies* dream.

"How adorable," Maggie commented. "Your mother was totally crushing on Clinton!"

"I would say they were crushing on each other," Grams agreed.

Maggie had lived that exhilaration of falling in love with the man of your dreams. Experiencing it once in a lifetime was a gift. She guessed Grams hadn't found another. Would she? Could she open herself up to love again?

"My mama must have written to Cécile about how to act properly around boys," Grams said. "In one of her letters, Cécile writes about not to be referred to as a wild girl, I think she called it." She pulled a letter from the stack and opened it. "Yes, here is what she wrote."

18, bis Avenue d' Italie
Paris 75013
France

7 October 1919

My dear little Yankee,

My dear I say like you, that men are foolish. I have observed when I am in the park Montsouris, that

I never am alone. I sit down on a bench and some minutes after on the other extremity of the bench a boy is sat too. If I read I go on to read, if I sew I go on too. If I do not, the man think I am a wild girl. He leaves and then, I am very quiet and glad.

Grams paused from reading, her eyes crinkling in amusement. "Cécile, like Ruth, took care to avoid being considered a 'fast girl' of her day."

"Does Cécile find her Clinton, Grams? Come on." Maggie couldn't help adding, "Like they would say back then, spill the beans!"

A shadow of sadness clouded Grams's happiness. "In good time, dear."

"All right." Maggie rearranged her blanket around her. "What park did Cécile mention?"

"Montsouris. I googled it."

"Grams, I love how you are tech savvy, googling away!" Maggie laughed appreciatively.

Her grandmother blushed at the compliment. "Who said you can't teach old dogs like me new tricks? They offer computer courses at the senior center, not only bingo games," she teased. "I'd love to sit on a bench where Cécile did at this park. Legend says the name Montsouris comes from an old windmill called the Moulin de Moque-Souris. In the eighteenth century, it stood not far from where the park is today."

"Moulin de Moque-Souris. What does that translate to in English?"

"Mocks the mice," Grams replied.

"How funny! What in the world?"

"According to Wikipedia—"

"Wikipedia," Maggie interrupted. "Impressive, Grams."

"Oh shush, you." Grams blushed a bit pinker. "According to Wikipedia, Moque-Souris was a typical name for windmills in France at the time, referring to millers who dared the mice to find and eat any grain inside."

"Moque-Souris," Maggie said sternly, waving her index finger as if scolding the mice.

Grams laughed. "It's good to see you being silly, granddaughter."

Maggie agreed It did feel good to temporarily forget her sadness. This trip could help heal her soul, she thought.

Grams continued to read the letter aloud.

My aunt De Tinteniac comes tomorrow, we received a telegram from her this morning. She is going into Alsace to try and send her husband's corpse who was buried there, when he died on the front. She wishes to have him buried near his home at Quimper. There she may visit his grave. She passes through Paris to change train. I think the effects of war don't end with the armistice, suffering continues for us that miss our one's we love so dearly.

Grams's voice shook when she read the last sentence. Maggie assumed her grandmother must be thinking of the grandfather Maggie wished she could have met—and the father her mother never knew. Each Memorial Day and Veterans Day, the three of them visited his grave. When Maggie was young, they had visited the Vietnam memorial in DC. All three made their own memorial etchings of his name on the wall. Those special tributes were framed and hanging in their homes.

Maggie took Grams's hand. "Cécile definitely understood. The effects of war never fade."

"No. They don't," Grams responded quietly. She returned her attention to the letter.

Well, it is 3 p.m. and I am going to the "Jardin des Plantes" to see the gallery of the museum where stands, mummies, diamonds, gold nuggets, etc...Good bye until again!

Kisses and au revoir,
Cécile

"We will visit the gardens too?" Maggie asked.

"Yes, it's on our itinerary. I mapped our sightseeing with a personal-tour-guide company your father recommended."

Maggie looked away, not wanting to think about her father. He had "changed his spots" like a leopard, her mother claimed. Her mother was wrong. A leopard never changed his spots. Maggie would not let her father worm his way back into her affections.

Her hand strayed again to her belly. No matter how much she might like to have an intact family and be in a loving marriage, she could never trust Cole again. She'd not accept his begging for forgiveness. His spots would never change either.

The plane took a sudden dip, and Maggie grabbed Grams's hand.

Grams squeezed hers, hard. "A little unsettled air," she murmured.

Maggie wondered if Grams was trying to calm her or herself. Maggie squeezed back. "I'm sure it's only a little rough—"

The pilot's announcement drowned out Maggie's words. "Ladies and gentlemen, we've hit a patch of turbulence. Please remain in your seats with your seat belts fastened. We should be getting to smoother air in a few minutes."

Grams took in a deep breath and let it out slowly. "A little turbulence. That reminds me of where we left off with Ruth. Both Dewdad and she were about to hit some rough patches of their own. And receive some dire news."

Maggie's eyes widened in curiosity as Grams continued.

CHAPTER TWENTY
RUTH

All day Monday, Ruth floated on cloud nine thinking about her Sunday outing with Clinton. However, she tumbled to earth when she walked through the kitchen door that afternoon, home from school.

The Quimper costume pieces were spread on the table, and the ironing board was open in the corner. Her mama pointed to a seat at the table before Ruth could tell her thank you for working on her costume.

"We must talk." Mama's no-nonsense manner meant trouble. "Sit."

Ruth sat.

"Mrs. Givens described reckless behavior on the drive back from Clinton's. He came close to running Phoebe over."

Ruth opened her mouth. Mama shushed her before a word could escape.

"I forbid you to ride in his truck ever again. Incidents like this with a boy ruin your reputation."

"Yes, Mama." Ruth provided an obedient reply even though she doubted she'd keep her word. If Clinton offered her another opportunity to ride with him or drive his truck, how could she say no?

"Let's get to work on this costume. Halloween is in ten days. We have quite a bit of sewing yet to do. Your grandpa ran an errand to pick me up some more thread and collect our mail. I've started a stew for supper. It will be a busy afternoon."

"Yes, Mama."

They were hard at work sewing when Ruth heard the crunch of gravel and crowing from Herkimer, announcing Dewdad's return. She hoped he was bringing her a letter from Cécile.

"How dare she?" Dewdad waved a document around in the air.

"Papa, calm yourself. How dare whom?" Mama asked, concentrating on her stitching.

"It's that woman. Mrs. Givens. She's gone and done it this time."

Dewdad opened the paper, read it, and folded it back multiple times. Ruth couldn't endure the suspense any longer. "Gee whiz, Dewdad. Spill the beans. What has Mrs. Givens gone and done?"

Mama quickly corrected her. "Ruth Calderhead. I have told you I will not tolerate such word choices."

"Yes, Mama."

"Papa, what has upset you?" Mama stopped her sewing to concentrate on Dewdad.

"Mrs. Givens followed through on her threat. She complained to city hall about Herkimer. She called him a destructive menace to the community. They ruled in her favor. They've ordered me to get rid of him."

"Oh, Papa. How awful. That rooster is special to you."

Mama's sympathy surprised Ruth. Mrs. Givens did have a point. Herkimer was a menace.

"That's not all. Some ordinance exists against keeping livestock within the city limits," said Dewdad. He perched on a kitchen chair, opened the letter, and read it again.

"That Mrs. Givens." Mama's aggravation was obvious. "She should spend more time minding her own business than ours."

Dewdad jumped from the chair. "Who says you can't fight city hall? They need to hear my side of the story. I'll negotiate with them, even if it means I'll have to give away Herkimer to keep my hens."

Give away Herkimer? Ruth couldn't believe her ears.

"You'd give away that rooster?" Mama stared at Dewdad with skepticism.

"If it means keeping my hens, I will have to." Dewdad rapped his knuckles on the table. "I'm off to city hall, ladies. Councilman Forrest is on the board at the factory with me. I'm going to plead my case with him. Wish me luck." He smacked the palm of his hand against his forehead. "I'd forget my head if it wasn't screwed on tight!" he exclaimed.

Mama's lips pursed in reaction to his choice of words. Ruth assumed what a girl couldn't say, a grown man could.

He pulled a spool of thread from his pant pocket and handed it to mama. "There's your thread." He fished from his inside vest pocket a piece of two pieces of mail. "Also, a letter came from Charles."

Ruth's sewing needle slipped at that news. "Ouch!"

"Thank you, Papa. Leave it on the table." To Ruth's disappointment, Mama expressed no sense of urgency about reading it.

"Ruth, the other mail is a letter from Lulu Cosquéric." Dewdad held it toward her. "Isn't that Cécile's brother?"

Ruth put down her sewing and plucked the letter from Dewdad's hand. "Yes! Cécile told me he wants a pen pal. Maybe he's writing me about finding him one."

She studied the meticulous and tiny handwriting on the envelope, different from Cécile's flowing cursive.

Mama resumed her sewing, making no move to read Pa's letter.

"I can't wait to read my letter." Ruth looked at Mama, hoping she'd show interest in Pa's. She didn't. "How about I ride with you, Dewdad, and I'll read it to us?"

"If that's fine by your mama, it's fine by me," Dewdad answered.

"Fine." Mama kept her focus on her sewing. "Hurry back, though. Dinner will be waiting."

Ruth doubted she'd have an appetite for dinner if Pa's letter remained unread.

Settling into the passenger seat for the ride, she examined the stamp on Lulu's letter, thinking about how far the envelope had traveled to reach her. "I've figured out exactly how to get to Paris from Oakland. Want to hear?"

"Yes, I would," Dewdad said.

"It takes about a week to go across the United States by train to New York. Once there, I'd set sail on a passenger ship to the coast of France. The travel onboard the ship requires five days, maybe a couple more. Once my ship reached the coast of France, I'd hop a train in the French port city of Le Harve and travel all night to reach Paris by the morning. If all worked to plan, it would take two full weeks of travel, give or take, to arrive at Cécile's door."

"Impressive." Dewdad tapped the letter. "Isn't that about the time interval for your letters to reach each other?"

"Yes. Unfortunately." Ruth knitted her eyebrows. "It's dreadful Cécile and I live so far apart."

"That distance will feel less once you read Lulu's letter," Dewdad suggested. "What does he have to share?"

She carefully unsealed the envelope. Unfolding the letter, she could tell it was short. He must not be a chatterbox like Cécile. She quickly scanned his news.

"Oh no." Her voice quaked. "Poor, poor Cécile."

CHAPTER TWENTY-ONE
MAGGIE

"**N**o!" Maggie blurted out in reaction to both her grandmother's last words and another patch of jarring turbulence. "What has happened to Cécile? Grams, tell me now!"

"Stay calm, Maggie. Let's catch our breath first." Grams snugged in her seat belt before reaching for the next letter.

Maggie glanced at the letter in her grandmother's hand with its tiny, carefully written words that were not Cécile's. "Why is that letter not from Cécile herself? What's wrong?"

Grams read the news slowly.

18, bis Avenue d'Italie
Paris 75013
France

10 October 1919

Dear Ruth,

Some lines to tell you that Cécile can't write you because she is very ill. She has not mentioned to you of her health, but she has been sick for a while. Sunday the seventh she went with father to church at the top of a hill called Montmartre in the north of Paris for mass. She was very hot in the church and when she went out the cold seized her. In the evening she ran a very high fever so we sought the doctor. In French her illness is called "Congestion Pulminaire."

"Tuberculosis." Maggie pronounced the diagnosis with a tremor in her voice. Grams handed her the letter, and Maggie read out loud, tears clouding her vision.

She must not move or speak it is very serious. You should be very kind to continue to write her, she loves your letters and your good heart. After few weeks I shall send you news from her.

Directly she can get up she will start in country perhaps in Switzerland in the mountains. In the next few days, the doctor can indicate to us where she will be the rest of her cure. I am not pleased to give you such news. I hope you understand my words and wish you and your family are quite well.

Lulu

Maggie clutched the letter, devastated at the news. She knew hardly anyone survived tuberculosis in that day and time. She recalled the facts she'd learned about the disease. During the sixteenth, seventeenth, and eighteenth centuries, more than 1 billion people died of tuberculosis, called consumption. It ravaged its sufferers, inflicting them with a hacking, bloody cough and debilitating fatigue. Patients sought "the cure" in sanatoriums located in a healthful climate, believing rest and clean air could make them well. They did not know that bacteria caused the sickness and that months of antibiotics were required to kill it.

The dreaded disease had taken the lives of many famous people: Chopin, Moliere, Chekhov. Jane Austen, Emily Brontë, Stephen Crane, Eleanor Roosevelt, Vivien Leigh. These names and others tumbled through her recollections.

"Grams, did Cécile die from tuberculosis?"

"Ruth feared that she would." Grams interlaced her fingers, her index fingers pointed prayer-like. "She understood what the diagnosis meant, having lived in Colorado Springs, where sanatoriums such as Cragmor housed patients." She trailed off before adding, "However, it wasn't only Cécile's news that upset Ruth at this time."

Maggie had several guesses about what Grams could be referring to. "Something about her pa? About Jesse? The secret?"

Grams took a deep breath before continuing the story of Ruth and Cécile.

CHAPTER TWENTY-TWO
RUTH

The words escaped from Ruth in a whisper. "Lulu writes that Cécile is sick. Congestion Pulminaire. She has consumption. Tuberculosis."

"Oh, Ruth." Dewdad patted her knee. "I'm sorry."

Ruth knew what going for a cure meant. Back home, people came to Colorado Springs for the "cure" of the pure mountain air. Some classmates of Ruth's had fallen ill with the dreaded sickness. Some of them got better and came back to school, after quite some time. Some never got better.

She had already lost Jesse. Pa wasn't with her. She couldn't bear to lose Cécile.

Dewdad steered the Chevrolet around. "I'll visit with Councilman Forrest tomorrow."

Once home, Ruth burst through the kitchen door, wanting to throw herself into her mother's arms and tell her about Cécile's illness. She wanted Mama to say Cécile would be fine. She wanted Mama to tell her that Pa's letter had said that he was moving to Oakland.

She found her mother in her bedroom with a steamer trunk open. Mable and Opal were walking around in Mama's shoes. Mama's clothes were spread out on her bed next to those of the twins and Florabelle. Florabelle sat among the clothes while Mama folded Opal's nightgown.

Shocked, Ruth stared at the scene for a moment before blurting out, "Mama! Where are you going?"

Dewdad followed Ruth into her mother's room. "Dolly, what's going on?"

"I'm heading to Colorado Springs." Her voice contained a lilt of excitement. "The farm has sold. I'm going back to help Charles pack up and return to Oakland with me."

All Ruth's breath left her body. The room started spinning. She leaned against the doorframe to steady herself. Her mind swirled with images: their farm, Pike's Peak, Jesse's grave. She had to go back for one last goodbye.

She started for the attic stairs. "I'll get my clothes to pack."

"Pack?" Mama followed her into the hallway. "Why, Ruth, you aren't going. I'm only taking the twins and Florabelle because caring for them would be too much for you and Dewdad."

"No! I have to go with you!" Ruth kept walking to her room, determined.

Mama grabbed her arm and swiveled her around.

"Ruth, we'll be gone for only ten days. We'll be back in time for Pa to see you in your Quimper costume for the Halloween party. There's no need for us to pay for your ticket and no need for you to miss school."

"Mama! Please! I need to go with you! I have to!"

"I said no. That is final." Her mother let Ruth go.

"You can't leave me behind. You can't!" Ruth clenched her fists. The words she had kept buried deep inside flew out. "You left Colorado to punish Pa and me because we didn't save Jesse. That's why you put so many miles between you and Pa. You can't forgive us."

Mama's jaw tightened. "Where did you get such a convoluted idea? I'm not punishing anyone. How dare you say such a terrible thing?"

"How dare you indeed, young lady." Dewdad marched into the hallway. "You apologize right this instant. I'll not tolerate disrespect to your mother."

Ruth clenched her fists tighter. Whenever she and Mama had been at odds before, Dewdad had helped calm them and convinced Mama to at least consider her point of view.

She searched her grandfather's face for a hint of understanding. She saw none.

Ruth grabbed Mama's hands. "If I'm not being punished, let me go with you."

Mama withdrew her hands and addressed Ruth square in the eye. "My decision is final, Ruth. Please understand."

"Mama!"

"Enough, Ruth," Dewdad interrupted. "You heard your mother. You are to accept her decision."

Mama walked back to her bedroom, her laced Cantilever shoes clacking all the way. Ruth knew from her mother's no-room-for-argument stiff posture that her decision was final.

Dewdad's attitude remained disapproving. If he ever found out the secret she held with Pa, he'd probably hate her. Like Mama would. Ruth started to shake. She was tumbling into a black hole, into that awful darkness that sucked her in when she let herself think about it.

The secret.

Ruth needed to tell Mama everything. She rushed to her bedroom.

Mama was nudging Florabelle off a stack of clothing to reach Mable's nightgown. The twins were chanting, "Pa's coming home. Pa's coming home." Florabelle was clapping.

"Mama." Ruth's voice trembled.

Mama stopped folding Mable's nightgown. "Ruth, dear. What is wrong? You're pale, as if you've seen a ghost."

Ruth opened her mouth. No words came out.

Mama hurried to her. "What comes over you with these spells of yours?" She lay her hand on her forehead. "No fever. Come sit on the bed with Florabelle." She led Ruth to the bed. "Rest until you feel better."

Ruth obeyed, pushing the secret back deep inside.

Everything would be better soon. Pa with would be with them again. He would adjust to living here, like they all had. He and Dewdad would enjoy each other's friendship. Maybe after a while, Pa and she would tell Mama their secret. Their family could heal, while still remembering Jesse.

Yes, everything would be better when Pa was back with them.

Now, Cécile had to get better.

She just had to.

CHAPTER TWENTY-THREE
MAGGIE

Maggie's spirit sunk. "Oh, Grams. Your mama had much sadness already in her life. For her dear, sweet Cécile to be sick is too much to bear."

"Yes." Grams shook her head, her sadness obvious. "After the loss of her brother, losing Cécile would be another tragic one."

Maggie let a moment pass before breaking the silence with a question. "How long before Cécile was well enough to write again to Ruth?"

"Her spirit remained remarkable. She continued the correspondence without much delay, writing even when weak and ill." Grams pulled out the letter that had come next. "Here's one she wrote right after Lulu wrote to Ruth about her illness."

Grams read the short letter.

18, bis Avenue d' Italie
Paris 75013
France

13 October 1919

My dear Ruth,

Thank you so much for telling me about Halloween and the Halloween greetings. I never heard about it. I never heard about it except as an exchange, a little branch of mistletoe. I hope my Quimper outfit will win you first place.

Lulu wrote you last week and tells you that I am ill. Now I am a bit better, I get up each afternoon and stay on a long chair. I received your serial letters and I thank you for being such a good chum for me. I do not know about my cure. I am not sure I go to Switzerland. I do know, I cannot stay in Paris where air is so bad and must go where the air is pure.

I send you a map of Paris. I would be glad if I could jump and play in meadow. But in Paris we have no meadow. I have not any space to plant flowers as you do, because in Paris the space is so narrow! When you are in the center of the city you never see gardens. Near the suburb you can see some, but they are not numerous. Behind my home is a small garden where lilac trees bloom in spring.

Bonjour to all your sisters and brother. My best wishes to your Momma,

With kisses from your sincere far friend,
Cécile

Maggie reflected over the closing: Bonjour to all your sisters and brother. "She mentions Ruth's brother. Hadn't Ruth written to her about Jesse's death?"

Tears gleamed in Grams's eyes. "Not yet."

"Because of this secret she's keeping about the day he died?" Maggie frowned. "How awful for a fourteen-year-old girl to carry such guilt. I'm sure no therapy or counseling existed back then like today."

Sessions with her counselor had been her lifeline while her parents were divorcing. Ruth could have benefitted from help, Maggie was certain.

"You're right." Grams touched the letter. "Cécile was her confidante, though, in other matters. They wrote to each other about their dreams, fears, and love."

"Thank heaven for her pen pal."

"Yes. And for Clinton. He does become another confidante of sorts. My mother's story of how he asked her to go steady was romantic." Grams's hand covered her heart.

"Tell me now!" Maggie related to romantic proposals.

Cole had planned out each special moment of proposing to her, beginning with the nonchalant way he'd asked her to go with him to Key Largo, where he had to be for business. "Why not mix business with some pleasure?" he'd suggested, and she'd agreed. While there, they'd gone for a stroll to enjoy a perfect sunset. She came across an ancient-looking bottle with a message inside and unrolled the parchment. On it, written in calligraphy, was his proposal. He dropped to one knee and asked, "Margaret Ruth Anderson, will you marry me?"

She stared at her empty left ring finger, remembering how he'd slid the engagement ring there, exactly the one she would have picked had she chosen it herself. He had known her well.

Or had he? He should have known infidelity would be a game-changer for their happily-ever-after. She needed to accept the end of their marriage, move on, and prepare for her life ahead, hers and— she swallowed hard—their baby.

"Yes, Clinton's proposal to go steady is one of my favorite stories about my parents," Grams said.

Maggie pushed her own memories aside and concentrated on learning more about the true love shared between Clinton and Ruth.

Ruth met Clinton for the morning walk to school to tell him that Dewdad would drop her at school later. "We're taking Mama and my sisters to the train station. Pa's selling the farm, and Mama is helping him pack up to move back here."

"You sound unhappy. That's good news, isn't it?" Clinton asked.

"Yes. It's a good thing." She shrugged. "I wanted to go with Mama, that's all."

She wanted to tell Clinton about how badly she needed to return to Colorado Springs and visit Jesse's grave, but if she started talking, she'd tell him everything.

She wanted to tell him about Cécile's sickness, but she couldn't bear to talk about that either.

"If I went with Mama, I'd miss the arithmetic contest today. I'm glad that it's after lunch. I'll be back from the train station in time."

"I'm glad you'll be there for it too. I can't wait for someone to win against Phoebe."

"I hope so. Promise me one thing."

"What's that?"

"One of us will win so that Phoebe Givens won't. Deal?" Ruth held her hand out to shake.

He took it and held it. "Deal."

Ruth's hand tingled. Only the fear of Mrs. Givens appearing from out of nowhere spurred her to pull hers away. "See you later."

All the way back home, her hand retained the warmth of his touch.

∞∞

The Western Pacific railroad station's immense columns, corniced with eagles, made Ruth feel tiny. Exhaust fumes from the trains mingled with smells of coffee, fried doughnuts, and hot dogs. The peculiar blend smelled like adventure.

People crammed the terminal searching for the right tracks to meet their trains. People jostled against Ruth, and one man who bumped into her shouted, "Hey, look where you're going."

She wanted to shout back, "*I'm* not going anywhere."

Mama had put her foot down when Dewdad offered to buy better tickets. She bought what she and Pa could afford. Mama and the twins had second-class seats, the cheapest way to travel. Florabelle would sit in Mama's lap or squeeze in with the twins. That meant the two-and-a-half-day trip wouldn't include sleeping accommodations.

Ruth pictured the trip through the scenic Feather River Route to Salt Lake City and on to Colorado Springs and home. She wished she could stuff herself into the steamer trunk and go with them.

Mama kissed Ruth's forehead as a goodbye. "Pa won't believe how much his little girl has grown when he sees you again."

"I'm a young lady now." Ruth's words were cross. "You said that yourself." She wanted to add, "I haven't been a little girl since the day Jesse died."

"Yes, you are a young lady." Mama placed a hand on Ruth's shoulder. "Act like one while I'm gone. I don't want to hear any disappointing tales when I return." She pecked Dewdad on the cheek. "We'll be back soon."

The conductor called, "All aboard." Her sisters and Mama boarded. Ruth couldn't help but be excited for her sisters.

"Bye-bye!" the twins yelled, waving.

She waved back. "Bye! I'll miss you!"

With a hiss of steam, the train chugged away. Ruth wanted to chase it and hop on it, like Jesse and she had hopped on that other train long ago.

Her entire family would be together in Colorado Springs. Except for her. After yesterday, Dewdad and she were on opposite sides, further apart than the ocean's distance between her and Cécile. He was on Mama's side, and without Pa, Ruth didn't have anyone on hers, until Pa was with them again.

She wished she could disappear without a trace, like the steam around her.

Dust floated up while around Clinton and Ruth took turns kicking a rock on their walk from school. Clinton burst out in laughter. "Phoebe was madder than a wet hen about losing that arithmetic contest to you."

Ruth giggled. "I must say that her red cheeks made her blonde hair look even blonder."

She took pleasure in the fact that Phoebe's ringlets didn't help her solve long division problems as fast as she could.

"Nope, she can't hold a candle to you." Clinton took his turn kicking the rock. "And not just in long division."

Ruth blushed. When they reached the cutoff to his house, Ruth gave the rock one last kick in Clinton's direction. "Well, see you tomorrow."

Clinton stopped and shifted his books from one arm to the other. "I'm taking my pigeons to Merritt Lake for exercise. Would your grand-father let you go with me?"

Ruth pursed her lips, unsure. Dewdad hadn't held a grudge about how she had behaved toward Mama, but things weren't the same between them.

"You can drive the truck again," Clinton said.

That did it. "I'll ask Dewdad."

"I'm sure he'll say yes." Clinton started toward his house. "I'll pick you up in about an hour."

Ruth hoped it wouldn't be a wasted trip.

She found Dewdad in the garage, polishing up the Chevrolet.

"How was school, Ruffis?"

She showed him her arithmetic contest first-place ribbon, hoping it would ease the way for her request. After he congratulated her, she took a deep breath and asked permission for the outing with Clinton. "He'll be here soon."

Dewdad answered with, "We'll see."

Whenever Mama or Pa said that, it meant no. Maybe Clinton could change Dewdad's "we'll see" to a "yes." Ruth didn't count on it.

When Clinton drove up in the driveway, she and Dewdad welcomed him.

"Young man, I need your help with something. Ruth, wait here. We will be just a minute."

Clinton and Dewdad disappeared into the garage, walking close to Herkimer's turf. Dewdad had let him out of the fenced-in yard for what he called "a little exploratory time." The rooster was strutting back and forth. His *brawks* dared them against getting too close.

Ruth did feel a little sorry for the bratty thing. Dewdad had struck a bargain that he could keep his hens if he got rid of Herkimer. The end-of-the-month deadline loomed, and Dewdad had yet to find the rooster a new home. Ruth secretly suspected her grandfather hadn't been trying hard.

The minutes crawled while she waited for Dewdad and Clinton. She checked out the pigeons in the back of the truck. There were two empty crates and one crate that held three pigeons. Each pigeon had a little cylinder contraption fastened on one leg.

She hoped that Dewdad would let her go. She wanted to observe Clinton releasing the pigeons, and she wanted to get behind the wheel and drive again. Not to mention they could spend time together, the two of them. No twins this time!

Mama's words rang in Ruth's ears. *Act like a lady while I'm gone.*
She silently promised that she would.

The sun faded behind the clouds, and the wind picked up, bringing the threat of rain. Ruth hurried into the house to grab her woolen shawl. When she returned, Clinton and Dewdad were shaking hands.

"Ruth," Dewdad said, "have a good time and remember what your mama told you."

Her mother's warning rang in her mind. *I don't want to hear any disappointing tales when I return.*

"Thanks, Dewdad. You can trust me." Ruth glanced at Clinton. "You can trust us both."

"Ab-so-lute-ly, Mr. Addison," Clinton added. Ruth was glad Mama wasn't there to hear what she'd deem his improper pronunciation of the word.

She sat in the truck, dizzy with amazement that Dewdad had allowed her this excursion with Clinton. When they reached the back roads around the lake, Clinton brought the truck to a stop.

He announced, "Your turn at the wheel."

Without hesitation, Ruth jumped out and raced around the back of the truck toward the driver's seat. A mess of majestic deep red, blue, and orangey-yellow feathers flew up in the air. Herkimer!

"Quick, grab him, Clinton!"

"You grab him!"

She dove for the rooster, who let out a squawk. Clinton got control of him, getting royally pecked in the bargain. "Ow! Throw your shawl over him," he yelled.

Ruth covered the rooster, and he stopped moving. She gasped, fearing the worst. How in the world could she ever tell Dewdad she had killed his rooster? She gulped the words out. "Is he alive?"

"Yes." With an aggravated groan, Clinton shoved the wriggling bundle of rooster into one of the empty crates. He unwrapped Ruth's shawl from it before locking it.

"He must have flown into your truck when I ran into the house for my wrap." Ruth laughed, taking her shawl from Clinton. "He loves cars as much as Dewdad. We've found him roosting in the back seat of the Chevrolet."

"Wasn't your grandpa supposed to get rid of this pesky old thing?" Clinton rubbed the spot on his arm where he'd been pecked.

"Yes." Ruth checked out the scratches on the back of her hand. Pulling the wrap around her, she asked, "You want him?"

Clinton's glare answered emphatically *no*. "Get in and drive, Ruffis."

Ruth frowned. "How did you learn my nickname?" She'd never survive if Phoebe ever heard it. She could imagine all the girls at school chanting it at her. She would die. Ab-so-lute-ly.

"Your grandpa let it slip." Clinton laughed. "Don't worry. It's safe with me."

Ruth stomped past him and sat behind the steering wheel. When he plopped into the passenger seat, she pointed at him. "You better not tell anyone about my nickname."

"My lips are sealed." He ran his finger across his closed mouth for emphasis.

Ruth drove with no lurches or sputters and no stomping on the brakes. She managed the clutch as if she had been born to drive.

"Stop here." Clinton motioned to an open area by the lake.

Ruth caught her breath at the beauty before her. She remembered Cécile writing about how she had no meadow or open space near her to breathe in fresh air that could help make her well. If only she could come to this most beautiful place.

The sun peeked in and out from behind the billowy clouds. The water glistened, its surface glass-smooth. Suddenly, the sun went into hiding and the wind blew. The surface of the water broke into choppy waves.

The changing weather reminded Ruth of her tumultuous moods. The calmness of the lake was like the calmness Clinton provided her. The sudden wind was like the change that came over her when she felt darkness overwhelm her.

"A penny for your thoughts." Clinton tugged on her sleeve.

Ruth opened the driver's door, quickly devising an answer to avoid the truthful one. "I was wondering how your pigeons find their way home."

"They have some sort of internal compass."

The image of Jesse's compass flashed into her mind. *To our barefoot boy. Love, Mama and Pa. 2/28/1915.*

"There's that look again," Clinton said.

She shrugged. "I'm not sure where my internal compass is directing me. Colorado Springs feels like a giant magnetic field pulling me back. After what happened, you'd think it would be the opposite and I'd never want to go back there."

"What happened?"

"Nothing." She shut the driver's door, angry that she'd referred to anything back home. She walked quickly to the water's edge, with Clinton following.

Flat stones shone in the brief moment of sun before the clouds gobbled the yellow ball up again. She picked a stone up and skimmed it across the water.

"You're pretty good." Clinton picked up a stone and also sent it skimming. It bounced a few times on the water's surface, traveling not much further than Ruth's. "Where'd you learn?"

"My older brother Jesse taught me." She took a deep breath, deciding on how much to confide. "He died in an accident this past April. After that, Mama moved us here." Saying it out loud brought a bitter taste to her mouth.

Clinton took her hand. "I am so sorry, Ruth."

"Pa stayed back in Colorado Springs to finish the harvesting and to sell the farm." She blinked back tears. "Things haven't been the same between Mama and Pa since the accident." She took back her hand from Clinton and ran it through her wind-tossed hair. "Maybe once Pa's here with us, I'll feel like I've found my way home again. I won't think that much about our life back in Colorado Springs." Or about Jesse in his grave there, she wanted to add. She'd only think about the flesh-and-blood Jesse, full of vigor and wanderlust.

"It is so hard to let go of someone who has died." Clinton looked up at the sky while he spoke. "My ma says that's why God lets us have memories. She says memories are held in your heart, not your mind."

Ruth's memories about Jesse weren't in a good place in her heart. They were trapped deep inside her in that awful place where secrets have to stay tucked away. Cécile had written that she knew Ruth's heart. Her pen pal couldn't. No one could.

"I don't want to talk about this anymore." Ruth started back to the truck.

Clinton walked past her, his longer legs outpacing hers. Reaching the truck, he waited for her to catch up. "Let's do what we're here for."

Without saying another word, Clinton lifted the crate that held the three pigeons. He unlatched the lid and opened it wide. One pigeon flew close to Ruth; the bird's wing fanned her face. Their purring trills comforted her like church organ music might. With nothing between them and the clear blue sky, the birds flapped their wings and soared south toward home.

Ruth could feel their yearning.

While Clinton drove the truck back to his house, Ruth searched the sky for the pigeons. "Where do you think they are?"

"Back on top of their hutch." Clinton shifted the clutch. "The pigeons will beat me back home for sure today since I promised your grandfather I'd drive safely and slowly."

They reached the cutoff road to Clinton's house, and he drove around to the back. To Ruth's relief, all three pigeons welcomed them back, cooing.

"See these cylinders attached to their legs?" Clinton asked her.

"Yes."

"They're called pigeon posts. During the war, soldiers wrote messages on cigarette paper and rolled them up and stuffed them inside to send."

"Like with Cher Ami."

"You've seen the newsreels about that hero bird?"

"Yes," Ruth answered. "Why did you put the posts on your pigeons? Were you sending yourself a message?" She giggled.

"No. I wasn't sending *me* a message." Clinton held one of the birds out toward her. "Open its post."

Ruth carefully pulled the top off the post and slid the paper out.

"Read it," Clinton said, putting the bird back into the hutch. He picked up another pigeon.

She read the neatly printed word. "Be."

He held out the other bird to her. Ruth retrieved its message and read it. "My."

He returned that bird to the hutch and picked up a third one. Ruth took out the message from the third cylinder and waited until Clinton had put that pigeon back into the hutch.

She unrolled the message and read it out loud. "Girl."

"Well, will you?" Clinton asked. "Be my girl?"

Before Ruth could answer, a loud squawk interrupted. The cage that held Herkimer flew open, and out came the rooster.

"Oh, no. Not again," Clinton groaned. "I must not have latched the lid good enough."

Herkimer strutted into the woods that led back up to the main road.

"We have to catch him!" Ruth started sprinting after the rooster. "Dewdad would never forgive me if Herkimer got lost!"

The two darted one way and the other, trying to catch the rooster. Ruth drew near and dove for him. He got away, leaving her with a mouth full of dirt and her hair covered in leaves and straw. Clinton rushed past her in the chase and wound up the same. Herkimer strutted up to the roadway.

"You look a mess." Clinton pointed at Ruth and howled with laughter.

She stood and gave him the once-over. "You don't look so great yourself." She couldn't help laughing while she brushed the dirt off and plucked leaves from her hair the best she could.

Together, they sneaked behind Herkimer. Ruth held her shawl out, ready to smother the crazy rooster. When they reached him at the roadside, Mrs. Givens came around the bend walking her tiny terrier.

Herkimer took off, heading straight for the tiny pup like a dive-bomber ready to attack.

"Stop him!" Ruth shrieked at Clinton.

With a scream, Mrs. Givens grabbed Teacup into her arms. Herkimer began pecking at her ankles. Reaching them, Ruth threw her wrap over Herkimer, and Clinton hoisted him from the ground.

Mrs. Givens's gaze examined every inch of Ruth and Clinton, covered in dirt, straw, and leaves. Without a word, she tossed her head and stalked away.

Ruth took Herkimer from Clinton. "I think I'll walk home."

A light rain began misting.

"Let me drive you," Clinton offered. "It's about to downpour."

"No, I don't want to give Mrs. Givens more ammunition against me." She tightened her grasp on Herkimer and began walking. At the turn in the road, she looked back. Clinton hadn't moved.

Ruth called out, "The answer to your pigeon posts is yes."

He clasped his hands together and waved them on either side of his head like a boxer who'd won a big match.

Mrs. Givens would be making a beeline to Mama when she returned from her trip. Ruth had managed, without even trying, to do something that would disappoint both her mama and grandfather. She cared, yet she didn't.

She walked home in the rain holding a crazy rooster in her arms and Clinton in her heart.

CHAPTER TWENTY-FIVE
MAGGIE

"I'm beginning to love that crazy old rooster," Maggie announced. "You and Ruth. My mother said Herkimer was one of a kind."

"Well, I haven't been around many roosters or chickens, but I think your mother had him pegged correctly." Maggie unbuckled her seat belt. "Now that the air is smoother, I will visit the restroom."

"Good idea." Grams unbuckled her belt and stood in the aisle, stretching. "Oh, it feels good to stand. Do you mind if I go before you?"

"Not at all." Maggie reached into the box holding the letters. "I'll read another letter."

"Go right ahead."

Maggie began reading, worried about what she would learn about Cécile's health.

18, bis Avenue d 'Italie
Paris 75013
France

17 October 1919

Ma chere petite Ruth,

Yesterday I went to the doctor. He tells me I need country's air and my country's air only, because the Bretagne is a good country and when the Bretons arrive in Paris they fall ill.

Lulu worries so. He thinks Papa has a marked preference for me. I know it is hard for Papa to see me so sick. We are all glad that Lulu leaves to be at Le Havre to study to be a dentist. I will miss him so. He will stay well near the sea because Paris air is so bad! Our houses are dark and sometimes black. Notre Dame is black, Le Louvre, the Arc of Triumph, the Chamber of Deputies too, and oh! When you walk along the quays you can see old monuments, old statues near a dark green river crossed by old dark bridges under a gray sky. Nice, very nice!! Paris is so old. Poor old city! And so dear city! Cause I like it very much.

Don't despair dear. Life is so droll and perhaps a day will come when you and I could see each other. Here's a French proverb: "Il n'ya que les montagnes qui ne se rencontrent pas" which means "There are none so distant that fate cannot bring together."

From your far friend, with kisses,
Cécile

P.S. Bidart is making "mew-mew"! I don't know what he wants for his plate is full of meat and he has milk and water in a cup.

Maggie reread the French proverb. *There are none so distant that fate cannot bring together.* She winced, reminded of the emotional chasm between Cole and her.

When Grams returned, Maggie headed to the restroom. The tight space always triggered her claustrophobia. She took slow breaths to fight the sensation. Washing her hands, she stared at her image.

"There are none so distant that fate cannot bring together," she stated out loud. Cole and she were too distant to ever be brought back together, fate or no fate.

This woman in the mirror did not resemble the one who had giddily accepted his proposal. Who had naively believed all the lies he told about working overtime. Who had decided to create a family with him.

She dried her hands and slapped the paper towel into the trash dispenser, thinking how her marriage had also gotten thrown into the trash. She fumbled with the door to exit, her heart feeling tighter than the space itself.

Returning to her seat, she found Brian giving Grams his rapt attention. They continued talking in low voice. Maggie slid around him and Grams, settling back into her window seat.

"Your story is fascinating. This trip to Paris will be memorable." Brian checked his watch. "We're only two hours out from Paris. You two haven't slept any. I hope you won't surrender to jet lag when we land."

"Not I." Grams glanced at Maggie. "I'm thinking we'll get checked into our hotel and go out right away."

Maggie pointed at Grams. "I'm with her."

They laughed quietly. Brian made his way to get them wash towels to freshen up before he would serve breakfast.

"We do have much to see." Maggie ticked the sites off her fingers: Notre Dame, Le Louvre, the Arc de Triomphe, the Chamber of Deputies. "Cécile was quite an ambassador for the city she loved so much."

"Yes, she was." Grams stifled a yawn.

"Should we take a little Bidart nap?" asked Maggie.

Grams chuckled at her pun. "I'd rather not." Grams shifted in her seat. "I would like to finish my story before we arrive in Paris. Unless you're too tired?"

"No, not at all!" Maggie angled sideways and reorganized her throw around her. "I am entranced by all of it. We left Ruth in quite the mess with Herkimer. I can only imagine how her mother will react when she returns home. Continue!"

CHAPTER TWENTY-SIX
RUTH

For the rest of Mama's absence, Ruth put forth her best behavior. Dewdad kept checking her temperature, worried that the absence of high-spirited activity and chatter meant she must be sick.

In truth, Ruth's was striving to make amends for how she had spoken to Mama. She was also planting seeds of good will. It was only a matter of time before Mrs. Givens would be spilling the beans on her. She suspected the busybody woman was waiting eagerly for Mama's return.

Ruth stitched on her Quimper costume to fill her time after school. Worrying about Cécile filled up her nights. She'd received a letter from her only a few days after getting Lulu's. Cécile had infused it with descriptions of better health, but Ruth assumed the optimistic message was to keep her from worrying. No one recovered from consumption quickly.

If at all.

She understood about Cécile needing pure air to breathe. That's what brought many people who were sick like her to Colorado Springs—the pure mountain air and freshwater springs. Ruth remembered their thin, gray faces and how Mama warned her to keep her distance from them. No matter what Mama would say, if Cécile were here by her side, Ruth would hug her tightly.

She hadn't finished the letter she'd started to her pen pal, wondering exactly what to include and what to leave out. She didn't want to relay more worry about Cécile's health. She wasn't sure how much she should tell her about all the good things in her own life—Clinton, driving, winning the arithmetic contest. Most of all, Pa coming to Oakland.

If only Cécile weren't sick, Ruth could be happy for the first time in a while—almost.

She had memorized the French proverb Cécile had quoted. "Il n'ya que les montagnes qui ne se rencontrent pas." How would fate bring the two of them together if Cécile died?

No. Cécile had to get better. She had to be cured. The two of them had to make this proverb come true.

The day before Halloween, Mama's telegram arrived. They would arrive on the four o'clock train that afternoon. Ruth prepared a wonderful homecoming dinner. She made Pa's favorite dish and kneaded the dough for homemade yeast rolls, setting them aside to rise.

When she couldn't choose what to fix for dessert, Dewdad convinced her to go with Mama's tried-and-true butterscotch pie. All the dishes would be ready to pop into the oven when they returned from the station.

Ruth planned to glue herself to Pa's side while their feast cooked. After dinner, she'd show him her Quimper costume and catch him up on Cécile's letters. She'd never had the chance to tell Mama about Cécile's sickness, and Ruth dreaded sharing that awful news. Maybe Pa would come with news of a new treatment being given at the sanatoriums in Colorado Springs. Ruth could write about it to Cécile, to help her get well.

Time came to head to the station. Dewdad invited Clinton to follow in his truck in case an extra vehicle would be needed to cart all the trunks home. In the station's lobby Ruth checked the track numbers posted and found the platform for their train. The three weaved through the crowd and waited for its arrival.

Ruth envisioned Pa stepping from the train and offering his hand to help Mama disembark. She couldn't wait to wrap her arms around him. Impatiently, she scanned each passenger car to look for her family. Finally, she saw Mama, holding a tired-looking Florabelle on her hip, and the twins stood on either side of her, yawning. Mama's posture drooped from exhaustion. Ruth's eyes searched behind them, for Pa's familiar face.

He wasn't there.

When they reached the railcar, Dewdad took Florabelle from Mama and stood her next to Ruth. He helped Mama step down. Clinton reached up and swung the twins onto the platform. When Mama reached to hug her, Ruth drew back. "Where's Pa?"

Mama grabbed her hand and held it tightly. "The sales deal fell through. But, good news. Someone else has leased the farm and says he wants to buy it. We went ahead and packed up our belongings. Pa is staying with Mr. White at his place above the diner until this sale goes through."

"Pa has to stay in Colorado Springs?" She flung Mama's hand away. "It's your fault! You don't want him to come here."

"Ruth, that's not true." Mama reached to grab her hand again. Ruth stepped away from her.

"I hate you." Ruth turned away.

"Ruth Calderhead!" Dewdad's shocked exclamation reverberated through her.

Ruth couldn't look at Clinton, feeling shameful yet furious. She had to get away from Mama and the train that was supposed to have brought Pa back. She pushed through the crowd, gulping for air. All she could think of was getting out of the station.

The willow tree by the creek beckoned to her. If she were propped against the trunk, its green curtain would be hiding her from everything and everyone. She could look up at the sky and daydream away her guilt and pain and unhappiness. In her daydream world, Jesse would be alive. They'd all be together again, in the shadow of Pike's Peak.

But Jesse had climbed that mountain into heaven, leaving her behind.

"Ruth!" Dewdad's hand clamped on her shoulder. "Where are you going?"

Ruth turned to find Clinton standing by her grandfather. She stepped away and avoided both of their gazes.

"Clinton, could you drive Ruth home for me?" Ruth detected anger in Dewdad's tone.

Clinton answered by taking Ruth's hand. She let him lead her through the station, and they rode home in silence. He didn't try to comfort her or reason with her or ask her any questions. Somehow, though, Ruth didn't feel he was judging her. She felt he understood.

When they arrived at Dewdad's, Clinton didn't say a word when she jumped out of the truck. She rushed up to her attic room, only wanting to be alone. She sat at her vanity and held Jesse's compass, remembering Pa's words. *He'd want you to have it.*

A vision came to her of Clinton's pigeons winging their way home. They knew exactly where they were going. Where did she belong? Not even the medallion she'd received from Clinton made her feel like she belonged.

She grasped the compass tightly in the palm of her hand, willing it to tell her what to do and where to go, longing for it to guide her out of her pain, to guide her family back together.

This time the trifold mirrors she stared into didn't multiply her image into a long line of Ruths. They didn't fracture her into uncountable pieces. They didn't pull her into their glassy surfaces. The longer she stared, the more her reflections faded, until she disappeared.

∞

Ruth woke to the smell of rosemary and thyme and the scent of freshly baked yeast rolls. She had fallen asleep at the vanity with her head resting on top of her folded arms.

She stretched the soreness out of her neck and back, avoiding her reflection. A tapping at the door surprised her. After the scene she'd caused at the station, she had doubted anyone would ever speak to her again.

"May I come in?" Mama asked.

Ruth's emotions tumbled around like the marbles she and Jesse used to play with. She had acted dreadfully. How could she face her mother?

Mama entered with a dinner tray. "You've outdone yourself, Ruth, with this delicious supper. I assumed you might be hungry, so I have brought you a plate."

"Thank you, Mama."

Her mother did not answer.

"I had no right to speak to you that way." Ruth's voice caught in a sob. "I'm sorry." Tears rolled down her cheeks.

"What you said came from your disappointment. I know you didn't mean it." Mama placed the tray on the night table. "We all must be more patient for your pa to join us. Eat your dinner and get some more rest." She exited the bedroom, pausing for a moment at the door to give Ruth an understanding smile.

Ruth's relief at her mother's understanding didn't help her appetite. She picked at the food, thinking how Pa would have enjoyed this homecoming meal. She thought more about what Mama hadn't said than what she had.

She hadn't said she was disappointed Pa didn't come back.

She hadn't said that the two of them had worked out their feelings about Jesse.

She hadn't said how long they'd have to be patient.

Worst of all, she hadn't said that she no longer blamed Pa for Jesse's death.

Pa had kept the secret.

ഗ‑ഗ

Herkimer's crowing woke Ruth up. She flung the cover off and sat on the edge of her bed. Her hateful words to Mama flooded back into her mind. She didn't look forward to facing her or Dewdad today.

Or Clinton.

The Quimper costume she'd finished for the Halloween party tonight hung from the outside of her closet door. The morning sunshine that streamed into the windows accented the costume's colors, making the reds redder and the blues bluer.

She wouldn't blame Mama if she said, "No party for you."

Another Herkimer crow reminded Ruth that today was supposed to be the rooster's last one with the family. Dewdad hadn't yet found a new home for him. He hadn't heard back from his rancher friend he'd written, asking for a home for the rooster. One thing was for sure, though. Mrs. Givens would not put up with Herkimer one day past his deadline.

Thinking of Mrs. Givens sent Ruth crawling beneath the quilt again. That woman surely would come calling on Mama to describe catching Clinton and her covered with leaves and dirt. She could only imagine what Phoebe's mother had concluded about their behavior. What kind of reputation would she have after Mrs. Givens's gossip started to spread? All because of that rooster. If she didn't care so much about Dewdad, Ruth would be thrilled if Herkimer ended up somewhere else.

Determined to explain to Mama what had happened before Mrs. Givens trumpeted her version of events, Ruth jumped out of bed and hurriedly dressed. The twins and Florabelle remained asleep despite Herkimer's loud crowing. Ruth found Mama sipping her coffee, probably glad for some time before the younger ones woke up. Dewdad was nowhere to be seen.

Sitting in front of the scrambled eggs and biscuits Mama served, Ruth lost her gumption to spill the beans. Ruth hoped Mrs. Givens wouldn't come by. She downed the breakfast and started off for school. "Bye, Mama."

"Bye, Ruth." Mama kept sipping her coffee, not looking up.

Dewdad was standing at the chicken coop with a basket of fresh eggs, watching Herkimer strut around the henhouse. After today, that could be a sight Ruth wouldn't see again.

She summoned the gumption to speak to him. "Good morning, Dewdad."

"Good morning." He brushed a hand across his mustache. "Are you feeling better, Ruffis?"

The use of her nickname made Ruth hopeful. Maybe his anger and disappointment in her had faded. "I'm trying to." She did want to feel better. But how? "Today's Herkimer's deadline. What are you going to do?"

He shook his head. "I'm hoping by tonight this rooster will be crated up and on a train north to my friend's ranch."

"I hope so, for both your sakes." Ruth handed him the letter to Cécile that she had finally finished. "Could you mail this for me?

"Of course. Your letter will brighten her day."

Ruth blew Dewdad a kiss and walked up the driveway toward the road. Mrs. Givens was rounding the curve, walking her terrier. A chill raced through Ruth. She should have told on herself to Mama. She'd be angrier finding out about her daughter's poor behavior from Mrs. Givens.

At least she could warn Dewdad of the incoming enemy. "Mrs. Givens is on her way," she called to him.

He responded with a slight wave.

To Ruth's relief, Clinton was waiting to walk with her to school.

"Hey. Was Mrs. Givens walking toward your house?"

"Yes. She's probably heading to tell Mama about seeing you and me chasing Herkimer. She'll describe us misbehaving . . ." Ruth trailed off.

Clinton looked away, embarrassed.

"Mama will give me a tongue-lashing for sure when I get home from school, even though Herkimer caused the entire problem." Ruth's chest heaved with indignation.

"I'm sorry, Ruth." Clinton positioned his books underneath one arm and motioned for hers.

How did she deserve such a good friend after her awful behavior? Or deserve to be his girl? "Clinton, about what happened at the station—"

"You were upset about your pa. We all knew you didn't mean what you said to your mother." He kept his hand held out toward her books. Drawn to his unshakeable confidence in their friendship, Ruth handed him her books. While they continued walking, Ruth came to the conclusion that like his pigeons, Clinton knew his way in life.

Now, if only she could find hers.

∞·∞

Ruth dreaded arriving home after school. Mama stood on the porch waiting, with Dewdad at her side. "Ruth Calderhead, march yourself right into this kitchen this instant," Mama said.

Ruth did.

Mama pointed to the kitchen chair. "Sit."

Ruth sat.

"Mrs. Givens shared quite the story about you. What do you have to say for yourself?" Mama's mouth formed a straight line.

Ruth hadn't ever seen her this angry. And she'd seen her mama angry a lot.

Dewdad's anger upset Ruth almost more than Mama's.

Ruth explained, starting slowly. "Clinton and I went to Lake Merritt to release his pigeons. Somehow, Herkimer managed to get in the back of the truck, and we discovered him when we got there. We penned him up into the crate. When we got back to Clinton's house and were checking on his pigeons, Herkimer got loose again."

She conveniently left out the sweet *BE-MY-GIRL* message.

Her words tumbled out, faster and faster. "When we chased the rooster, we both tripped and fell in the woods. Herkimer reached the roadway exactly at the moment when Mrs. Givens and her dog walked by. I covered him with my shawl, and Clinton grabbed him. Mrs. Givens looked us up and down, and I walked home the rest of the way with Herkimer." She breathed in a sharp intake of air. "That's the truth, Mama. I promise."

Mama's skeptical look did not comfort Ruth.

"What do you suppose Mrs. Givens is saying to everyone after seeing the two of you coming out of the woods?" Mama leaned toward her. "Incidents like these cause gossip, which in turn will have people thinking you have no virtue. They will think that you are"—she took a breath— "an easy girl. A hussy!"

Dewdad breathed in sharply at the word. He didn't come to her defense. Mama put her hands on her hips. Ruth braced for more tongue-lashing.

"I've tried to explain to you that perception, for most people, is reality. Mrs. Givens's perception of this incident is not to the benefit of your reputation." The room fell silent. Mama spoke her next words quietly and firmly. "Perhaps I have been far too lenient with you. You will no longer walk with Clinton or ride in his truck or release his pigeons. You are forbidden to have anything to do with Clinton. Do I make myself clear?"

Dewdad's harrumph gave Ruth a glimmer of hope that he'd be her ally. "Dolly, perhaps you should wait until you're calm before you dole out discipline."

Mama waved her hand at him dismissively. "I love you, Papa, and I appreciate you allowing us to live with you. Ruth is my daughter, though, and I will discipline her as I deem fit."

There was no changing her mind. Ruth knew that about Mama. "May I go now?" she asked.

Her feelings were all mixed up. She didn't want her reputation to be ruined, especially since she and Clinton had done nothing wrong. It wasn't fair. She didn't want to stop being his girl.

"One more thing," Mama said. "You may go to the Halloween school party, but under no circumstances will you have anything to do with Clinton. I'm sure Mrs. Givens has spread her vicious gossip, and all attention will be on you two."

How could she ignore Clinton? He meant too much to her.

She answered, "Yes, Mama."

But she knew she would disobey her mother, reputation or no reputation.

CHAPTER TWENTY-SEVEN
MAGGIE

"Good gracious. What a mess." Maggie sighed. "I certainly hope your mother didn't get herself into even more trouble at this party."

Grams nodded knowingly. "My mother is about to make even more of a mess of things. We Ruths are all alike—strong-willed and quick to act. Especially if we believe we have been wronged."

Her grandmother's words hit close to home for Maggie. She had definitely not hesitated to cut Cole out of her life that morning after she had allowed him back in her bed. The redhead had texted that she'd missed him at a corporate dinner. Good grief. She'd dismissed any of Cole's attempts to explain. How stupid did he believe her to be?

Like Ruth, Maggie had been the wronged party. Grams had said Ruth made a mess of things. Maggie disagreed. Those around her had made the mess.

"In this letter, Cécile accidentally gave my mother an idea for quite an adventure," Grams read it out loud.

18, bis Avenue d 'Italie
Paris 75013
France

19 October 1919

My dearest Ruth,

My health is better but I am very weak from my illness as I write to you already. I write again so soon because I start to the country soon for my cure. I don't want to leave Paris, Maman, and Papa. Already I miss Lulu.

I know it is best but I don't like it. I like to stay in Paris with Bidart. I know the air isn't pure here but I hope to see again Paris very soon.

I will write you long letters daily almost as I will have much lazy time in my cure. Write to me in Paris and Maman and Papa will bring you letters to me when they visit me.

This means I think like you when you had to move to Oakland, it is difficult to leave a home which you loved and grown and made memories. I am like you that we have not had choice of this change and must endure. Now we will both think in our dreams at night of Paris and Colorado.

What I think in French and write in English is to give you with my heart the best kisses I can give; I can make it in all languages.

Au revoir, Cherie! with kisses,
Cécile

Maggie marveled at Cécile's insights. "Cécile certainly related to Ruth's feelings about being homesick for Colorado Springs. Does her family reunite back there? Or in Oakland? Come on, Grams. Tell me!"

"It's good you're buckled up. You are heading on quite an adventure with my mother, who takes reconciling her family into her own hands."

CHAPTER TWENTY-EIGHT
RUTH

Ruth did not keep her distance from Clinton at the Halloween party. How could she? He was adorable, dressed like Charlie Chaplin's Little Tramp, complete with baggy pants, black bowler, oversized shoes, cane, and hand-painted black mustache above his top lip. Cécile, such a lover of the Hollywood star, would have loved Clinton!

The Little Tramp approached Ruth, doing the side-to-side walk and swinging his cane. "You look great. Um, what is your costume supposed to be?"

Before Ruth could explain about Quimper and Cécile, Mary Pickford, also known as Phoebe Givens, appeared, trailed by her group of girlfriends. "Clinton, can't you tell that Ruth is a clown?"

Anger rushed through Ruth. While her mind scrambled for a saucy retort, Clinton jumped in first.

"Shut up, Phoebe." Clinton turned his back on her. "Ruth, tell me about your costume. If you'd like."

Phoebe snickered and walked away, a triumphant sneer on her face. Ruth blinked back tears of embarrassment. Phoebe had passed the condemning judgment on Ruth's costume, and no one would dare cross Phoebe. Ruth wished she had never come to the dumb Halloween party, much less dressed up like a Quimper girl. What had she been thinking? Why hadn't she come dressed in a princess costume?

"So, are you going to tell me, Ruth?" Clinton swung his cane and twitched his mouth to make the mustache move back and forth.

Ruth couldn't help but giggle at his impersonation. Clinton could always cheer her up. "It's a costume from Quimper, France, where Cécile grew up."

"You look great. You want to go bob for apples?"

"Sure."

They passed by Phoebe, whose attention was riveted only on Clinton. To Ruth's delight, Clinton paid her no attention. Together they walked around to the different activities at the party. He imitated the actor with the trademark side-to-side, dance-like steps while swinging his cane. When everyone laughed, he'd bow. They bobbed for apples and went through the not-so-scary haunted house set up in a classroom, squeezing peeled grapes that were meant to pass for eyeballs and dodging the black balloons that were pretend bats.

The night unfolded perfectly, until Miss Newton called for their attention.

"And the winner of the best girl's Halloween costume is . . ."

Ruth held her breath.

"Miss Phoebe Givens, dressed as America's sweetheart, actress Mary Pickford!"

Phoebe floated up to the front of the auditorium. The ruffles of her pink and cream satin and crinoline dress flounced with each bounce. A matching satin headband held up her perfect ringlets that tumbled down her back. A long rope of pearls, knotted midway, and her shiny cream ballerina-like slippers added Hollywood glamour.

Even Ruth had to admit it.

Phoebe was a dead ringer for the star.

Miss Newton placed the envelope holding the five dollars in prize money into Phoebe's hand. Disappointment stung Ruth. She had badly wanted that prize money to fix the bike and give it to Clinton.

It wasn't only about the prize money. Winning would have given her a reason to explain about Quimper and Cécile. The other students would find out she had a French pen pal and think she was more interesting than dumb, boring Phoebe.

Who was she kidding?

Even if Phoebe hadn't looked so terrific, Miss Newton would have made sure she won the award. Ruth could tell by Miss Newton's icy stare at her that Mrs. Givens must have bent her ear. Girls with dicey reputations shouldn't be rewarded.

"I can't believe she won," Clinton whispered into Ruth's ear. "Anyone can dress up like a movie star. Who else dresses up like a girl from wherever you said."

"It's pronounced 'Kem-pair.'" What difference did the pronunciation make now?

"Attention, students," Miss Newton called out over the applause for Phoebe. "The winner of the boy's costume is Clinton Carlock, dressed as Charlie Chaplin, the famous movie star and comedian."

Everyone clapped and whistled.

"Go on, Clinton. You won!" Ruth pushed him toward the stage. He imitated Charlie Chaplin's walk, twirling his cane, on his way to collect his prize.

Miss Newton presented the envelope holding the winnings to Clinton. Ruth's happiness for him danced within her. If he wanted to use the money for fixing the bike, she would give it to him in an instant.

On the stage, Phoebe stood close to Clinton, grabbing his arm, posing like the real Hollywood stars, while Mr. Higginbotham readied to take their photograph. The flash went off. Everyone clapped and whistled even louder. Except Ruth. Through the smoky haze of the photographer's popping flashbulbs, Ruth saw Clinton bending his head close to Phoebe's mouth, listening to whatever she was saying.

Humiliation spread through Ruth. How could she ever have believed she would be the one Clinton would like? She could never compete with Phoebe "Mary Pickford" Givens.

She took one last look at Clinton—smiling at Phoebe, posing for more pictures—and rushed out the door. Dewdad wouldn't be waiting for her yet. She didn't care. She ran to the cloakroom and grabbed her shawl. She would walk home. Alone.

She tugged her shawl around her against the October chill. Back in Colorado, there would be snow by now. They'd be celebrating Halloween with ghost stories around the bonfire. Jesse's stories had always been the scariest. He'd loved Halloween.

"Ruth, slow down."

She glanced over her shoulder. Clinton was running toward her with the Charlie Chaplin cane in his hand. This time she didn't laugh. She didn't slow down either. She sped up, trying to make it impossible for him to catch her. He reached her anyway. Perspiration dotted her face, flushed from walking fast—and from anger.

Clinton grabbed her hand. "Why did you leave the party like that?"

She snatched her hand from his and wrapped her shawl more tightly to try to control her shaking.

"You're freezing." Clinton took off his coat, draping it around her shoulders. "Why did you run out?" he asked again.

"What does it matter?" She started walking again.

He walked next to her, his legs falling into stride with hers. "It matters to me because you're my girl. You're wearing my necklace, aren't you?"

She quit walking. He stopped too.

"I am? Your girl?"

"Yes."

"Even though you're Charlie Chaplin and Phoebe is Mary Pickford?" He started laughing.

"It's not funny."

"Phoebe. She's such a troublemaker." He took her hand. "She's gossiping about you. About us."

Tears rushed into Ruth's eyes. "Mama said I can't be friends with you because of all that gossip."

"We have to change her mind. Explain that Mrs. Givens was wrong."

"Mama's anger will prevent her from listening to anything I say." Ruth turned from Clinton, not wanting him to see her brimming tears overflow.

They walked on in silence. When they got to the cutoff to his house, Ruth whispered, "Bye, Clinton."

"No, I'll walk you the rest of the way."

He took her hand. She let him. After tonight, she wouldn't be able to even talk to him again, much less hold his hand. Not with Phoebe's unwavering spying and Mrs. Givens's wagging tongue. If she even gave a sideways glance at Clinton again, Mama would hear about it.

They reached her driveway and stopped. Ruth's mind whirled with a crazy idea. "Would you go with me to talk with Mama? Maybe if we explained together that we hadn't done anything reputation-ruining, she'd understand."

"You think she would?" Clinton didn't express hopefulness.

"Ab-so-lute-ly." Ruth forced confidence into her voice.

"Ruth?" Clinton pulled her close, his strong arms holding her. She stood on her tiptoes, turning her face up toward him. His breath smelled like the sweet cotton-candy treat they'd shared at the party. His face grew closer, until it blocked all else from view. At this moment only Clinton filled her world.

For all of Mama's talk about manners and protecting one's virtue, she hadn't said anything to Ruth about protecting one's heart. Hers fluttered like the wings of a bird when Clinton's lips touched hers. She wanted the two of them to stay that way forever, in an embrace and kissing.

Rays from Dewdad's headlights illuminated them, breaking her magical moment. Ruth pulled from Clinton's arms. Her throat closed up in horror. She couldn't breathe. She let Clinton's coat fall from her shoulders and drop onto the ground.

Dewdad sat behind the wheel with Mama by his side. The twins and Florabelle poked their heads out the back window. They had all set out together to pick her up from the Halloween party. Mama stepped from the passenger seat.

Dizziness overtook Ruth, partially from happiness over her first kiss—and over the dread of being caught. Clinton's kiss had set off stirrings inside her. Was she the hussy Mama had accused her of being? Would Pa believe her to be a "fast girl?" If she were a proper young lady, would she have allowed Clinton to kiss her?

Mama was nearing them. A survival instinct overtook Ruth. She swung her arm at Clinton, her hand connecting against his cheek. The loud slap stung her hand. She ran toward her mother, who gripped her arm tightly and half-dragged her to the automobile and pushed her into the back seat.

Dewdad emerged from the driver's side. His words came out like lashes from a whip, sharp and crackling against the night air. "Young man, you are to leave Ruth alone." He returned to the driver's seat.

Steering the car into a three-point turn, its headlights swept across Clinton's startled face. Ruth saw his hand remained on the spot where her slap had landed. Sobs rose in her and came out in soft hiccups.

Dewdad parked his automobile in the garage. In silence, they entered the house.

"Ruth," Mama said, her tone warning of the reprimands to follow.

She ran to her attic room, away from Mama's ladies-don't lecture and Dewdad's hurt expression. Slamming the door, she threw herself onto it. Clinton's bewildered face kept flashing through her mind. How could she have slapped him? He had not forced the kiss upon her. She had desired it.

She sat up on her bed and caught her reflection in the mirrors. The room started spinning. Her breathing grew shallow, and her vision narrowed into a pinhole until the room darkened.

∞⟡∞

Her nerves in her body snapped at the same instant, jolting her awake. Snatches of her awful nightmare came back to her. Cécile in a sanatorium. Pa running beside a train, shouting, "Wait for me!" The gypsy lady calling out the letters. *"G-O-B-A-C-K."* Mary Pickford with her long blonde curls. Charlie Chaplin swinging his cane. Birds flying in circles, lost and searching for their home.

She had fallen asleep in her Quimper costume. It was wrinkled from her tossing and turning. Her nightgown rested on the back of her vanity chair. A tray sat atop the vanity with a glass of milk and a sandwich on it.

Mama must have come to check on her wayward girl—or more likely to give her a bigger piece of her mind. Wriggling out of the costume, Ruth slid on her nightgown and attacked the sandwich. After her first bite, she noticed the edge of an envelope underneath the tray. It had to be a letter from Cécile! She gobbled the rest of the sandwich before moving the tray to retrieve the letter. To her delight, not one, not two, but three letters from Cécile awaited her!

She placed them in postmarked order. The oldest one was postmarked from Cécile's home address. The two more recently dated ones were postmarked from a different address. Ruth opened the oldest letter first, dated October 19. Holding her breath, she skimmed Cécile's news, which focused on her having to leave home for treatment.

This means I think like you, it is difficult to leave a home which you loved and grown and made memories. I am like you that we have not had choice of this change and must endure. Now we will both think in our dreams at night of Paris and Colorado Springs.

Cécile was right. Neither of them had a choice in what was happening to them. Unlike poor Cécile, though, Ruth could make her own choice, couldn't she? Cécile's parents were taking care of her by placing her in a sanatorium. Ruth's parents were making her life worse by making her stay in Oakland, apart from Pa.

A plan took shape in Ruth's mind. She stared at herself in the vanity's mirrors, wondering if she could follow through with it. She kissed Cécile's letter, deciding to save the other two to read later. Her resolve over her plan strengthened.

First, a disguise would be required. A boy would draw less attention. People didn't think twice about boys traveling alone. Ruth crept downstairs to Jesse's trunk. Opening it, she chose two of Jesse's shirts, two pairs of his overalls, and two of his belts before shutting it quietly. Stealing into the kitchen, she located the large scissors Mama used to trim her hair.

She sneaked back upstairs and changed from her nightgown into one of the shirts and pulled on the overalls. She rolled the too-long pant legs to prevent tripping.

The mossy scent of the outdoors Jesse loved clung to his clothing. The release of his spirit surrounded her; she heard his laughter and remembered his gentle touch with animals. She took his compass from the vanity and tucked it into the front overall pocket.

One last thing remained for her to do.

Sitting in front of the vanity, she pulled her hair into a ponytail with one hand and held the scissors in the other. Clenching her teeth, she severed the ponytail with a single cut. She braided it into a long strand, tied bows at either end to hold it together, and hid it in her vanity drawer.

Clinton's necklace shone in the dim light of the room. She removed it and kissed the medallion before placing it in the drawer. *Goodbye, Ruth. For now.*

Checking herself out in the trifold mirror, she almost couldn't breathe. *Welcome back, Jesse.* Mama or Pa would think her to be his ghost, so strong was the resemblance. More lines came to her from "The Barefoot Boy," the poem that Mama had loved to recite about him. *Hand in hand with her he walks, Face to face with her he talks.*

She straightened the patchwork quilt on her bed and spread out Jesse's other clothing, her underwear and nightgown, her stationery and pencil, Cécile's two letters she'd yet to read, and the railroad brochure and map she'd saved from their trip to Oakland. She rolled all of it up into the quilt and secured the bundle with Jesse's belts, creating a shoulder strap.

In the kitchen, the clock read midnight. She gathered biscuits, a jar of green beans, carrots, and peaches and packed it all in the picnic basket they had taken to Idora Park. She filled up Jesse's old canteen that she'd found in the cupboard and hung it across her chest. Digging around in the flour canister, she searched for the tiny jam jar Mama kept hidden. She kept her rainy-day fund in it. There were only a few coins, but better than none.

Ruth slipped out the kitchen door, careful to ease it shut behind her. The moon cast eerie shadows, and at any minute she expected Dewdad or Mama to place a hand on her shoulder and ask her where she was going. What would Clinton think when he heard she'd run off? After the way she'd slapped his face, would he even care?

She made her way across the yard to the garage. The doors were heavy, and she grunted with effort to push them open. Dewdad's keys and checkered driver's cap were hung in place on the pegs on the garage wall. Grabbing them both, she slid into the driver's seat. She tossed her bundle onto the passenger seat and placed the picnic basket on the floorboard.

A distant train whistle boded a good omen for her journey. Tugging Dewdad's driver's cap over her bobbed hair, she stuck the key into the ignition and pulled the lever on the steering wheel. The engine revved up. She backed out and accelerated up the driveway toward the road.

Like one of Clinton's pigeons, she started winging her way home.

⸰⸰⸰

The gravel and rocks crunched from the weight of the motorcar. When she reached the dirt-road cutoff to Clinton's, she wanted to turn the steering wheel in the direction of his house.

She could still feel his lips on hers. The memory made her tingle.

Why in the world had she slapped him? She knew the answer. Because she feared Mama would believe her to be a "hussy," kissing a boy under the stars. Remembering the shock on Clinton's face, she kept driving past his house. He'd probably never speak to her again, much less go on the lam with her.

Brawk! The squawking erupted from the back seat. Herkimer! Her hands flew up to cover her face. The car drifted to the right. Ruth grabbed the steering wheel and swerved the car back onto the road, barely missing a tree.

"You good-for-nothing stupid rooster!" Braking to a stop, she got out and opened all the car doors. "Get out now, you stupid bird!"

Herkimer flapped his wings and bounced around the interior of the car, relieving himself. "Stupid, stupid thing. Dewdad should have thrown you into the pot and cooked you! It would have served you right!"

She angrily shut the doors and plopped back into the driver's seat, slamming that door. She was losing time and losing this battle. She drove faster, racing to the train station with Herkimer flapping around again.

The stone eagles stared from high upon the massive columns of the station's entrance. "If they were real, I'd send them swooping to snatch you up in their sharp talons, you filthy thing," she hissed at Herkimer. His beady eyes blinked at her.

Dewdad was going to be furious that she had driven his car. He'd be even more furious if she left Herkimer locked inside it until someone found the car. She couldn't live with her conscience if she let the bird loose to make its own way in the night. Or even worse, if the bird should die locked in the car. Only one answer came to her.

She got out of the car and went around to open the front passenger door. She strapped her bundle to her back and grabbed the picnic basket. She retrieved a biscuit to coax him closer. She slid into the back seat, calling out, "Here, birdy-birdy, here." He pecked at the biscuit and she lunged for him. With his quick instincts, he dodged her. The more she lunged, the more he dodged.

She doubted that when people called the back seats of cars "struggle buggies," they were thinking of this type of struggle. Clinton would be howling for certain at this lively matchup between girl and rooster. She wished he were there to help.

Herkimer went for the last bite of the biscuit. This time, her hand moved faster than his peck. She grabbed him and stuffed him, feathers flying, into the wicker basket and latched the lid. His beak kept poking through the basket's weave before he finally calmed.

Ruth headed for the same track that had been used for Mama's trip to Colorado. Once the train pulled in, she'd hop an empty boxcar like she had with Jesse.

Not many people were milling around. Ruth slipped behind a tall pile of steamer trunks that would be loaded onto the train once it arrived and sat to wait. The chimes of the station clock struck two in the morning. With Herkimer settled in the basket, Ruth rested her head on the back of the trunks and waited for her real adventure to begin when the 7am train arrived.

The sharp train whistle and chugging engines jolted Ruth awake. The sun had arisen. Herkimer started squawking, and the basket danced around on the ground.

"Shush. Quit moving," she sputtered.

The train halted amidst waves of steam, and the terminal jumped to life. People swarmed toward the passenger cars. Porters hoisted trunks and luggage. Ruth grabbed the basket and made her way toward the caboose, hoping for an open boxcar.

What if she'd come all this way and couldn't get on the train? If only she had the money to buy a ticket. Mama's rainy-day coins were hardly enough to buy a coffee and doughnut, much less a ticket to Colorado Springs.

She reached the last boxcar, next to the caboose. The door had been left open about two feet. A uniformed railroad detective stood near with his back to her.

"You keep quiet," she whispered sternly to Herkimer. A loud noise out of him would ruin her chance to hop on the car.

She shrugged her blanket roll off her shoulders and placed it into the boxcar, followed by the basket. Hoisting herself up and into the car, she crouched on her knees to peek out the door. The detective had not seen her actions.

"Well, you nasty old bird," she whispered, sliding the basket into the corner of the boxcar toward a stack of crates, "you and I are going to be riding the rails together."

The inside of the boxcar stunk worse than bird droppings. The vinegary smell of rotting potatoes in the crates filled the air. The hay on the floor stunk of manure. No wonder this boxcar had no occupants. It wasn't fit for even a hobo. It certainly wasn't fit for a girl and her bird.

The train jerked and steam hissed. The conductor called out, "All aboard!" Ruth could make out the silhouette of the detective, moving toward the boxcar door. Ducking behind the crates, she held her breath against the stink and against the fear that Herkimer would give them away. The detective poked his head in and took a quick glance around. He shoved the door shut. The train started to roll.

Her journey had begun.

CHAPTER TWENTY-NINE
MAGGIE

"She ran away!" Maggie lowered her voice and added, "Hopping a boxcar all alone."

"No, not alone." Grams chuckled. "She was with that darned old rooster."

Maggie rolled her eyes. "I cannot imagine what she was thinking, putting herself in danger like that!"

"I know!" Grams frowned. "She actually was quite lucky when it came to the danger she confronted and how she managed to stay safe."

"Cécile must not have believed all this when Ruth finally wrote her about it!" Maggie clasped a hand to her forehead, still in shock over this latest turn in her great-grams's life.

"Much happened to my mother during this journey to her father. I'm not sure how much she wrote about it to Cécile. Actually, Cécile accompanied my mother on the trip since Ruth had brought her recently received letters." Grams pulled out those letters. "And my mother was on Cécile's journey to the Health House too. They both were facing the next stage of their lives."

Maggie took the letters from Grams and examined the return address. Cécile had written them from a Health House at Bligny Fontenay. "Did you research about the Health House? Was it far from Cécile's home?"

"I did google the address, and I found out that the Red Cross opened it to be a sanatorium in 1918. It was about twenty miles from her home address. It's now a private hospital."

Maggie gave a low whistle, imitating Dewdad. "I am telling you, Grams, that you missed your calling. You should be a cyber detective."

"Oh, you." Grams's reply couldn't hide her delight over Maggie's compliment.

"You will find this letter interesting, Maggie. A bored Cécile wrote more details about living through the bombings and drew Ruth a map of where the bombs hit."

Maggie needed no further tease to turn her attention to the letter.

Health House
Bligny Fontenay
France

22 October 1919

My Dear little Ruth,

I begin to habit myself here. I am in a Health House we are about 100 girls. We have a large park around the house. My room is on the second story. There is a lift but we go upstairs by ourself. Each girl has a room for herself and all the window open on a wide valley, the famous "vallee de Chevreuse" where air is so pure. On the lawn in front of my window is a croquet game. There is a piano in the hall and I played a little song on, yesterday. We have cinema each Friday, at night.

I bless you for all you go through if you can understand this writing. Excuse my pencil, I have an inkstand and a penholder but I cannot write with ink in my room and I don't like to write in the hall. I write you as I sit on my long chair because this hour is the hour of repose. We have many hours of repose in a day. Morning-1. Afternoon- 2. Evening-1.

I like very much to get up here. By the large window I see the trees, fields, sky and hear such a beautiful concert with the birds! That's different of Paris life. My long chair is on my balcony. When I hear a wheel noise I watch the part of the road I can see from my balcony and I see the carriages or the motorcars pass. Sometimes I see pedestrians or bicycles, men or horsemen.

I like to watch the clouds like you now. Sometimes they have nice shapes. During the war watching the sky was make me afraid.

Today I work for you darling; as the time is long, very long to stay all the day on a chair. I draw you a map.

During the war many bombs drop from the sky. The little marks are bombs of Gothas and cannons Berthas. The nearest bomb dropped near our home is on the Italy place.

Sometime, during war, I would look to the sky and instead of cloud I would see zeppelins dropping bombs on Paris. Zeppelins look like a cloud that makes a great shadow.

Nighttime was afraid, too, at 2 am all the siren in the city sounded and we go to the cellar, as was an air-raid of the Boches. For the first time I hear exploding shells and barrage fire. So loud! The next day Big Bertha fired shells, "blockbusters" from the forest outside Paris, eighty miles away! Everyone looked up in the clouds for the Gotha.

Soon we could know the schedule of Bertha. Every fifteen minutes for many days. So Maman and Lulu could leave home to get our food. They would wait for the sound of the big gun and would hurry home ahead of Bertha.

The most bad day was day our neighbors home was demolished, I mark it on map closest to Italie place. They all die. We were glad to be not harmed and our home not bombed.

*The Boches drop many bombs near the rail to try to take it out.
You can also see I draw the fortifications that circle the city of Paris.
Sometime we go to school but our numbers were not great.*

*Write me many letters dear Ruffis as I you. I bring here your
past letters and that is a distraction to read them. So au revoir
petite amie.*

*With kisses,
Cécile*

Maggie found herself speechless at the first hand description of the
attack on Paris. The map was an amazing artifact, sketched by a young
girl whose world was literally exploding around her. Anger surged within
her. "After all Cécile has lived through during the war, how unfair she
would fall ill with tuberculosis." Her voice shook with emotion. "She and
Ruth both were experiencing such terrible events in their young lives."

Grams answered softly. "Yes, I think that is what Cécile means when
she writes of the fate that connects the two. While Cécile is on a journey
to get better physically, Ruth's journey is for the sake of her emotional
health. We all have times in our lives that we fight for that, don't we?"

Grams's pointed question caught Maggie by surprise. If she were to
be honest, she had to admit her anger was hurting her emotional health.

Grams broke the awkward silence by asking, "Shall I tell you more
of your great-grandmother's story?"

"Please," Maggie replied, glad to return to someone else's problems
and leave hers buried.

CHAPTER THIRTY
RUTH

Never before had Ruth been all alone with no one to care for her. She shivered from both fear and excitement.

After the train had been going for a little while, she unlatched the picnic basket to let Herkimer out. He ruffled his wings and strutted around in the hay, exploring his new temporary home.

The boxcar grew colder. Ruth's teeth chattered. In her haste to leave, she had forgotten a coat. The warm weather in Oakland did not require her to wear heavy overcoats, mittens, scarves, and boots. Without all her bundling-up clothing, she was going to freeze in Colorado!

She unrolled her blanket to use the quilt for warmth, placing her belongings next to her. Wrapped in the patchwork patterns, she leaned against the railcar wall, remembering the night in front of the vanity mirrors, falling into pieces. Now she was traveling in a stinky, cold boxcar with a rooster, running away from Mama and toward Pa. Maybe she *had* gone crazy.

Herkimer nuzzled against her. Although she resented him for all the trouble he always caused, she had to admit his company weirdly comforted her.

The breeze of the blue-misted high Sierra summits wafted in through the gaps of the car's slats and helped sweetened the foul boxcar air a bit. Through the slats, Ruth glimpsed the landscape slipping by under the sun rising higher in the sky. She spread the brochure and the map out in her lap and concentrated on trying to get her bearings. From what she could determine, she was traveling through the Feather River Canyon, whose many gorges widened out in some places into gentler terrain.

She continued to peer out from the slat openings. The train was hugging a stream's edge. Ruth saw men trout fishing, and upstream, she could make out a bear and several deer. Jesse would have loved the heavily timbered country, isolated yet somehow welcoming.

The morning sun slid across the sky and turned into afternoon sun. Ruth's stomach rumbled from hunger. Herkimer had eaten all the biscuits. She opened a jar of peaches, fished out the pieces with her fingers, and ate them hungrily.

Herkimer bobbed his head at her, and she threw a few pieces onto the hay. His pecking dance around them showed his confusion at this new kind of morsel. He finally managed to eat most of his peach bits. She sipped some water from Jesse's canteen and poured a dribble onto her fingers to clear away the stickiness.

With her stomach somewhat filled, she read one of the letters Cécile had written from the Health House. Cécile's positive description couldn't hide her homesickness. Ruth studied the map that showed the bombs that had dropped around her pen pal's house, and she read over and over her description of Gothas and Berthas. She studied the drawing of fortifications that circled the city of Paris.

Ruth wanted to open the other letter she had received but decided to save it. She needed something to look forward to during her long and lonely journey.

The train slowed. According to the route map, Ruth figured that they had reached the first stop near the state line between California and Nevada. Portola served as the junction for passengers who wanted to change trains for Reno, Nevada. She rolled her belongings back into the quilt and slipped the bundle onto her shoulders in case she had to jump off quickly to avoid any more railroad detectives. She grabbed

Herkimer, shoving him under her arm, and moved back into the shadowy corner by the crates.

The train jerked to a stop. Over the noise of passengers getting on and off and trunks and luggage being loaded and unloaded, she could make out the voices of men standing outside the boxcar's door. The door slid open.

"Hey. This one's empty."

Herkimer's heart beat hard against her fingers. Ruth's own heart beat even faster. She crouched back to avoid the bindle on a stick that came flying through the door of the boxcar, followed by another. Two hobos entered the car and flopped on the floor.

One was tall and beanpole thin. If he turned sideways, he would disappear. His long, tangled black beard was speckled with gray and his stringy long hair reached his shoulders. The other man was short. The way his clothing hung off him, a second body could fit inside with him. His red scruffy beard bushed out in wild frizzles of curls that match his curly hair. They smelled like they hadn't had baths in a month of Sundays. Ruth tried to hold her breath against their stench.

"Looks like we're set for Salt Lake," Beanpole said.

"Looks that way," Scruffy answered.

"Close the boxcar door, why don't ya?" Beanpole said.

"All right, all right." Scruffy scrambled to his feet and managed to pull the heavy door shut.

The whistle blew, and the loud hissing of steam announced the train would depart soon. Ruth pressed against the railcar's wall to better balance herself. Herkimer squirmed against her. The combination of the rotten potato stink, dirty hay, and Herkimer's feathers took hold of her. Her nose started tickling and burning.

A Ruth Calderhead sneeze was coming.

She clamped one hand against her mouth to try to stop it. Herkimer squirmed against her. He let out a soft *brawk*.

"Did ya hear that?" Beanpole asked.

"Yea." Scruffy walked toward the crates. Ruth sunk lower. Her sneeze was building, building, building.

Scruffy inched closer and closer.

Ruth's nose burned hotter inside.

Herkimer and she exploded at the same time.

A —choo! Brawk!

Ruth opened her eyes and found Scruffy staring at her. "Well, if we don't have ourselves a rail kid aboard," he sneered. "He's holding on to his dinner!"

The whistle blew again. "All aboard!" the conductor yelled.

The train would be pulling out of the station in a matter of minutes. She couldn't be stuck with these two!

Leaning to get a better look at Herkimer, Scruffy asked, "Is that rooster a fighter?" His breath smelled of hooch. Ruth remembered that smell from the night Jesse died. On that night, Pa drank himself into such a stupor that Mama had to help him into bed. It had been the only time in her life she had ever seen Pa drink.

Was Herkimer a fighter? Once, when a fox crept around the hen-house, she'd seen Herkimer push one of his wings to the ground and strut in circles. Dewdad had called it his cockerel waltz. He said roosters behaved that way when they were serious about fighting.

The answer to Scruffy's question was yes. Herkimer *was* a fighter. He had to be. He was her only weapon against these hobos. He'd better waltz for real now.

"Get him, Herkimer!" She threw him straight at Scruffy's face. "Attack!"

The hobo stumbled backward, waving his hands. "Get away, you stupid bird!"

Herkimer hit the nasty floor of the boxcar, and one of his wings went down. His feathers bristled up high, making him double in size. He started his cockerel waltz against Scruffy's legs, pecking at them and squawking at him full throttle.

Yelling, the hobo backed away until he reached the boxcar's door. He jerked it open. The lurch of the departing train pitched the hobo right out of the car. Ruth let out a victory yell.

Beanpole scrambled to his feet and grabbed both bindle sticks. Herkimer made a direct launch against his chest, and the man waved the bindles against the bird.

"Call him off, kid. Call him off." The squawks coming out of Beanpole were louder than Herkimer's.

"Go, Herkimer! Go!" Ruth yelled.

Beanpole ran for the door and jumped off the slowly moving train. Ruth stuck her head out of the half-opened door. The dazed hobos remained sprawled on the ground. She grabbed hold of the door and struggled to close it.

Herkimer walked around the car in circles, primed for more fighting. She would forever tolerate his pecking, grateful for his protection against those threatening hobos.

"Hurray for you, ya old rooster." Ruth sunk into the stinky hay, feeling shaky. "For once, you've earned your keep. Dewdad had it right. You *do* have spunk."

She leaned against the wall of the boxcar. Herkimer settled at her feet.

"Thanks, Herk," Ruth whispered. "Friends?"

His beady eyes blinked, "yes."

He fell asleep, and soon the rhythmic clack of the train traveling the steel rails lulled her to sleep also.

Ruth awakened to the slowing of the train. Between the slats of the boxcar, she could make out the name of the station they were approaching: Palisade, Nevada. She needed a restroom visit. When it came to going to the bathroom, she was a girl. She'd have to sneak in the ladies' room.

She strapped the bundle on her back and picked up Herkimer. He didn't put up much of a fight when she pushed him into the wicker basket. The train came to a stop, and she pulled the boxcar door open enough to slip through. She waited until the hurly-burly of passengers claiming their luggage had slowed to a trickle before jumping.

Her left foot didn't clear the landing, and she went flying forward. She hit the ground with her foot pinned under her. Pain came in waves, washing through her again and again. With gritted teeth, she forced herself to stand and limp into the station like a pirate on a peg leg. She made her way to the ladies' room. A gasp from a woman exiting reminded Ruth that she was a "boy" who shouldn't be entering!

She darted into a stall and did what she needed to do. When the bathroom emptied, she ventured out to wash. Before leaving, she peeked out the door to be sure no one was outside to observe her exit. She hobbled to a bench on her throbbing ankle and sat. How in the world would she be able to hop a boxcar now?

Herkimer rustled in the basket. She shifted her bundle and looked around the station. A ma and pa and their children were gathered at the entrance to one of the passenger cars. The confused conductor counted off a passel of squirmy kids pushing and shoving each other while boarding. Limping over, Ruth merged with them in making their way up the steps. The conductor didn't noticed her. She was on board.

Ruth settled in a window seat behind the mama and two of her children. She turned away when the conductor came through the aisle to check each person was seated before the train pulled away. Herkimer cooperated by staying quiet in the basket.

"Thanks, Herk," she whispered.

The woman seated next to her shifted in her seat, sniffed at the air, and pulled her handkerchief from her bag to breath into it. Ruth could hear Mama: *Ladies don't give off terrible odors.* Good thing the lady believed her to be a boy. A boy was supposed to be smelly.

The conductor called, "All aboard."

They were off.

Ruth's ankle throbbed in rhythm with the clacking of the train on the tracks. She shifted her weight this way and that, trying to get it in a position that would hurt less. She was lucky to have a seat, yet how she longed for a sleeping berth.

Her empty stomach rumbled. The lady sneaked a look sideways at her. Ruth pretended not to notice. With the landscape slipping by, Ruth was relieved to be getting closer to Pa. But, her growing anticipation couldn't keep her mind off her growling stomach and her aching ankle.

The train slowed slightly in its approach to Elko, Nevada. From her window, she saw the engineer stick his arm out in the evening shadows to hoop a message while they came around a curve.

On their trip to Oakland, Mama had explained how hooping worked. If a station needed to get a message to a train that wasn't going to stop, they'd clip the message to a large loop at the end of a long pole. The train's engineer snared the loop with an extended arm and retrieve the message without ever having to stop the train.

Ruth wondered what was in the message the engineer had hooped.

The train gained speed after passing through Elko. The conductor walked back and forth between the passenger cars, dining car, and first-class sleeper cabins. He had a preoccupied look on his face.

"These all your children?" he asked the pa.

Ruth held her breath.

The father put his arms around two of his children's shoulders like a bird spreads its wings to protect its brood. "Yes, sir," he boomed in a proud voice.

"We received a message that a family is looking for their runaway daughter, fourteen years old. We are on the lookout for her," the conductor announced.

Ruth tried to shrink herself from view, realizing that the hooped message must have been about her. She tugged on Dewdad's cap and tightened her grip on the wicker basket.

Her conscience reprimanded her. Running off had been a bad idea. How scared Mama and her sisters must've been when they discovered she had gone. Dewdad too. He must have been angry about his messy car and worried about Herkimer. Did Clinton miss her too? Had he forgotten their kiss? She hadn't. She never would. She regretted slapping him. She hoped he wasn't kissing Phoebe now.

Her stomach groaned loudly. She couldn't pretend the noise away. Tugging the cap down further, she mumbled, "Excuse me" while making her way into the aisle. Ruth wished she could apologize for her awful odor. Dewdad would describe her as odiferous.

She limped to the dining car, took a seat, and studied the menu. Herkimer shifted in the wicker basket. "Shh. Be patient. I'll feed you something."

She ordered a bowl of soup. It cost a nickel. Ruth hated to spend the money when she had food in her basket, but she couldn't risk opening it. She either spent the nickel or keeled over in a faint brought on by starvation. At least crackers and a glass of water would come free with the soup.

When the soup came, she spooned up the first taste, blew on it, and slurped it down hungrily. After all, she was a boy, and boys slurped, didn't they? She sneaked bits of crackers to Herkimer through the openings in the wicker basket.

Ruth could have eaten another bowl or two of soup. She filled up on more crackers while gazing out the window at the Great Salt Lake, surrounded by the peaks of the Wasatch Range. Islands dotted the lake. She remembered Mama telling her the abundance of salt in the water created such buoyancy that a swimmer couldn't sink. Pa was like the salt in their family's lake. They needed him to keep their family from sinking. She needed him to keep her from sinking.

When Ruth returned to her seat, the lady let out an irritated *harrumph*. Ruth didn't care because the next stop would be Salt Lake City. She would be half-way to Pa!

The next morning, when the conductor walked by, singing out, "Next stop, Salt Lake City," Ruth cheered up at the announcement. Her night had been long and miserable. At some point, the lady who had been sitting next to her had moved to another seat. Ruth assumed her stink or her moaning had run the woman away. Ruth had been glad for the room to stretch out her ankle. She could tell it had swollen to twice its size.

The mama of the large brood to whom Ruth was pretending to belong started waking up her children.

"We're home!" the youngest called out.

Ruth couldn't wait to be saying the same thing when the train pulled into Colorado Springs. Pa would be shocked she'd made her way to him. What if he wasn't pleased? She pushed that doubt away. Of course he'd be pleased.

The train came to a stop at the station. The family gathered their belongings and started toward the exit.

"Hold up there." The conductor stopped the pa. "Aren't you forgetting one of your youngsters?" He pointed to Ruth.

She couldn't breathe.

She'd been caught.

◌⁘◌

Ruth hated the smell of the Union Pacific infirmary, where the conductor had led her. It reeked of rubbing alcohol. The walls' ugly lime green color repulsed her. She sat on a gurney while a young doctor wrapped her ankle. Each time he moved it, she winced over the pain and the disappointment that she wouldn't reach Pa.

Mr. Cooper, the man the train's conductor had placed in charge of Ruth, wrote something on the clipboard in his hand and poked the pencil behind his ear. "You're in good hands here. I'm going to notify your mother that you have been located. You'll soon be on the next train back to Oakland."

Herkimer squawked and rustled around in the basket. The doctor jumped, and the bandage slipped from his hand. He cocked his head toward the basket. "What do you have in there?"

Mr. Cooper raised the lid, but Ruth slammed it down again. "My grandpa's rooster is in there."

The two men exchanged confused looks.

She shrugged again. "It's a long story. If you're sending a telegram to my family, could you please let tell them Herkimer is all right? My grandpa will be worried."

Mr. Cooper pulled the pencil from behind his ear and licked the point. "How's that spelled?"

She spelled out Herkimer's name. He scribbled on the clipboard.

"We don't let animals travel in passenger cars." He frowned. "I guess you've gotten this far with a rooster in a picnic basket. We'll let you keep on traveling with him." Shaking his head, he left the room. Ruth heard him mutter, "A rooster in a picnic basket. A girl dressed to be a boy. What else will this day bring."

The doctor finished the bandaging. "You have a bad sprain and don't need to be putting much weight on that foot for at least a week." He rummaged in a supply closet and brought out a pair of crutches. "Try getting around on these."

Ruth hobbled a few steps using them. Her ankle throbbed, but the tight bandage helped.

The door burst open, and two men rushed in carrying a rail worker whose arm was covered in blood.

"Wait out in the waiting room until Mr. Cooper returns," the doctor instructed her. He handed back her bundle and the basket. "Good luck."

"May I use the restroom?" She rubbed her hand across her face. "I need to wash up."

He pointed down the hallway. "Right that way, and hurry back."

She leaned the crutches against the wall and struggled to slip her bundle over her shoulders. If she used one crutch, she could manage the basket with Herkimer. She started in the direction he pointed until the door to the infirmary closed behind her. She scanned around for Mr. Cooper but didn't see him.

Time to make her getaway.

Hobbling as quickly as she could, Ruth made her way through the crowd of busy travelers and out the main door of the station onto the street. Drifts of plowed snow covered the curbs. A blast of wintry cold air sent flecks of snow swirling around her. Why hadn't she brought a coat?

Herkimer was restless and trying to peck the basket lid open.

"Stop it, or I'll let you out right here in the middle of wherever we are in Salt Lake City," she warned him, her words sending visible puffs of breath into the cold air.

A tiny woman bundled into a full-length fur coat crooked her neck when passing Ruth, her curiosity apparent. The lady's navy-blue hat with multicolored feathers sticking out of it reminded Ruth of Herkimer.

"My boy." The woman approached Ruth. "Why are you speaking to a picnic basket?"

Herkimer let out a squawk and thudded his head against the lid.

"Oh my. It appears your basket is speaking to you." Her warm and friendly manner settled Ruth's nerves about talking with a stranger. "What's your name, young man?"

Ruth didn't even stop to think. "It's Ruffis. Ruffis Addison." She held onto the basket. "My grandpa's silly old rooster is in there." She started to hobble away, fighting against pain shooting up her leg at even the slightest weight placed on the injured ankle. Growing woozy, her knees buckled.

"Let me help you." The woman took the basket from her. "Is there anyone coming to pick you up?"

"No, I've traveled here alone." Ruth let out a moan. The loud street noises started to fade away, and the people on the sidewalk blurred.

"All alone?" The woman frowned. "How old are you?"

Ruth took a chance that her height would allow her to pass for older. "I'm fifteen."

"Well, fifteen and all alone. That can't be good." The woman waved her gloved hand above her head and cried, "Yoo-hoo!"

A motorcar pulled up to the curb.

"Sister, this poor boy has no one. And he has no coat! He's hurt and needs help."

Ruth leaned more on the crutch, hoping she could remain standing.

"Yes, sister," the driver said. She wore a red hat with its netting covering her forehead. "He does look pretty cold and pathetic."

Her ankle's throbbing finally won out. Ruth slumped toward the sidewalk, and the crutch fell from her.

The driver called out, "Catch him, sister, catch him!"

Before Ruth hit the ground, the woman caught her and helped her to the motorcar. Ruth reclined in the back seat with the crutch across her lap and the basket with Herkimer beside her. The feather-hatted lady sat on her other side.

"You appear to require a place to rest and a good meal to eat," the driver said. "Would you allow us to help you?"

Ruth shrugged.

"That means yes." The feather-hatted lady waved her gloved hand in the air. "Drive on, Mrs. Beard."

"Ab-so-lute-ly, Mrs. Butterick," the driver answered.

That fun pronunciation from a grownup would horrify Mama.

"Where are we going?" Ruth asked

"To the Glory Bee Tearoom on Thirteenth Street, one half block from the university," Mrs. Butterick answered.

"We are the proprietors," Mrs. Beard added.

A tearoom. That meant food. She could eat and rest before setting out again for Colorado Springs.

She had come too far to turn back now.

CHAPTER THIRTY-ONE

MAGGIE

"Oh, Grams! How lucky Ruth made it that far without being attacked—or worse!" Maggie shuddered. "I'm grateful for Mrs. Butterick and Mrs. Beard!" She giggled. "They remind me of the characters from *A Wrinkle in Time*—Mrs. Whatsit, Mrs. Which, and Mrs. Who."

"You always did love that book, dear. These two ladies were lifesavers for my mother. She kept in touch with them until they both passed. If not for them and what happened when she was in their care, your great-grams would never have found any peace about her brother's tragedy."

"Okay, you have to finish telling me Ruth's story. What could possibly happen at a teahouse that would bring her peace?"

"Let's not skip too far ahead. Remember, Ruth took with her the letters from Cécile." Grams pulled out an envelope whose contents appeared thicker than a letter. "Cécile had sent photos!"

"Oh, let me see!" Maggie's words came out in a squeal.

"First, would you like to read the letter?"

"Well, of course I would." Maggie began reading it out loud.

Health House
Bligny Fontenay
France

23 October 1919

Dear little Ruthey,

*I write you much because it makes the time pass
for me and I hope you enjoy my letters. The bell
has tinkling for the repose from 10:30 to 11:30.*
*I saw the doctor yesterday. He says it is better to take of oneself in
a Health House than in Paris, so I can get fat and strong. I am so
bloodless when I come here. So, my dear, I will stay here the whole
winter, until March.*

*The stagecoach started today with girls and women of our health
house to Paris. We wave our handkerchiefs to them. The next railway station is Limours, a pretty little town. The stagecoach is like
this. When it snows, they are obliged to come here with sleigh. I
will be happy to travel in a sleigh, as I never do? Have you? It must
be so funny to glide on the ice. It is raining today and so cold. My
radiator is heating but as my window-door is open it is just same
as if the radiator was cold and the window shut! I could not live
with my window shut, and day and night, it is open.*

*We are making a stock of chestnuts with my friends and we eat
them as we are always hungry. I eat as a man who has not ate since
36 days. My friend Mimi has very short hair all curly. I like very
much short hair but Maman will never let me cut mine. I cut you
a bit of my long hair. Maman will not know because I will not tell
her! But by way of it you can see my hair is very long.*

*Mr. Marius the photographer took pictures. The other girl on
the picture is Jeanne. You can see her too on my right in the other
picture. She has a little bouquet of flowers too. On the picture we*

are reading one of your letters I brought with me. You can see the Health House behind it is difficult to see my window.

We had a fete for our doctor. I dressed as a Spanish girl. My complexion was painted yellow and it was difficult to clean my skin after. The doctor did not recognize me at first. He says, "Who is she?" My knight was Julienne, who was dressed like a boy of Africa. What is your opinion about colored men? Have you a sort of hate with the Negro, or have indifference for them? I know in U.S.A. the colored men are not loved, but I desire having your opinion. I do not make any difference of a pale face and a Negro, cause I think "the both are men, and all the men are same."

I had a dream that you were coming and see me with your Mama. I was speaking to you in English. This is very rare to dream in English! Do you know about putting a looking glass under the pillow? You see in your dreams the boy who will be your husband. I don't believe this but I do it to laugh. I put it under my pillow and I didn't dream as usual, so I said I should not marry! A girl saw her fiancé and another saw a boy she knows, and I saw... nothing.

People say that when you dream during the night of Thursday to Friday it will surely be right, so dream on these nights of our meeting to be sure it will be right! A good kiss for Mable, Opal, Florabelle and your mama, and, of course,

kisses for you, little sweetheart,

Cécile

Maggie folded the letter, a pensive look on her face. "How interesting that Cécile would ask about race relations. And how she believed all to be equal. That attitude in Paris brought the young writers and painters and other creative types—and those with alternative lifestyles—to the city in the twenties."

"The Lost Generation. Cécile reached adulthood while they were nurturing their creative spirits."

"We are all broken. That's how the light gets in."

"What?"

Maggie shrugged. "Hemingway. That's a famous quotation attributed to him." She did wonder at its meaning. If it were true, why wasn't any light getting into her? Her life had been derailed by her husband's infidelity. She put her hand to her belly. Was her little one the light in her pain?

"Did you ever do that?" Grams asked.

Maggie frowned. "Do what?"

"Put a looking glass under your pillow to dream about the boy you would marry, like Cécile wrote about."

"No, I didn't, Grams." Maggie knew if she had done that, she would have only dreamed about Cole, the only boy she'd ever loved.

"Aren't superstitions interesting?" asked Grams. "Like tossing spilled salt over your left shoulder to strike against the devil lurking there."

"Or not stepping on a crack because it would break your mother's back," Maggie added.

Grams laughed. "It would require more than stepping on a crack to break your mother's anything. She's a tough cookie."

"True." Grams's spot-on description of her mother conjured up Maggie's self-accusations: why couldn't she be strong? forgiving? willing to reconcile with a straying spouse?

"Remember, Maggie." Grams's demeanor turned serious. "Toughness runs through all of us Ruths. My mother's story bears that out."

Startled, Maggie couldn't help wonder once more if Grams read her mind.

"Shall I continue with more?" Grams asked, eyebrows raised.

Maggie nodded. "Yes! I can't wait to find out what happens at the teahouse with Mrs. Butterick and Mrs. Beard. And if there's any tesseracting about to happen, I'll be upset that I'm only now finding out I've inherited the power to wrinkle time!"

"Don't we all have that power, my dear?" Grams eyes twinkled with her reply.

Maggie folded her hands in her lap and squeezed them together. Her grandmother's message was not lost on her. Grams failed to understand, though, that not even wrinkling time could erase the damage of betrayal.

Could it?

CHAPTER THIRTY-TWO
RUTH

Mrs. Beard drove them down a tree-lined avenue. Ruth believed it to be one of the prettiest streets she'd ever seen. Quaint bungalows were sandwiched between English cottages and Tudor estates.

Mrs. Beard pulled up in front of a white two-story clapboard cottage that had two dormer windows and a shingled roof. Its white picket fence gave it a cozy appearance. Ruth loved the large trees in the front yard. Even though their bare branches were powdered by snow, she could imagine the shady canopy the leaves would create in the summer.

A hand-painted sign attached to the house featured a beehive and large letters that proclaimed, "Glory Bee Tearoom. Open Monday–Friday. 11 a.m. to 7 p.m."

Mrs. Butterick tapped the crutch against the car's window. "Welcome to the Glory Bee."

"The two of you own this place?" Ruth asked, surprised. She was aware of women who worked outside the home. Nurses. Teachers. Seamstresses. Even laundresses, like Clinton's mom. She wasn't aware of any lady who actually owned a business.

"We own it lock, stock, and barrel, young fellow," Mrs. Beard answered. "Most around here call us the Busy Bees." She opened the driver's door and slid out. Ruth recognized the woman had good height and was of slim build, with large feet. Mrs. Beard and she could be kindred spirits.

"Let's get settled inside." Mrs. Beard's gloves muted her snapping fingers. "We've cooking to do for the evening crowd, sister."

"Oh, yes." Mrs. Butterick chuckled. "Without you, sister, I'd run amuck." She helped Ruth out of the car and onto the crutch, whispering to her with a conspiratorial wink, "At least, that's what I let Mrs. Beard believe."

With the tall Mrs. Beard on one side of her and the tiny Mrs. Butterick on her other, Ruth made her way into the Glory Bee. From the front lobby, she glimpsed arched entrances to four rooms, each filled with hand loomed rugs, calico curtains, fireplaces, and assorted wicker and wood tables.

Mrs. Beard tugged her gloves off and pushed them into her pockets. She whisked into the left front room to light a fire, and Mrs. Butterick eased Ruth onto a bench next to a coat rack. She returned to retrieve Herkimer, who was banging against the basket's lid.

"Poor rooster." Mrs. Butterick peered through the basket weaving to check on him. "I think he needs some fresh air."

Mrs. Beard passed them with matches in hand, heading for the right front room. "Why not settle him into the old rabbit hutch in the back? Good thing we left it there when we bought this place."

"Excellent idea, sister." Mrs. Butterick directed her attention to Ruth. "Ruffis, you stay right there, resting that ankle of yours, and I'll settle this rooster back there. Does he have a name?"

"Herkimer," Ruth answered.

"Herkimer? Interesting name." She headed down the hallway. "I'll give him some water and bread crumbs. You wait right there." Her voice faded while she disappeared into the back of the house.

The bench sat opposite three stairs that led to a landing. More stairs continued up to the second floor, which Ruth assumed led to the location of the living quarters. She rested her head against the wall, noticing the roses that covered the wallpaper. Her mind drifted to how good a bed would feel. Soon she drifted off to sleep.

"Well, well," Mrs. Beard said, causing Ruth to leap up. "A sleepy gus, are you?"

The woman hung her coat on the coat rack and placed her red hat on the shelf next to it. She wore her black hair streaked with silver in a tight bun on top of her head. Ruth guessed her age to be younger than Dewdad and older than Mama. Mrs. Beard gave a little sniff, like the lady who had sat next to Ruth on the train. "We have a spare bed and bath. You are welcome to wash up and rest."

"A bath would be swell." A nice hot bath to rid herself of the boxcar and rooster stink would be delightful.

Mrs. Butterick appeared without the basket. She slipped out of her fur coat and hung it up, placing her feathery hat next to her sister's red one. She patted her bun gathered at the nape of her neck. Unlike Mrs. Beard's, Mrs. Butterick's shiny dark brown hair had no silver streaks. Ruth guessed she was the younger sister, yet her crow's feet and slightly sagging chin hinted that she wasn't too much younger.

"Your rooster is all settled in," Mrs. Butterick announced. "I hope you don't mind that I tossed the contents of the basket. I'm afraid that the basket itself may be ruined." She held her nose to make her point.

Ruth groaned. Mama would definitely not be pleased.

The two ladies helped her up the stairs. The attic bedroom reminded her of her own in Dewdad's house, with slanted low ceilings and narrow windows. Homesickness flooded Ruth. She wondered if Mr. Cooper from the railroad had sent the telegram to Mama. What had happened when he discovered she had escaped?

At least Mama and the rest of her family had been informed she was among the living. Ruth hated causing such concern. She was only a day's train ride away from Colorado Springs. Once she reached Pa, he'd get in touch with Mama.

After a warm bath, Ruth spread her belongings out on top of the bureau and folded her quilt at the foot of the bed. She dressed in the other pair Jesse's overalls she'd packed. Finding the bureau drawers empty, she placed her belongings into the top one.

Cécile's letters made her feel as if Cécile were with her on the trip. Ruth had one more letter she hadn't yet read. She took it out. The return address of the Health House reminded her of how sick Cécile was.

A hum of activity downstairs grew louder with dinner service in full swing. Ruth couldn't make it to the lower level without the ladies' help. The way her ankle was throbbing, she hoped it wouldn't be another night of no sleep. At least she could stretch out and rest until either Mrs. Beard or Mrs. Butterick came for her.

She climbed into the bed and put Cécile's letter beneath her pillow to read later. Closing her eyes, the vision of Pike's Peak appeared and she tumbled down, down, down into a soft layer of snowy dreams.

Herkimer's cock-a-doodle-doo awakened her. The sun shone through the dormer window. She bolted straight up in the bed. Where was she? This room wasn't hers!

Yesterday's events rushed back into her mind. Her ankle was propped up on two pillows. One of the ladies must have come In to check on her, elevating her foot and covering her with the quilt.

Her empty stomach reminded her that she had fallen asleep without having eaten. Her aching ankle reminded her that the doctor could be right; it might be days before she could walk on it. That meant days before she could hop a train again.

"Ruffis?" Ruth recognized it was Mrs. Beard at the door. Her mannerisms reminded Ruth of Mama's no-nonsense one.

"Come in," Ruth called out.

Mrs. Beard bustled in with a tray of food. Ruth blinked at the woman's blindingly white starched apron.

"Mrs. Butterick and I prepared you a little breakfast," said Ruth's hostess.

Ruth leaned back against the pillows. "Thank you." She fought against tearing up from appreciation, reminding herself boys hardly ever cried. They were supposed to suck in their feelings, for some reason.

"Our pleasure." Mrs. Beard placed the tray on Ruth's lap. "What goes around comes around, we always say."

Ruth's mouth watered over the waffles, scrambled eggs, and sausage. On one side of the plate was an extra tall glass of milk. On the other was a pitcher of warmed blueberry syrup. Pa's favorite.

"Mrs. Butterick and I will check on you in a bit. We must prepare for our lunch opening." Mrs. Beard scurried out the door.

After sending up a quick prayer of thanks for her rescue, Ruth scarfed down the food. Every bite tasted better than the one before it. She cleaned her plate and drained the last sip of milk from the glass.

She placed the tray on the bed table and shifted her weight in the bed. Pain throbbed through her ankle, catapulting her flat onto her back.

Ruth retrieved Cécile's letter, hoping that reading it might distract her from the pain. From Cécile's comments, she appeared to be feeling better. The photographs enclosed with the letter brought her friend closer than ever.

Both she and Cécile were in new places, and both were hoping for cures—Cécile from consumption, Ruth from the ankle sprain that was keeping her from Pa.

Cécile's questioning Ruth's opinion about colored men made her think. She agreed with Cécile. All men were the same, pale faced or colored. Ruth giggled about how Cécile had put a looking glass under her pillow. If she put one under her own pillow, Ruth knew she would dream of kissing Clinton again. If she ever got another chance to kiss him, she wouldn't slap him, no matter who saw them.

A tap at the door interrupted Ruth's daydreaming. She placed Cécile's letter under her quilt for safekeeping. She didn't want to explain how she, "Ruffis Addison," had letters from a pen pal named Cécile that were addressed to a Miss Ruth Calderhead.

"Come in."

Mrs. Butterick entered, her eyes lighting on the empty plate. "You were hungry, like the growing boy you are. Unfortunately, from the looks of your ankle when I rewrapped it last night, you aren't going to be up and around for a few days at best."

"No, I'm sure I can walk." To prove it, Ruth sat up and swung her feet to the side of the bed. A groan of pain escaped through her clenched teeth.

"Oh, dear." Mrs. Butterick fluttered around her, helping her settle back in bed. "You must rest and let Mrs. Beard and me care for you until you've healed." She patted Ruth's arm. "Is there anyone you want us to contact about your whereabouts? Your grandpa perhaps?"

The faces of her family and Clinton crowded into her mind. She pushed them away. "No, there's no one. I was coming here to find a job. I have no one, only my grandpa's rooster that he left me."

Ruth cringed, waiting for the roof to cave in on her for telling such a whopper. When it didn't, she didn't feel any better about being deceitful.

"You poor thing." Mrs. Butterick picked up the tray. "Don't worry. I have an idea that will help both you and us out."

She hurried out and shut the door behind her.

೦೦⌒೦೦

Mrs. Butterick's idea was to hire Ruth to be employed as their dishwasher, busboy, and all-around "gopher." The fact that she could drive once her ankle healed increased her value to the sisters. Thank heaven Clinton taught her how!

Working at the Glory Bee Tearoom meant that Ruth didn't have to feel guilty about letting the Busy Bees provide her a place to sleep and food to eat until her ankle healed enough for her to depart.

Ruth made a countdown calendar. Thanksgiving was three weeks away. If she caught the train on the Monday before that, she would earn three weeks of pay for being an assistant Busy Bee. She would have the money to buy a ticket to Colorado Springs. No more hopping boxcars or sneaking onto passenger cars.

By the third day of her stay, her ankle had healed enough for her to get busy. She learned how to set up the rooms for lunch and dinner according to Mrs. Butterick's standards. She learned how to bus the tables and how to wash the dishes to meet Mrs. Beard's standards. She learned how to wash and starch the table linens, napkins, and aprons to satisfy both the Busy Bees.

To Ruth's surprise, running a tearoom appealed to her. She observed how the sisters planned the menu according to their budget and how they set each meal's price. She observed how meticulous they were about their recipe file and how protective they were of their famous, closely guarded recipe for melt-in-your-mouth lemon tarts.

Their tarts were the item most in demand. Ruth squeezed more than a pint of fresh lemon juice each day in order for the Busy Bees to make enough of the treats. When she'd try to glimpse the recipe, she'd get a slight slap on the hand, and it would be hidden from her view. The Bees took their lemon tarts seriously, which Ruth didn't mind. Who was she to question their insistence on secrecy when she was keeping secrets of her own?

She began daydreaming about running her own tearoom. Maybe Cécile could move to Oakland and help her run it. They could call the tearoom CeCe's. That had a French ring to it. They'd serve French food like crepes. She made up a menu and decorated it to put in the letter she was writing to Cécile.

What would Mama say when she told her she wanted to be a business lady? Maybe if she served Mama's own best desserts—butterscotch pie and cinnamon cake—and made them famous, her mother would approve.

On day five of her stay, Ruth convinced Mrs. Beard her ankle had healed enough for her to get behind the wheel. During the drive around the block, Ruth kept a stiff upper lip when the twinges of pain would come. After all, she was a boy, and didn't boys always tough it out? To Ruth's delight, the trial drive went well. She begged to drive the sisters to Mr. Hess's farm, where they purchased their fresh eggs and vegetables.

The next day over their breakfast of buttery croissants and black-berry jam, Mrs. Butterick didn't project her typical calm. She and her sister kept exchanging glances. Ruth worried she'd been found out. She couldn't withstand the suspense any longer. "Is there something wrong?" she asked.

Mrs. Butterick answered. "Ruffis, before we head to Mr. Hess's farm, Mrs. Beard and I have to discuss a little matter with you. Well, it's a big matter, really." She stirred her coffee for the umpteenth time and sloshed a little into the saucer. "Oh dear, sister. You must be the one to tell him."

Ruth found it difficult to swallow her bite of croissant. Was she about to be sent home without ever seeing Pa?

"Sister, I am sure Ruffis will understand," Mrs. Beard said. "It's about Herkimer."

Relieved, Ruth managed to swallow the croissant. "What about Herkimer?" Herkimer was a handful. She wouldn't blame them if they wanted to put him in a soup pot. At one time, Ruth would have agreed. Not now. Not after all she'd been through with the rooster.

"What we are trying to explain, Ruffis," Mrs. Beard said in her matter-of-fact way, "is that our neighbors have been complaining about Herkimer's loud crows. Mrs. Butterick and I were thinking . . ." She paused for a sip of her coffee.

Mrs. Butterick blurted out the question. "Would you be fine if Mr. Hess gave Herkimer a home on his farm?"

Ruth started laughing. Mind? Dewdad would be pleased!

"I think my grandpa would approve," she answered. "Herkimer is a rooster with spunk. He needs a farm life."

Mrs. Butterick relaxed back into her chair, relief spreading across her face.

"Problem solved," Mrs. Beard said, summing things up in her usual efficient manner. "That is, if Mr. Hess agrees."

⌒⌒⌒

Mr. Hess did agree. Packing the rooster into his stinky basket for his trip to his new home, Ruth's sadness about giving Herkimer away surprised her. He'd been such a pest, but he was the only family she had around her. And he *had* saved her from the hobos.

Ruth pulled on a winter coat, boots, and gloves that Mrs. Butterick had picked up at a thrift store. The ladies wore warm tailored driving coats and gloves with scarves wrapped around their heads and necks. Mrs. Beard sat in the front passenger seat and Mrs. Butterick in the back with the basket holding Herkimer beside her. Ruth could see her in the rearview mirror.

They stopped at a filling station and paid fifteen cents a gallon for gasoline, three cents higher than Dewdad paid in Oakland. Ruth could hear him muttering about "highway robbery."

The Wasatch Mountains loomed high, the snow topping them like ice cream on giant cones. They reminded her of the Rocky Mountains surrounding Colorado Springs. Like Oakland, Salt Lake City was not without towering modern skyscrapers. Mrs. Beard pointed out one building that was twenty stories high! Mrs. Butterick pointed out the Beehive House. "It's a symbol of the Mormon Church," she explained.

Ruth wondered about the name of their teahouse, the Glory Bee. "Are you both Mormons?" she asked.

Mrs. Butterick laughed. "Well, have you heard that old saying 'when in Rome'? It means that you adapt to the culture around you. That's why we call our tearoom The Glory Bee."

Mrs. Beard added, "Not everyone who lives in Salt Lake City belongs to the Mormon Church. We are, in fact, Methodists. However, we have found Salt Lake City welcoming to us and our tearoom."

Ruth had no reason to doubt that, because these two had been generous and kind to her.

"We settled here after we lost our husbands," Mrs. Butterick added. "They both died in the war."

"They were too old to enlist," Mrs. Beard said. "They were determined to serve, so they went overseas as medics. They died in a bombing outside Paris."

Paris! Ruth remembered Cécile's description of the terrible bombings. "How awful."

"Thank you, dear." Mrs. Beard's voice thickened. Ruth hoped she wouldn't cry.

"We had lived in New England on the coast," Mrs. Butterick said. "We wanted a change of scenery and traveling West appealed to us. When we got off the train at Salt Lake, we fell in love with the mountains and the friendly people."

The city blocks eventually turned into a winding road leading out of town. Ruth had never driven for such a long stretch. If only Clinton could see her!

By the time they arrived at the farm, Ruth concluded that the valley farmland would be a paradise for Herkimer. The Busy Bees introduced her to Mr. Hess and explained that Ruth would be running the daily errands to him for supplies. Mrs. Butterick told him about Herkimer, and the farmer fawned over him, like Dewdad always did. Ruth knew Herkimer would love his new home. Mrs. Beard showed her how to inspect the eggs and vegetables to be sure the order was up to her standards.

The time soon came to bid Herkimer goodbye. "I'll miss you, crazy old bird. I wonder if you'll find another Mrs. Givens to pester," she whispered.

Right when she was getting all misty-eyed, Herkimer started strutting and plumping out his feathers, revving up to go for her ankles. She moved away from him as fast as her bad ankle allowed, but she understood that he wasn't trying to hurt her. He was being a rooster.

On the drive back, Ruth couldn't keep her mind off her family. Letting go of Herkimer had been like letting go of her last connection to them. The passing countryside lulled her into memories of her family's life in Colorado Springs before Jesse's death. She wondered if the Busy

Bees ever wished they could turn back time to the days before they lost their husbands.

A car passed them, and its engine let out a loud backfire. Ruth jumped and her hand jerked, causing the car to swerve.

"Whoa there, Ruffis!" Mrs. Beard grabbed the wheel. "Steady as she goes, now. It was the noise of the engine."

Mrs. Butterick caught Ruth's eye in the rearview mirror. "You look like you've seen a ghost! Do you need Mrs. Beard to drive?"

Ruth pushed away the memory of Jesse, his red blood flowing from him. "No, I can do this."

She wasn't talking about finishing the drive. She was talking about finding Pa and convincing him to let her tell the truth.

"I can do this," Ruth repeated.

CHAPTER THIRTY-THREE
MAGGIE

When Brian interrupted to offer breakfast, Maggie discovered how hungry she'd become while lost in Grams's tale. "I'd love some. What about you, Grams?"

"I would enjoy a Bloody Mary. I need to wet my whistle to be able to keep talking." Grams glanced at Maggie. "Don't tell me. You would like the tomato juice only, right?"

Maggie reddened. "Actually, I'd like a glass of milk, please."

She ate with appetite the scrambled eggs and biscuit Brian served, pushing the bacon aside. She never turned away bacon, yet now its greasiness repulsed her. She patted her mouth with her napkin between bites. "It's a shame to admit that airplane breakfasts taste better than ones you cook yourself." She rolled her eyes. "Too bad I can't boil water without burning it. That cooking gene somehow skipped me."

"For all intents and purposes, your mother also lacks that gene. Except for her lasagna."

Maggie burst out laughing. "Keen observation, Grams. That's definitely her only specialty."

"Well, it's never too late to learn how to cook, dear. I'll be glad to share some of my mother's recipes from her Busy Bees Two tearoom. She loved running that place in Oakland. I enjoyed working there growing up."

Maggie shook her head. "All these years and I never knew where that name came from. I knew Great-grams ran a tearoom, but I had no idea how she came up with the idea. Or the name." She took a sip of milk. "You hated selling the place."

"Well, after your grandfather died, I couldn't make ends meet running it. Selling it provided me with a nest egg that helped put your mother through law school." Grams sipped her drink thoughtfully. "My mother may never have opened a tearoom if she hadn't been taken in by those kind women."

"Tell me more about Ruth's great adventure. I can't believe all that has happened to her. At fourteen, I was lucky if I could go unsupervised to a mall, much less hop a train, pretending to be a boy."

"Times were different back then." Grams took another sip of her drink. "One thing remains the same. Family is family. And father-daughter relationships are important."

Grams's words weighed on Maggie's spirit.

The silence settled for a few moments before Grams resumed speaking. "Bear with me, dear, for I am about to share with you the hardest part of my mother's story."

Her own mother's words came back to Maggie. *Skeletons in closets. Unspoken secrets. Tragic misdeeds.* What was Grams about to explain?

CHAPTER THIRTY-FOUR
RUTH

Ruth's days with the Busy Bees were drawing to a close. The Friday before Thanksgiving had arrived, and she planned to leave on Monday. Her ankle was a little sore, but she knew she could make it the rest of the way, especially since she had earned enough money to buy a ticket. No more hopping boxcars.

While Mrs. Butterick washed up the breakfast dishes, Ruth dried them. Mrs. Butterick held on to a serving platter for a moment before she handed it to Ruth. "Don't be shocked at what I'm about to tell you, dear."

Ruth took the dish, her interest piqued.

"Each Thanksgiving time, Mr. Hess holds a turkey shoot, and this year's falls today. Sister has participated each year since we moved here. She's quite a markswoman. Her husband taught her how to shoot."

"I guess you could say I'm a regular Annie Oakley," Mrs. Beard announced, entering the kitchen with her rifle.

The sight of the gun startled Ruth. Her nerves rattled, the serving platter slipped through her fingers to the floor, and it exploded into shards. She burst into tears.

"There, there. No need to cry over spilt milk, as they say." Mrs. Butterick patted her shoulder. "It was an accident."

"It's just a platter." Mrs. Beard handed Ruth the broom. "Sweep up. When you're done, we'll be off to Mr. Hess's." She added, "You'll hold on to wet dishes more firmly next time. Mistakes are how we learn."

Ruth knew she could live with a mistake of breaking a platter. What she didn't know was how to live with a mistake so horrible you couldn't bear thinking about it.

∽∽

When they arrived at the farm, Ruth maneuvered carefully around all the cars and trucks to park. She breathed in deeply the welcoming aroma of hot cider, simmering in the kettle hanging over a fire.

"Welcome," Mr. Hess called from a table on the porch.

A sign hanging from the table advertised, "Turkey Shoot Begins 9 A.M. Tickets $1."

"I'll catch up with you later." Mrs. Beard became the lone woman in the line of attendees waiting to buy tickets. The men tipped their hats to her with an unwelcome attitude.

"Mrs. Butterick, may I check on Herkimer?" Ruth asked.

"Of course, dear." Mrs. Butterick shifted her shopping basket from one hand to the other. "I'll collect our order of eggs and vegetables."

Ruth hurried through the gate and looped the rope around the nail to latch it back before entering the hen yard. The rooster strutted and pecked, happy with his new harem to protect.

"I can't wait to tell Dewdad what a happy home I found for you." Ruth dodged the pecks at her ankles. She scrambled from the yard and latched the gate behind her. Herkimer strutted against the gate, knocking it ajar.

Ruth latched it again. "I'd better get Mr. Hess to make this more secure, Herk."

He flapped at her and strutted off.

She headed back to join Mrs. Beard, standing next in line to pay for the shoot.

"Well, Mrs. Beard, you're back again, I see." Mr. Hess spoke out of one side of his mouth, his words muffled by a huge hunk of tobacco. "Do you think you'll get the winning bird this year?"

"We'll see, Mr. Hess." Mrs. Beard handed him her money and cradled her rifle while waiting for her ticket.

"How about you, young fellow?" Mr. Hess asked Ruth. "You taking part in the shoot?"

Her knees buckled. She regained her balance and shook her head.

"I can lend you a rifle. Ever shoot before?" Mr. Hess spat tobacco juice into a bucket by him.

"I'm going to put the eggs and vegetables in the car," Mrs. Butterick called out.

Ruth followed her. "Let me help you." She had to escape before Mr. Hess tried to put that rifle in her hands.

When they returned from the car, the men and Mrs. Beard were lining up. Mr. Hess stood at the head of the line, a revolver in his hand.

"The rules are the same," he said. "There are twelve turkeys, weighing from ten pounds up to the prized one at twenty-five pounds. Whoever gets the twenty-five pounder wins the ten dollars in prize money, not to mention winning a lot of turkey to share come Thanksgiving. Good luck. May the best shooter win."

He cocked the gun and shot it up in the air. Ruth flinched at the sharp, reverberating crack of the bullet. The men and Mrs. Beard went off in different directions through the woods.

"Would you like some hot cider, Ruffis, to warm from the chill?" Mrs. Butterick asked. They walked to the kettle. Mrs. Butterick ladled some cider into a cup and handed it to Ruth.

Before she took it from her, Ruth heard Herkimer's familiar *brawk*. She worried that the gate might have come ajar again. "I'm going to check on that dumb rooster," she said.

As she suspected, the gate had swung open and Herkimer had strutted outside the chicken yard. He was pecking the dirt in Mr. Hess's plowed fields. Ruth rushed toward him, waving her arms like Dewdad always did. "Herkimer, get back in the yard."

He strutted into the fringe of the woods that bordered the fields. "That's the wrong way!" Ruth ran after him. "Come back, Herkimer!"

A turkey flew out of the underbrush, gobbling and squawking. Ruth screamed and ducked. Herkimer pushed one of his wings to the ground, preparing to do his cockerel waltz like he'd done on the boxcar when he saved Ruth from the hobos.

"No, Herkimer! It's okay!" Ruth yelled.

Gunshots ripped through the air, and Ruth fell to the ground, her chest heaving. She curled into a tight ball, pressing her hands against her ears. More gunshots came in quick succession.

Ruth squeezed her eyes shut. Red splattered against the darkness. Once again, she witnessed Jesse slowly, slowly falling to the ground. She curled her body more tightly, pressing her hands harder against her ears, until no more shots rang out. When she raised her head, Herkimer lay in the underbrush, the wind rustling his feathers. She crawled to him.

He wasn't moving. He wasn't breathing. His brilliant orangey-red breast feathers were matted with a reddish black ooze. Sobs caught in Ruth's throat, strangling her screams. The ghastly scene before her swirled around and around before her world went black.

Ruth opened her eyes. She lay on the couch in the Busy Bees's cozy cottage, a wool throw spread on top of her. A roaring fire gave off a warm, rosy glow. A teapot and cups were set up on the low table in front of the sofa.

Mrs. Beard sat in one of the winged chairs across from her, folding napkins in her typically crisp manner. Mrs. Butterick was ironing aprons.

Ruth sat up, wondering what had happened. They had been at Mr. Hess's. At the turkey shoot. The horrible scene flashed into her mind.

Gunshots.

Herkimer.

Poor, poor Herkimer.

Another one she loved, dead because of her. She whimpered softly. Tears flowed unchecked down her cheeks.

"There, there, dear." Mrs. Butterick stopped ironing and perched on the sofa by Ruth. Mrs. Beard sat on Ruth's other side and handed her a handkerchief. Ruth wiped away her tears, wishing she could wipe herself away. Hide from the kindness of these ladies.

"Ruffis, we grieve with you over Herkimer," said Mrs. Butterick. "His death resulted from a senseless accident. That poor hunter feels dreadful."

Ruth looked up. "Please tell him I understand. He didn't do it on purpose. It was . . ."

She hesitated before finishing her statement. "It was an accident."

An accident.

Jesse's body sprawled on the ground flashed again and again in her mind. Her brother's death, like Herkimer's, had been because of a terrible accident.

Her voice came out trembly. "I promised my pa that I would keep our secret about what happened the day my brother died. But I can't anymore."

Confusion painted the faces of both ladies. Ruth realized they had no idea what she was talking about. How would they react when she told them?

"We are here for you, dear," Mrs. Beard said. "You can tell us anything."

"Yes, Ruffis," Mrs. Butterick said. "Whatever you may say will not change how we have grown to care for you."

Ruth winced. She risked losing their friendship if she told them the truth. Risked losing her mama's love if she learned the secret. Her mouth felt cotton-dry and her body grew chilled, as if ice pumped through her, not blood. Yet, the time had come. She had to free herself.

"First, I have to tell you that my name isn't Ruffis." She ran a hand through her short hair. "And, I am not a boy."

Mrs. Butterick exchanged a knowing glance with Mrs. Beard. "We've suspected since we first met you outside the train station," Mrs. Butterick said.

"I'm afraid, my dear, you don't make a terribly convincing young man," Mrs. Beard said.

"What is your name?" Mrs. Butterick asked.

"Ruth Calderhead." Ruth took another deep breath. "I left Oakland for Colorado Springs to find my pa. My family lived there all together until . . .It was all my fault!"

She quit speaking. The room fell quiet.

Mrs. Butterick patted her arm lightly. "What was your fault? Perhaps if you tell us, you will feel better."

Ruth's insides quaked. She must stop talking. "Never mind." She shook her head. "I promised Pa."

"Your pa would not want you to keep a secret that pains you." Mrs. Butterick took Ruth's hands in hers.

"I agree with Sister," Mrs. Beard said.

Ruth withdrew her hands from Mrs. Butterick and covered her face. After a moment, she let her hands fall to her lap and looked first at Mrs. Butterick, then Mrs. Beard. She found strength in their compassion. She started to tell her story, her voice quaking.

"Jesse was my big brother. He was my best friend. He took care of me. Mama adored him. He was kind and gentle. He loved going barefoot and reciting poetry."

The mirrored tiles that framed the fireplace reflected multiple images of Ruth. The images were fractured like the reflections had been on that night she had sat at her vanity. The shimmery glass drew her into the world of that tragic April afternoon. Her present fell away into her past. She spoke as if in a trance.

"That April day started out with a chill in the air, like April days do in Colorado. The bright sun in the blue sky promised it would get warm quickly. Pa announced plans for Jesse and him to do the spring deer scouting to prepare for hunting in the fall. I had never been allowed to go. I didn't want to be left out of the adventure, especially the part where we'd get to look for shed antlers. Last year, Jesse had returned with antlers shed by a buck that he'd found, and he still bragged about them.

"Over breakfast, I begged to go. Mama said no. I had no business traipsing out in the woods with them, like a tomboy. Pa gave in to my begging." Ruth choked up. Her next words came out thick with emotion. "What would be the harm, he said."

She fought back the tears that were desperate to flow. If she started crying now, she'd never finish telling what happened.

"We set out, Pa driving the buckboard, clicking the reins and calling out giddyap. Our breath showed in the dry, crisp air when we spoke. We followed a trail deep into the woods before Pa reined the mule to a stop. He explained to me that we were searching for signs where bucks rutted. Their rub signs marked where they bedded and where they fed. Tracking these signs would tell us where to hunt for deer during the fall hunting season. We would know if our deer stand needed relocation. I was so full of pride to be helping with such an important family chore. Jesse teased me with his brags about finding even larger shed antlers than he had found last year."

A slight smile tugged at Ruth's lips. "He was always bragging, trying to take me down a peg. Teasing me like a big brother would." She fell quiet, thinking how she missed that. Would always miss that.

"When I jumped off the buckboard, my skirt caught on a nail. My hem ripped. Jesse let out a hoot, saying how mad Mama would be. He said whoever heard of going deer scouting in a skirt, anyway? How I wished I could have been in overalls and high leather work boots like him." Ruth looked at her clothes. "Like I'm dressed now. These are his clothes I've been wearing."

Mrs. Butterick and Mrs. Beard both nodded. Ruth laced her hands together and pressed them hard. If only what happened next had never happened. How was Pa to know what was to come? How was she to know?

"Before we started off into the wood, Pa handed Jesse a Savage hunting rifle he'd brought for protection, in case of bears or mountain lions. He handed me the smaller Winchester. Jesse showed me how to hold it with the barrel down, even though Pa said it wasn't loaded."

A wave of sadness swept through her. Why had she agreed to carry that rifle? She should have said no, but she had wanted to be like her father and brother. Grown-up. Brave.

She continued her story, her voice dropped low. "We shuffled through the forest. Its floor smelled sweet with compost. The underbrush was thick. The rifle grew heavier and heavier in my arms. Every now and then, Pa stopped and pulled his map of the property out to write his observations from our scouting. We rested in the dip of a knoll and shared the beef jerky Pa had packed. I kept taking sips of water from the canteen because I had worked up such a thirst. My arms were aching from carrying the rifle, and my feet were sore from stepping on all the roots and stones.

"After our rest, we started out again to locate the deer stand that Pa and Jesse had used last year. I'd never been up in a deer stand. When we found it, I asked Pa if I could climb up and look out. Jesse teased me, saying I only wanted to go up in it because I was too tired to keep scouting."

She breathed in deeply, ragged sobs catching in her throat. Those were the last words Jesse had spoken to her.

"Take your time, dear," Mrs. Beard said.

"Yes," Mrs. Butterick added, handing her a cup of the hot tea. "Sip this, and when you're ready, share the rest of your story."

With shaking hands, Ruth accepted the cup and managed to sip a little without spilling it. She returned the cup to Mrs. Butterick, took a deep breath, and continued her story.

"Jesse started up a trail to the left of the stand. I climbed up the deer stand, balancing the rifle the best I could. Reaching the platform top, I knelt and held the rifle like a hunter, my finger on its trigger. I peered down its barrel, pretending some wild animal was in my sight. Suddenly, a hawk swooped out of nowhere. I remember dodging from it, hearing a crack of a gunshot, sprawling backward from the kickback of the rifle. My ears rang. I couldn't understand what had happened. The gunshot couldn't have come from my rifle. It couldn't have. The rifle wasn't loaded. Pa had said so. But the smoke streaming from my rifle's barrel told me differently. It had gone off."

Ruth stared straight ahead, as if the scene was playing out in front of her.

"A terrible scream echoed through the woods. I scrambled up and looked out. Jesse lay crumpled on the forest floor."

Bile crept into Ruth's mouth. She pressed back against it, making herself swallow hard. In a shaky voice, she went on.

"I scrambled from the deer stand, screaming my brother's name. By the time I reached him, Pa was holding my brother on his lap. Jesse wasn't moving. He wasn't breathing. He stared, unblinking, into the sky.

Ruth clenched a fist to her mouth, her breathing coming in shallow bursts. Mrs. Butterick pulled her into her arms. Mrs. Beard leaned in to them and wrapped both into her arms. Together they huddled, their trio made into one through their embrace.

Once Ruth's breathing slowed, the two ladies loosened her from their hug. "Perhaps rest now," Mrs. Beard whispered.

Seeking out a hand from each to hold, Ruth shook her head. "I leaned against Pa, who kept rocking back and forth with Jesse in his lap, telling Jesse he loved him. The clear sunny day shrunk into darkness. All I wanted was for it to suck me into death with Jesse." Ruth trailed off.

The cozy room in which she sat narrowed in her vision until she viewed it through a pinprick. The blackness of that tragic day shrouded her once again. Suddenly, a kaleidoscope of memories burst with brilliance, illuminating the darkness sucking her away: hopping trains with Jesse. Sneaking away to Cragmor. Reading books at the mercantile. Being protected from Mama's wrath by his silver-coated tongue. Hearing Mama recite *The Barefoot Boy.*

"My dear, are you faint?" Mrs. Beard asked.

Mrs. Butterick fetched a cool cloth and held to Ruth's forehead. "There, there, my dear. Just breathe," she said in a comforting tone.

Ruth took the cloth and wiped her face. "Thank you."

"Perhaps you rest now." Mrs. Beard patted her shoulder. "We'll talk more later."

"No." Ruth twisted the damp cloth in her hands. She re-entered the reality of the day that changed her family, herself, forever.

"A flock of wild geese flying overhead startled me from the darkness into which I had floated, or fainted I guessed. Pa helped me stand, his hands still sticky with Jesse's blood."

At that memory, Ruth tightened her grip on the cloth being twisted in her hands.

"Pa spoke in a fierce tone I'd never heard from him before. He said, 'Ruth, it was my gun that went off, not yours. Do you understand? This was my fault.' When I started to argue, his slap across my cheek stopped me. 'Do you understand?' he asked. 'Tell me. Who shot Jesse?' I answered back in a faint voice, 'You did, Pa.' He motioned for me to follow him. I didn't want to leave Jesse alone, yet I knew I wasn't strong enough to help Pa move the body. We needed help. We hiked through the woods to the buckboard.

"Pa hoisted me onto the seat and wrapped the reins in my hands. 'Tell your mama to send help. And remember, Ruth, to keep the secret. Never tell a soul. Never.' The wagon wheels creaked and groaned on my trip home, mourning Jesse with me."

Once her last words were spoken, Ruth's heart hammered against her chest. She had told the truth. Told the secret Pa demanded she keep.

Exhausted, Ruth collapsed against Mrs. Butterick, who gathered her once more in her arms. Mrs. Beard kneeled beside her, stroking her hair. They stayed that way until the fire turned to embers and the room grew chilled.

CHAPTER THIRTY-FIVE
MAGGIE

Maggie realized she had been barely breathing, caught up in Ruth's agonizing confession, shared by Grams. No wonder Ruth suffered panic attacks and worried that she was unworthy of her mother's love. In trying to protect her, her pa only caused Ruth more grief.

Maggie couldn't organize her jumbled reaction into coherent sentences. The only words she could manage were "Poor, poor Ruth."

Grams took a deep breath, as if coming out of a spell. She murmured, "Yes, my poor dear mother. She had suffered from guilt for so long. However, she finally accepted the awful truth. It had been a terrible accident. She needed to forgive herself and forgive her father for trying to protect her. He also needed to forgive himself. They needed to tell their family the truth."

"Did they?" Maggie whispered.

CHAPTER THIRTY-SIX
RUTH

Although Ruth no longer trembled, a hollow coldness ached within her. Mrs. Beard busied herself by stoking the fire back to life while Mrs. Butterick cradle Ruth in a comforting hug.

Mrs. Butterick spoke quietly. "What happened to your brother was like what happened to Herkimer today, Ruth. A horrible accident. Neither you nor your Pa should continue holding onto this secret and this guilt."

Mrs. Beard added, "Your pa was only trying to protect you by taking the blame."

Ruth nodded.

"Perhaps you should rest now," Mrs. Butterick said. "We'll prepare you a nice supper and bring it to you."

"Thank you." Ruth headed toward her room.

"One minute, dear." Mrs. Beard put the poker back with the other tools beside the hearth. "First thing tomorrow," she announced in her efficient manner, "I will send telegrams to your mother in Oakland and your pa in Colorado Springs. They must be worried sick about your whereabouts. We'll put you on the train to Oakland. I'm sure your pa will join you there once he understands what you've been through. You'll work everything out."

Ruth had seen that same look of concern before on Dewdad's face. It said, "We only want the best for you." The best for her wouldn't be going back to Oakland without seeing Pa in Colorado Springs. Without seeing Jesse's grave one last time. She was too close to Pa, too close to convincing him to tell Mama the truth.

If she returned to Oakland, there would be no way of knowing if Pa would ever reunite with them. If their secret would ever get told. She also owed it to poor Herkimer to finish what they had started when they set out together on this journey.

No argument would change the Busy Bees' decision to contact her mama. For now, she would pretend to agree with their plan to send her back. "I'll never be able to thank you enough for taking care of me," she said. "I do think I'll go upstairs and rest."

Her plan for escape catapulted her into motion. Reaching her room, she pulled out the letter that she had started writing to Cécile. Her friend had been wondering about Ruth's sudden move to Oakland. Ruth would write her the truth. She would hold no more secrets inside.

Ruth wrote fast and furiously, telling her pen pal what she had told the Busy Bees. She also wrote about poor Herkimer. Next, she wrote a note of thanks to the Busy Bees. In it, she asked them to mail the letter to Cécile.

Spreading out her patchwork quilt on the bed, she traced its jigsaw pattern with her fingertips, remembering how the secret had made her feel pulled apart, disjointed like the quilt's patched-together design.

Ruth pulled Jesse's compass from the bureau drawer. She knew without a doubt that it was pointing her to Colorado Springs. With her belongings bundled up, she sneaked down the steps. She heard the soft murmurings of the Busy Bees in the kitchen preparing dinner. The aroma of the lemon tarts baking made her mouth water. She pulled on her coat, gloves, and boots and slung her bundle onto her back.

She propped Cécile's letter and her note to the Busy Bees on the bench by the front door, remembering how cold, tired, and hurt she had been when she sat there on the day the Bees took her in. She had been a bird with a broken wing. Now, she was strong and ready to wing her way home.

ᑎᕐᑎ

In a purchased seat with her blanket roll in her lap, Ruth exhaled with relief. No hopping a boxcar for this last leg of her journey. She viewed the landscape out the window while the train traveled through flat pastures, over rivers by way of trestles, through tunnels, and, finally, over the Rocky Mountains, past the majestic rock formations in the Garden of the Gods.

"Next stop, Col-o-ra-do Springs," the conductor called out.

Her stomach tightened, and her mouth went dry with anticipation. Soon she would be with Pa, wrapped in his arms.

The train shuddered to a stop, and Ruth stepped onto the platform, her roll on her shoulders. After making her way out of the station, she paused on the sidewalk. The frozen air stung her lungs. In the distance, the snow-covered Pike's Peak looked awash in the corals and pinks of the sunrise.

She was home. Pa was near.

"Excuse me." A man hurried past her, brushing against her shoulder. "You'd better bundle up. It's only nine degrees, young fellow."

Her disguise as Ruffis fooled him, even if it hadn't completely fooled the Busy Bees. She pulled on her gloves, tugged on Dewdad's cap, and pulled the hood of her coat over it.

What would Pa say about her wearing bobbed hair and Jesse's clothes? What would he say when he found out that she had told the Busy Bees their secret? That she had written it all in her letter to Cécile? Ruth had betrayed his trust. Would he understand?

With her stomach growling, she tramped through the snow for four blocks to White's Diner. Mama had said Pa was staying with Mr. White until the sale of the farm. Ruth hoped when she walked into the diner, Pa would be there.

He wasn't.

She stood at the counter and watched Mr. White deftly scrape a mound of hash browns around on the large griddle and flip thick slabs of bacon. The smoky smell of the food made her empty stomach ache.

Mr. White scooped up the hash browns and landed them on a plate already loaded with ham and eggs. He placed it on the counter in front of the man next to Ruth. "What'll it be for you?" Mr. White asked her, pouring steaming coffee into the man's cup.

She couldn't believe that her pa's best friend, who'd known her since she was born, didn't recognize her! She pushed her hood back, took off Dewdad's cap, and stared at Mr. White, waiting for him to say, "Ruth Calderhead!"

He asked again, "Made up your mind yet?"

"Mr. White, it's Ruth Calderhead."

He froze like a funny statue, holding the coffee pot in one hand and resting the other on his hip. "Well, I'll be doggoned. Ruth Calderhead?" He pushed his cooking hat back further on his head and scratched his balding scalp. "I'll be dog..."

Ruth interrupted him. "Where's Pa? Mama said he was staying with you."

"Well, that he is, girl, but he's not here right now."

The disappointment turned Ruth's knees rubbery, and she grabbed the counter's edge to steady herself. "I've come all this way. I must see him."

"Well, first things first, Ruth. Let's get you warmed up." He snapped into action, grabbing a cup and pouring her some steaming coffee. "Have a swig of coffee. You must be hungry. What would you like to eat? On the house, girl."

"Thanks, Mr. White." She glanced hungrily at the food he'd served the man next to her. Facing Pa would be hard enough. She would fortify herself with food before seeing him. "That all looks fine to me." She pointed to the man's breakfast.

"I'll have it up for you in a jiff. Then, we'll get you to your Pa."

Ruth perched on the stool, not shedding her coat and blanket roll. She sipped the hot coffee. It warmed her from head to toe. Within minutes, she was gobbling up eggs, ham, and hash browns. Mr. White served other customers while he kept his eye on her and kept her coffee cup filled to the brim. She ate until she could fit nothing else in her full stomach.

"Now that you're warm and full, it's time for you to do some explaining." Mr. White plucked the plate from her and leaned across the counter. "Everyone's been searching for you. Your pa got a telegram saying you'd gone missing and another saying you were seen in Salt Lake City. He's been hoping you were making your way here."

"Where is he?" Her question came out breathlessly.

"He's up at Cragmor."

Cragmor? Why would Pa be at Cragmor? Unless he had fallen ill with consumption. Like Cécile. *That* must be why Pa hadn't come back with Mama.

Mr. White hurried from behind the counter. "You look like you're about to faint. Sit for a few minutes."

The diner buzzed with people talking and laughing loudly. They didn't have a care, while Pa suffered at Cragmor. She walked toward the door.

"Ruth! Where are you going?" Mr. White called after her.

Outside the diner, Ruth tugged Dewdad's cap back on and pulled the hood over her head. Sets of snowshoes sat on the sidewalk. She grabbed a set that looked to be about her size and ran down the street.

Once she traveled far enough from the diner to be out of view, she stopped to strap on the snowshoes. Snowflakes melted against her cheeks, which were already wet with tears. Her shoes crunched against the snow. Each step would bring her closer to the sanatorium. To Pa.

❧

Ruth knew the way to Cragmor. It was located about six miles from the center of downtown, high on a hill. Ruth calculated traveling that distance in the snow would take her most of the day.

She had no way to measure the mileage she covered. She remembered from math class that it took around two thousand steps to walk a mile. Counting her steps would help her keep track of the distance she had covered. And keep her calm.

Ruth adapted to walking in the snow, leaning forward slightly and taking firm and deliberate steps. She trudged to the edge of town, past homes with smoke curling from their chimneys. At her first two thousandth step, the bundle on her back weighed her down like a fifty-pound bag of sand. Her sore ankle started to throb.

The snow began falling with blizzard strength. She moved toward the fence that lined her path, keeping one hand on it to keep from losing her way in the blinding whiteness.

The second two thousand steps left her exhausted. She could barely place weight on her ankle. Leaning against the fence for a rest, she tried to conjure the warmth of the fire blazing back at the Glory Bee. Her teeth chattered.

She started counting again. One, two, three, four . . .

The snow slackened into a light flurry. At step six hundred and one, Ruth could hear a rattling over the rushing wind. She kept going, not wanting to lose count. Six hundred and two, six hundred and three . . .

The rattling got louder. A buckboard whose driver sat hunched against the cold came into view. She could beg for a ride! She scrambled away from the fence to flag it down. The driver pulled on the horse's reins, and she rushed to speak to him. In the back, a pale woman lay bundled in blankets covered with snow. She was hacking into a bloodied handkerchief pressed tightly against her mouth. Ruth cringed. Would Pa be that ill? Was Cécile?

"Are you going to Cragmor?" Ruth asked, already sure of the answer.

"Yes, though I'm not sure Cragmor will accept her as a patient." The driver squinted at the woman. "She may be too sick. She's my wife of twenty-five years. What I will do if I lose her to this sickness?"

His words struck a nerve with her. How many times had she feared losing Cécile? Now she feared losing Pa. She forced out hopeful words. "Maybe she will recover."

The man shrugged.

Ruth could tell the man was bracing himself for the worst outcome. She hoped he wouldn't mind her asking for help. "Could I bother you to give me a lift to Cragmor?"

He searched her face. "Are you sick too?"

"No."

"Didn't think so. You don't have that gray, haggard look about you. Why are you heading to Cragmor?"

"I need to visit my pa," Ruth answered.

He nodded, his face relaying sympathy.

"Thanks." Ruth climbed into the back wagon of the buckboard. He jostled the reins, and they resumed the journey.

The bumps jostled Ruth. It didn't exactly feel like she was gliding over the ice in a sleigh like Cécile described, but the wagon ride was better than walking. She leaned against the side rail, her blanket roll buffeting its hardness.

The woman's ongoing hacking spiked Ruth's worries. In what condition would she find Pa at Cragmor? Was Cécile getting better or worse at the Health House? Were they coughing blood into their handkerchiefs? How could two people she loved become ill from the same awful thing?

It wasn't divine providence. It had to be a curse. Or punishment for Jesse's death.

Please, God, she prayed, *don't let me lose either Pa or Cécile.*

By the time Ruth arrived at the gates of Cragmor, the sun had started to come out from behind the snow clouds. The freshly fallen snow glistened, pure and clean. Ruth found it hard to believe that in such a spotless setting, people—like Pa? —lay inside the sanatorium sick and dying.

The man reined the horse to a stop in the circular drive at the steps to the sanatorium's front doors. He leapt from the seat and held out his hand to help Ruth. Gathering his sick wife in his arms, he took the steps two at a time. Ruth followed him to the door and lifted the brass knocker, banging it for someone's attention.

A woman in a nurse's uniform opened the heavy, tall door. "May I help you?" she asked. Her name tag said, "Miss Park."

Ruth had always heard that even those who worked at the sanatorium were sick. Was Miss Park's gauntness proof of that?

"It's my wife. She's in a bad way," the man said, his voice flat and sorrowful.

"Please help her to the first room on the right." Miss Park pointed to a room off the huge marbled lobby. The man rushed off quickly. Ruth didn't have a chance to thank him for the ride or wish him good luck.

"Are you with him?" Miss Park asked.

"No. I'm here to visit a patient here by the last name of Calderhead." Ruth choked up when she said her family name.

Miss Park frowned with confusion or pity—or both. Ruth couldn't tell. "We don't have a patient by that name," she answered.

Fear squeezed Ruth throat shut, preventing her words from flowing. What if Pa had already died? She looked past Miss Park into the sanatorium, wondering where to begin searching. So many doorways led to so many rooms.

She took a deep gulp of air and forced her words out. "Tell me what room he is in."

"I said we don't have a patient by that name here." Again, the nurse looked confused. "Mr. Charles Calderhead is here. But he's not a patient. He's a maintenance worker."

"Maintenance worker?" Ruth repeated. "He's not sick?"

"That's right." Miss Park pointed. "If you look behind you to the left, you'll find him. He's shoveling the snow off the walkways."

Ruth whipped around. Pa was tossing shovelfuls of freshly fallen snow over his shoulder. Its crystal-like whiteness sparkled in the sun.

"Are you his boy?" Miss Park asked.

"No," she answered, flying down the steps. "I'm his daughter, Ruth."

She slid the blanket roll from her back and ran toward him, her hood flying off. She clamped her hand on Dewdad's driving cap to keep it from blowing away.

"Pa!"

He looked up and stopped shoveling in midair.

"Pa!" Ruth ran closer to him. "It's me!"

"Ruth?" He studied her closely from the top of Dewdad's cap to the bottom of Jesse's boots, relief washing over her face. "How you favor Jesse." He dropped the shovel and held his arms out wide.

She threw herself at him. They both lost their footing and fell into the snow. Pa struggled to his feet and held out his hand. He pulled her up and grabbed her in a bear hug.

"Pa," Ruth cried out. "I can't breathe!"

He loosened his hug, keeping his arms encircled about her. "Where have you been? Are you all right?" She detected irritation in his voice. "You have worried your mama and Dewdad to distraction. I've been worried sick. We feared that you were—"

Ruth knew he was about to say "dead."

"It's all right, Pa. I'm all right. I need to talk to you about Jesse."

"Let's walk, Ruth." He held Ruth's hand, and they started walking on the newly shoveled sidewalks.

"Pa—"

"Ruth—"

They both started to talk at the same time.

Pa squeezed her hand. "Let me go first."

"All right," Ruth agreed.

"When your mama came here with your sisters, you were all she could talk about. She told me you think she's punishing me for Jesse's death, that you believe she broke our family up because she couldn't forgive me—"

Ruth interrupted. "Oh, Pa, I said some awful things to Mama."

"Shh." Pa dropped Ruth's hand and put his arm around her waist. "It was the accident that broke us apart."

"It *was* an accident, Pa." The memory of Jesse sprawled unmoving in the dirt sent a shudder through her. "A *terrible* accident. You believed the gun was unloaded. I was startled by a bird. The gun went off. It happened, Pa. It just happened. And, it's been hurting me too badly, Pa, keeping our secret about it. We must tell…we must begin forgiving ourselves."

He pulled her into him, hugging her tightly again. "I guess you're no longer my 'same old Ruth,' are you?" he asked, choking up. "Your photograph I received showed you to be such a pretty young lady, but when did my little girl become so wise?"

Images ran through Ruth's mind. Of Jesse's compass. Clinton's birds. The Busy Bees. Herkimer's death. Cécile's letters. Maybe it was all of these—and the passing of time—that allowed her to accept the truth at last.

And forgive herself and Pa.

She pulled away from Pa's hug and looked at him eye to eye. "I'm not that wise. I only figured out that living with lies means you live without happiness."

They walked arm in arm through the snow; no more words were needed between them.

She retrieved her blanket roll. Pa informed Miss Park he would be gone for the day. Together, they went to Western Union to send a telegram to Mama. Ruth listened to Pa dictate the message:

DEAREST DOLLY STOP RUTH IS WITH ME STOP WE ARE TAKING THE TRAIN TO OAKLAND TOMORROW STOP WE WILL ALL BE TOGETHER STOP MUCH LOVE STOP CHARLES

Ruth gasped. "Pa! Do you mean it?"

"Absolutely." He drew her into a hug. "Absolutely, my dear girl."

They made their way to Mr. White's apartment above the diner. Ruth returned the snowshoes she'd taken. She helped Pa pack his few belongings. Mr. White cooked up a hearty dinner for them. For dessert, Ruth spooned down a hot fudge sundae dessert while listening to Pa arrange for Mr. White to oversee the sale of their family farm.

The next morning, she went with Pa to purchase the tickets to catch the evening train. "How about a sleeping cabin with bunk beds for the trip back, Ruth?" he asked.

"Perfect, Pa." She gave him a hug.

Her trip back to Oakland would be far different than her trip coming to Colorado. When they'd arrive back home, she and Pa would tell Mama about the day Jesse died. She would no longer be that scared and guilt-ridden girl, convinced she didn't deserve any happiness.

She had one more thing to do before they caught their train.

Visit Jesse's grave.

Ruth settled into the buggy Pa had borrowed from Cragmor and snuggled under a blanket. Fog swirled from the horse's nostrils while he trudged through the ice and snow, pulling their wagon. The mountains stood like a line of frozen sentinels on either side of Pike's Peak.

Once home, she would have so many things to tell her family—about bobbing her hair and passing herself off to be Ruffis Addison. About driving the Chevrolet and finding the stowaway Herkimer. About hopping the boxcar and about Herkimer saving her from the hobos. About hurting her ankle and about the Busy Bees taking her in. About how skilled she had gotten behind the wheel of a car. About how she wanted to become a businesswoman and run a tearoom.

She had to give Dewdad back his cap. And tell him about Herkimer. Should she protect his feelings and say she had found his rooster a good home with Mr. Hess? Or should she tell him the truth? That dilemma helped Ruth understand why Pa demanded they keep their secret. Hiding the truth *could* be a tempting option when it would bring pain.

What would she say to Clinton? She'd ask his forgiveness for that awful slap. She'd ask if she was still his girl. She sure hoped to be. She couldn't wait to wear once more the necklace he'd given her during her birthday celebration at Idora Park.

She hoped that a stack of letters from Cécile would be waiting for her. Would they be full of good or bad news about her health? For those few horrible hours until she'd found him, she believed Pa might be at death's door. He was sitting here beside her, though, strong and healthy. Please, she prayed, let that be how she'd find Cécile. Recovering. Strong. Healthy.

The horse struggled up the incline toward the markers and monuments at the top of the hill. "Let's stop here. We don't want to exhaust the horse," Pa said, pulling back on the reins.

"May I have some time alone with Jesse, Pa?" Ruth asked.

"I'll wait here for you." He jumped off the wagon and helped her down. She hugged him and climbed the hill. She paused at the entrance to the cemetery, a lone archway with thorny rose canes climbing and twisting over it.

She knew where she'd find her brother, behind the cluster of evergreen trees to the right. The paths were newly covered in hay in preparation for a graveside service. Freshly dug earth was piled in a heap in the distance. She paused to catch her breath. She shaded her eyes against the sun's rays to read the headstones.

"Glockner."

"Mathews."

"Adams."

When she reached "Calderhead," she stood at the foot of Jesse's grave. The branches of the tree they had planted for him were winter bare. His simple gray headstone read

Jesse Calderhead
Our Barefoot Boy
1903-1919.

Ruth had prepared herself for the moment, even rehearsed a prayer. Now that she was there, the prayer would not come. "I'm sorry, Jesse," she whispered. "I love you. I'll never forget you."

A warmth radiated inside her. Jesse understood.

Some movement in the woods beyond the graveyard caught her attention. A family of deer was slipping through the trees, foraging for food. They paused, sniffing the air. A young deer broke away from them, its spindly legs trudging through the high blanket of snow. It approached Ruth, eyeing the hay at her feet.

Ruth picked up a handful and took a step toward the deer, exposing the hay in her open palm. It stared at Ruth. Ice crystals stuck to its eyelashes that framed its soft brown eyes. Its body let off a slight steam of warmth against the frigid air.

Behind it, a ten-point battle-scarred buck snorted. How Jesse would have admired his antlers. The buck reared up in a bolt, warning the small deer against coming too close to a human. In a flash, all the deer except the young one scattered helter-skelter into the woods.

Determined, it inched closer and extended its long neck. It curled its tongue around the hay and ate from Ruth's hand, showing a courage that none of the others had, not even the mighty buck. The bravest one, it remained, giving itself the best chance to survive the harsh winter.

"Be strong, little one," Ruth whispered. "Be strong."

CHAPTER THIRTY-SEVEN

MAGGIE

"You were right, Grams." Maggie's tightened throat made it difficult for her to speak. "I come from a line of strong Ruths. Your mother, facing such unbearable tragedy and yet being able to forgive herself and reconcile her family. You, losing your husband, who gave his life in battle—yet you carried on, never losing your love for our country. And my mom, who somehow found a way to love my father again."

"And you? Our brave and beautiful Margaret Ruth, who is expecting my great-grandchild. Ruth's great-great-grandchild. I am sure you have the same strength to pass on to your child, my dear."

Maggie felt the color rushing into her cheeks. "I suspected you knew." Relief surged through her at being able to confide her secret. "I haven't been ready to tell anyone."

"Not even Cole?" Grams asked.

"No!" The word exploded from Maggie. "This baby will be mine to raise. He doesn't deserve this child—or me, for that matter."

"You're angry. Rightfully." Grams spoke quietly. "However, you say he is sorry for hurting you. You say he has begged you for a reconciliation. Could you consider trying again? For your child's sake? Take little steps and see where they lead."

"Let's not talk about me right now." Maggie blotted her remaining tears. "Did Ruth arrive back home to more letters from Cécile?"

Grams eyes flooded with tears. "Yes. Remember the letter Ruth left for the Busy Bees to mail for her?"

Maggie nodded.

"In it, she told Cécile about what happened to Jesse and how she was going to try to bring her family back together. Cécile's reply awaited Ruth when she returned home to Oakland. It is my favorite of all Cécile's letters."

Grams began to read.

> *Health House*
> *Bligny Fontenay*
> *France*
>
> *5 December 1919*

My dear Ruth, (or should I call you Ruffs, a "boy" adventurer, yes?)

I was very happy to receive your letter. I had a nice November. On All Saints day I sang at church a nice solo. The priest says I have an angel's voice. Do you know what is the Saint Catherine's day? It is the festival of all the girls of 25 years old who don't marry. Each girl of 25 receive a nice bonnet and they make a procession. They sing, dance and etc…it is very funny. We enjoyed ourselves with the prospect of pleasure. We danced very much and made a walk in the park, at night my white shoes were dirty and I was tired. We sang and drank Champagne. I was offered cigars, but I could not smoke it.

Now to seriousness.

You speak in your letter with love of the kind ladies and their tea room. I hope to one day visit and you will pour for me!

Mainly, petite amie, I write today about your plan for the joyous occasion of the reunion of your family. That you could tell me your truth—to tell as friends do; I love you more than ever. You are a dear dear friend. I was thinking long ago when you moved to Oakland was a surprise and I did not know how big was the problem. I am admiring your heart. I say I know your heart. It is so big I hear the sound of it in France!

You say your family planted a tree for the remembrance of Jesse at his grave. When my auntie husband die in the war, before she can move him back to Quimper she could not visit his cemetaire, and this was hard for her so she planted a tree for him. You see our hearts are the same.

I think like you that trees are like a family. Their branches are each like a member in the family. A tree needs branches, like a family needs all the people in a family. But sometimes a tree breaks a branch; a family loses someone they love. But do not to be angry; no bitter root should grow and hurt the tree. We must graft God's branch to the tree and it will grow stronger.

So, my dear, be strong as the tree is strong. God knows your heart and he forgives you. I will not speak of this to anyone as you have asked. I love you dear Ruth more than ever.

A girl new at the Health House who speaks English better than I teaches me to pronounce your name: Rootss. So my dear "branches of a tree in the ground," I shall now call you Roots, the sweet name of my best friend.

Bonne Annee with a million kisses from your sincere far friend,
Cécile

"Roots," Maggie repeated. "How perfect. We Ruths are strong, as the tree is strong."

"Yes. Cécile was wiser than her years. She advised Ruth that she should not to be angry. No bitter root should grow, Cécile wrote, for that would harm the tree. Such profound wisdom from a young lady, don't you think?" Grams held the letter to her heart.

Maggie understood. Her grandmother was advising her to listen to Cécile's wisdom. Do not let bitter root grow within her. Yet, how could she not feel bitter about her father's actions? About what her husband did? Would Cécile have felt free from bitterness had she experienced such betrayal?

Grams eyes glistened with unshed tears. "Cécile had hoped for good health in the new year. Alas, she lost her battle."

"Lost her battle? Grams! No! She loved life...she had too much remaining she wanted to do!" *That* was Cécile's betrayal. Her body had betrayed her, her illness slipping her from the bonds of earth all too soon. She must have known her fate, yet she held no bitterness.

Grams reached for Maggie's hand. "Each time I read her letters, I lose her again. Visiting her grave was something my mother always wanted to do, to say a proper goodbye. Now, we will do that for Ruth."

"Yes." Maggie squeezed Grams's hand. "We will send your mother's kisses to Cécile."

"Please place your tray tables and seats in the upright position and secure your seat belts. We will be touching down at Charles de Gaulle airport shortly."

Maggie took advantage of the announcement to try to shift the mood. "Finally, Grams! We're in Cécile's Paris. I can't wait for us to enjoy the city she loved."

The look in her eyes told Maggie that the conversation would soon find its way back to Cole and the baby. She hoped not. To fully embrace Cécile's Paris, she needed to suspend her depressing reality.

The plane's chimes alerted that they had arrived at the terminal gate. She helped Grams gather their belongings. On the way out, she stopped to give Brian a quick hug. "Thanks for a terrific flight."

"You two behave yourselves. Maybe I'll be working the return flight you are on. If not, Adieu."

Grams shook her head. "Not *Adieu,* young man. *Au revoir.*"

Maggie echoed, "Au revoir."

They mingled into the chaos of De Gaulle airport, found their way to the baggage claim area and into a taxi. Maggie announced, "Grams. I could use a nap. What about you?"

"Perhaps a tiny power nap, my dear." Grams craned her neck to view the sights from the cab window. "I've always heard that the best way to fight jet lag is to immediately adjust to the time zone you've flown into." She glanced at her watch. "We have a full day ahead of us, and I have planned exactly what I want us to do first."

Maggie laughed. "Why am I not surprised?"

Grams waved off her comment. "We will check in at the hotel and get refreshed. Then we'll be off to the Boulevard du Montparnasse and the Parisian café La Closerie des Lilas. It's where Hemingway read Fitzgerald's draft of *The Great Gatsby* and where he wrote some of *The Sun Also Rises*."

Maggie remembered the ending of *The Sun Also Rises,* how the two main characters acknowledged their love could never be. She remembered the scene well and the line that Brett delivered: "Oh Jake, we could have had such a damned good time together." *Oh Cole, we could have had such a damned good time together.*

A light poke to her ribs made her jump.

"Wake up, sleepyhead." Grams was gathering her belongings. "We're almost at the hotel."

"I'm awake, I'm awake." She shifted in her seat when they pulled up to the front of the Paris Marriott Champs Elysees Hotel. Her father had used his points to book adjoining rooms for them. "Nothing but the best for my favorite gals," he'd said.

She remembered all those years when she, her mom, and Grams weren't his favorite gals at all. Why did her mind always travel to those hurtful memories? Could she ever let all that go like her mom had done? Cécile's words encouraged her to follow that path. If only her stubborn spirit could relent.

Each *bonjour* that greeted them in the hotel helped ease some of that stubbornness. Their hotel was a beautiful choice, in the center of the Champs-Élysées area. She *should* thank her father. She'd send a text when they were settled in their rooms. Reconciliation could begin with one step at a time.

The rap on her adjoining door told her Grams truly had meant a *tiny* power nap. Maggie opened the door and used her unpacked suitcase to keep it from shutting. "Entrez, Grand-mère," she said, sweeping her hand toward her room.

With a chuckle, Grams came in. "Our rooms are identical. So nice of your father!"

"I texted him my thanks and sent a photo," Maggie hastily reported. "Little steps."

Grams gave her a thumbs up. "Are you ready to meet Hemingway?"

"If only we could. I'll settle for his Parisian spirit." Maggie stretched. "I actually could have slept the day away. Then I reminded myself, *I'm in Paris! Who needs sleep?*"

"Exactly!" Grams shrugged her shoulder bag into position and announced, "Let's begin our adventure. First, lunch and next . . . well, I'll tell you during lunch."

"How mysterious. I bet it's something to do with meeting Cécile—or her ghost."

Grams locked arms with Maggie. "How I wish we could meet her ghost. Did you bring a Ouija Board, by chance?"

"I knew I had forgotten to pack something!"

"We're off to Boulevard du Montparnasse. Remember how Cécile wrote about traveling there for work?"

"I do. She could have passed many famous Lost Generation writers and not even realized."

They headed to the lobby, and Maggie flagged a taxi. After all, Hemingway was waiting.

At the end of the ride, they found themselves at the Café Rotonde instead of La Closerie des Lilas.

"No matter what café in Montparnasse you ask a taxi driver to bring you to from the right bank of the river, they always take you to

the Rotonde," Maggie stated after they settled at their table in the Café
and ordered the baguette toasts and large Café Crèmes.

"What do you mean, they always bring you here?"

"Oh, it's a line from *The Sun Also Rises*." Maggie shrugged. "And
here we are."

Grams pulled some envelopes from her bag. Maggie knew exactly
what they were. "Grams, you were holding out on me! More letters!"

"Yes, she actually became well enough to return to Paris before her last
relapse. She became a nanny for a while." Grams handed Maggie a letter.
"Here's what she wrote a few months after she left the Health House."

18 bis Avenue de Italie
Paris 75013
France

Paris le 6 April 1920

Dear little one,

Excuse me…I am late…and I promised to write
you more often! So much happen since I come
home to Paris. Yes, it is good to be home! I work
since the 17th of March. I am a governess at Mrs. Hartman's. She
is American and her husband is a major in your army. They have
a baby boy, Dudley; he is six. I teach French to Dud, he improves
in reading, and Mrs. Hartman says I am able to teach him how to
read in English, because he doesn't know. Yesterday I went for a walk
with him and his friend Melkon. Melkon doesn't speak French and
I have to speak only English with him. That's well but the awfuller
is, that I can speak but I can't understand.

They are coming from Washington but the town where Dud
was born was Watertown. I'll probably go with them to Germany
for their vacation.

I received your letter with the pretty card for Easter. Thank you so much for it. You ask what "should I do with a million dollars?" I know, I immediately take the railway, to the steamer, and the railway to Oakland and I go to Mrs. Calderhead's and I kiss my dear unknown and well known Ruth.

When Mrs. Hartman asked me for going with them in U. S., I thought of you but as Washington is so far of Oakland I shall never see you by that manner. If I ever accept it will be to further in U.S. than Washington, to approach of you.

I spoke with a French governess who would like to go in U.S, and she gave me the address of a certain club: the American Women's Club. I went there and asked for a governess situation with American people which live in San Francisco they say they do and gave me an address, if I wish to write to the family and learn more. So I write a letter and am waiting news from the family. So, perhaps you'll have the surprise to learn I go in your country. How far is San Francisco to Oakland?

Yesterday night I sang Breton songs at a club of countrymen. Charlie Chaplin is visiting Europe. I enclose a photo of me dressed up like him for a fun costume party. I should like to run into him. That would be jolly good! Since I am in Paris I walk all day so I am tired. I bought two pairs of shoes with high heels so every time I wear them I get a pain in my feet. Ooh! la la, my dear, it hurts!

I dance last Sunday and I taught Lulu. He knows the one step and the Scottish and on Saturday I think he will be able to dance with my friends. Soon we'll have a ball and I'll go.

I am sorry, for myself, to be so lazy to write my dear Ruth. By waiting, my dear, I send you many kisses. I don't promise to write you as soon as possible, because when I do not, I am a liar. So I think I keep it and just say…

With kisses from your loving little friend, Cécile

"Oh, Grams. Cécile had such plans." Maggie glanced back at the end of the letter. "How excited your mom must have been about Cécile possibly moving to San Francisco."

"Yes, if only the two could have met. Cécile's was a life cut too short," Grams whispered. She took a deep breath. "Now, to our itinerary. On our way back to our hotel, I would like for us to go by Cécile's home address."

"Oh, yes, Grams. A perfect start," Maggie commented.

"We'll let Cécile determine our other must-visit places in Paris." She reached in her bag and retrieved another letter. "I'll read again what she wrote to my mother, describing plans for what they would do if Ruth visited."

Last night I dreamed you came to Paris and I was so happy! After dinner we sat on terrace of Musee de l'Orangerie. The terrace is near the Seine, in the garden called the "Tuileries." From that terrace I show you the Museum "Le Louvre", "The Concord Place", the two arcs of triumph, "The great, and the arc of Carousel" built by Napoleon to celebrate military victories. I show you the parliament "Chambre des Deputes", the Eiffel Tower, the "Great Wheel", and "The Invalides." It is a nice view and you liked it very much. We go to top of Eiffel Tower and ride the Great Wheel and you love it!

"We will love it all," Grams added upon completion of reading. "I have asked the concierge to arrange a VIP tour guide of these places starting tomorrow, including the Louvre and Eiffel Tower. That way, we'll bypass the tourist lines and see what Cécile had planned to show Ruth. Or at least see the sites that still exist for us to see, one hundred years later."

"Brilliant, Grams!" Maggie sighed. "The Great Wheel is no more. What a fabulous sight that must have been!"

"If only we could go back in time." Grams winked. "Oh, I also had the concierge book us a Seine dinner cruise one night."

How Maggie had dreamed of doing that cruise with Cole. Her hand rested instinctively on her stomach. A twinge of conscience over her anger she nursed against Cole panged her. Being in the City of Love must be wearing down her grudge against her soon-to-be ex. That and Grams's gentle prodding to consider reconciliation, as well as Cécile's wise words.

Communicating in a friendly manner with Frank was enough reconciliation for the moment. Perhaps she would be ready to fully forgive him one day.

Anger flamed in her again when she considered that Cole had done to her the same thing her dad had done to her mom. Why did anger feel more comfortable than forgiveness?

She determinedly redirected herself to their plans at hand. "Let's get started, Grams. On to 18 bis Avenue de Italie." Soon, Maggie stood next to Grams in front of the address from which Cécile had written many letters to Ruth. "It's surreal, Grams."

Grams agreed. "It's a dream come true, my dear. For me, and for my mother's memory."

A black cat stretched before them on the sidewalk, sunning himself. Maggie nudged Grams. "Could that be a descendent of dear, sweet Bidart?"

"Perhaps." Grams laughed. "We must take photos and after that, I confess I'm ready to get a good night's rest. Tomorrow begins our sightseeing in earnest."

The next morning, bright and early, Maggie met Grams at the concierge desk.

"Our tour guide awaits!" Grams announced.

After brief introductions, the guide ushered them out to a waiting car, and the sightseeing began. Maggie checked their schedule. "First stop, the Louvre and meeting that woman with the mysterious smile, Mona Lisa. Tomorrow, the top of the Eiffel Tower. The day after that, we'll visit the Ménagerie du Jardin des Plantes and Montmartre, ending with the Seine Dinner Cruise."

The mention of Montmartre reminded Maggie of how Cécile had fallen ill in the cold night air when visiting Sacre Coeur there. Had she lived, she could have become a famous artist or author. She could have married and had her own children. Again, Maggie's hand found her stomach, and this time joy filled her. She was going to be a mother.

Maggie let herself be caught up in the whirlwind of sightseeing. Touristy and clichéd as the choice might have been, the dinner cruise on the Seine was enjoyable. They took in the quays and the many famous bridges while they drank and ate. Maggie tried to ignore the couples at the other tables holding hands, obviously in love. They reminded her of what she had imagined for her and Cole.

"Franc for your thoughts, my dear." Grams held up her glass of wine.

Maggie reluctantly clinked her water glass against it. "Oh, Grams." She glanced around at the other couples and looked back at Grams. "I'm trying to let go of my romantic dreams."

Grams took a sip of wine, set her glass down, and leveled her gaze at Maggie, who braced for another reconciliation lecture. She wasn't disappointed.

"Remember, Cécile didn't get a chance at love or marriage or carrying her husband's child."

Maggie winced.

Grams reached out and patted Maggie's hand. "Count your blessings, Maggie. Not Cole's sins. Let this City of love and lights open you up. You'll be surprised at what will happen."

The Eiffel Tower, awash in lights, came into view. The couples rushed up the stairs to the ship's upper deck for a better look. For the first time, Maggie wished she were leaning into Cole's arms with his hands resting on her bump. Her throat tightened. To her surprise, her heart did not. Instead, it opened up to a new rhythm.

One of forgiveness?

Midweek, they had their tour guide drive them to the Bligny Fontenay Health House, where Cécile had sought treatment, now a modern public hospital. Grams beckoned Maggie to join her on a bench in the hospital's front yard, where they sat in silence for a few minutes.

"Cécile described this place being located in the country. That's hardly true now." Maggie looked around. "I'd love to identify the exact places on these grounds where she posed for the pictures she sent to Ruth. If only we could step back in time during Cécile's stay."

Grams nodded absentmindedly. After a moment, she reached into her bag to retrieve another of Cécile's letters. "Cécile did have a spell of remission, and her letters were full of happiness and joy during that time when she nannied. After the American family, she worked for another family, the Paillys, and she spent quite a bit of time with them at Longueville."

"That's where we're traveling next. I assumed our visit to the Normandy area was because of what occurred there during World War Two. I didn't realize the connection to Cécile."

"Yes." Grams handed the letter to Maggie. "Think of how another world war would soon bring violence, destruction, and great loss of life. The Dieppe Casino that Cécile writes about visiting was destroyed in the D-Day invasion. We will see this historical setting through her viewpoint, before the destruction World War Two would bring."

As Maggie began reading the letter, her pulse raced.

Chateau de Bois Robert
Longueville, France

7 June 1920

My dear chum,

I now am caring for Guy, the Paillys' son. I have been enjoying Bois Robert with them. We are going on Saturday to Osmond Castle for a fortnight or a month. We shall go in the morning and we'll reach Osmond in the afternoon. I hope the weather will be nice because the car is a sport motor car and we have not a roof.

I went dancing last week to Dieppe's casino. It closed last Sunday because of the high sea and yesterday I did not see anybody at the beach. I bought naughty books, very shocking but I did not know when I bought them. One is nearly all right but the others ... Ooh la la !!!

We had a lovely trip to Chateau d' Osmond in the car. Osmond Castle is a big place. My room is charming. I have got a lot of animals all over the walls in paintings. The furniture is old and nice. Behind the castle is the wood; in front are the lawns with pretty flowers, a small river and the hills. This house is a new one but in another part of the park is the old original castle. We went there today. Guy and I looking for a croquet game in the empty rooms. Near the garden is the pond but it is absolutely dry now and the island looks very funny in the center.

I went to the beach all by myself yesterday. I sat there. I love being alone some times. I could then think of life. I am happy here and each day is a good day especially those days when a letter arrives from my dear Ruffis.

We are just coming back home. We started this morning at nine, had lunch in Rouen. I saw a statue of Joan of Arc. Don't you know she was burnt in Rouen?

It is late, I am sleepy. My best kisses to you, dear old Ruffis, R-oo-th my sweetheart. I am your own, Say good night to all. Give my love to your Mother, Flora, Mable, Opal and for you sweetheart a huge kiss from your old chum,

Cécile

"She writes, 'Each day is a good day.' Their letters to each other were precious gifts they exchanged." Maggie returned the letter to Grams.

"Cécile loved life! She definitely shared her true confessions with Ruth—dancing at casinos, drinking champagne, flirting. Ooh la la." With a laugh, she added, "I bet we'd find the naughty book *Fifty Shades of Grey* on her Kindle."

"Maggie, really!" Grams's eyes widened. "Oh my. Imagine her in modern times. Ooh la la, indeed."

Maggie's mood turned serious. "Visiting Normandy will mean much more to me after seeing the area through Cécile's point of view. She sat alone on the beach where too many soldiers not much older than she gave the ultimate sacrifice."

Maggie remembered the map Cécile had drawn to show where the bombs had dropped around her home and the fortifications that circled Paris. If only Maggie had realized the bomb aimed for her, in the person of Hayley Huntington. She had been so full of resistance to starting a family that she hadn't thought about building fortifications against another woman's attack. She had been too targeted on Cole's mistakes to clearly examine her own. Had she pushed him into another's arms?

Her anger began to drain. Her heart beat with that new rhythm it had found a few days ago when she had daydreamed of Cole during the dinner cruise.

Maggie had accompanied Grams to Paris in order for her grandmother to grow closer to Cécile and Ruth. Maggie had never dreamed that it could be Cécile and Ruth who would help her grow closer to Cole. Could she chance another reconciliation?

She walked hand in hand with Grams to their waiting car, leaving Cécile's sanatorium memories—and maybe her own bitter ones—behind.

∞‑∞

The Normandy visit left Maggie emotionally spent. She'd cried many tears over both the past and present. Now, her emotions needed to heal during the journey to Quimper and Penmarch. The trip there from

Longueville took about a day, traveling through beautiful French countryside with a private driver.

They checked into their quaint bed and breakfast in time for a quick dinner before bedtime. Dreams of seeing Cole again when she returned home filled Maggie's sleep. When she awoke, her heart did not weigh heavily in her chest, for the first time since discovering Cole's infidelity. Where her new-found optimism would lead her, she couldn't predict for sure. She wouldn't rush into any plan of action.

The next day, they enjoyed the Cornwall Festival, held each July in Quimper. They'd specifically timed their visit to attend. The Great Sunday Parade showed off the traditional costumes.

"This is what Ruth must have looked like for Halloween!" Maggie commented to Grams while they enjoyed the parade of the girls in their Breton costumes.

On the last day of their stay in Quimper, they had the driver take them to Penmarch. They stood where Cécile had on that day long ago, watching the sea. Maggie reread Cécile's description of the place: *The sea is quite dangerous at Penmarch where I have been. There is a large stone where five persons have been taken by one of that dangerous waves.*

Maggie said a prayer for those Cécile described who lost their lives there a hundred years ago. Her bitterness and unhappiness washed away with the tide, leaving her cleansed with optimism.

∽⊙∾

To Maggie's dismay, the incredible trip had reached its end. Yet, her pulse did skip with anticipation at what returning home might bring.

"One last stop," Grams said during breakfast at Café de Flore.

Maggie recognized the irony of eating at another café where the Lost Generation had gathered when she finally had begun to feel "found" again.

She had crafted multiple texts to send to Cole to ask for a meeting when she returned, only to delete them all and deciding to wait until returning home to reach out. She would ask him to meet for a coffee. They would start off slowly. Test the waters. Determine if she could sustain this feeling of forgiveness.

She hadn't told Grams of her plan. She sensed her grandmother somehow knew—even without a Ouija Board between them.

"I have a few last letters to share, my dear." Grams reached into her bag.

"Oh, how I love these letters, Grams. I will always treasure them," Maggie said. "Reading what will be the last ones from her will be too devastating."

"Yes," Grams agreed. "Although poor, sweet Cécile knew that her health had started to fail again, she wanted to keep up her correspondence with my mother. Here's the last letter Ruth received from her friend."

Maggie took the letter, her spirit sinking. Cécile used her remaining precious strength to write it.

18, bis Avenue d' Italie
Paris 75013
France

29 September 1920

My darling Ruth,

I am at home since a few weeks not well at all. Now I am feeling a little bit better and I think I shall write you a long letter very soon.
I had some letters from you and I wanted to answer them but… that awful fever did not allow me to do as I wanted for some time now. Write me always nice letters as you do, they make me feel so glad when I read them.

Love and Kisses,

"Oh, Grams, this shatters me. Cécile had the rest of her life ahead of her." Maggie paused, thinking of what lay ahead for her and

Cole, parenting their child. "She had a lifetime of more love to give and receive."

Grams's eyes clouded with sadness. "Her brother, Lulu, kept my mother informed about Cécile's health." She held out another letter. Maggie recognized Lulu's handwriting. "I think he was trying to prepare her for the eventuality of Cécile's death. In writing Ruth, I suppose he also was preparing himself."

Maggie exchanged Cécile's final letter for that of Lulu's. With a heavy sigh, she opened it and read it.

> *18, bis Avenue d' Italie*
> *Paris 75013*
> *France*
> *Paris le 2 December 1920*
>
> *My dear dear Ruth,*
>
> *Please forgive me my long delay, you have so good a heart. The principal reason is, Cécile is so much ill, she is very ill and we despair to save her; she is abed since the first days of September and is very very thin and skinny and nothing interests her but your letters.*
>
> *In your next letters don't say you know Cécile is so ill. Cécile is in her bed…25 feet from me but she is so feeble she never does hear me. So good bye and I kiss you for Cécile, for my parents… and for me.*
>
> *Lulu*

Through her tears, Maggie reread the letter, this time more slowly, picturing Cécile in repose, craving with determined spirit more news from her dear pen pal while the illness ravaged her body. "This news must have broken Great-grams's heart," she said. "It's breaking mine for sure."

"Oh, yes, this letter from dear, sweet Lulu truly did." Grams placed another letter on the table, and Maggie let it remain there untouched.

After a long moment, she whispered, "I don't want to read it. I want to picture Cécile full of joyous life. Dancing. Masquerading as Charlie Chaplin or a Spanish girl. Holding her sweet Bidart in her lap. Walking barefoot by the sea."

"We will always have that Cécile, Maggie, like my mother always did." With trembling hands, Maggie opened Lulu's letter.

18, bis Avenue d' Italie

Paris 75013

France

January 20, 1921

Dear small friend,

I think you have received Cécile's death notice. She died during the night of January 3rd and was buried January 5th. I would have liked you to have been able to see her procession (funeral). There were a lot of people and a lot of flowers. At the church there was a very pretty service with organs and singers.

Our dear Cécile is buried at the Gentilly cemetery in the out-skirts of Paris, which is one mile from our house (11 minutes from home). For several days we kept thinking that Cécile was lost, but we weren't thinking that it would happen so fast. We thought she would last till springtime.

Up until the last days, she always had hope of recovering, but the last four or five days she understood that she was going to die. On the eve of her death she said, "adieu" (final goodbye) and was very courageous. She died without realizing it was happening; without stirring—like a lamp that extinguishes when it runs out of oil.

She had always been happy to receive your letters, and in these last days if she didn't write to you, you will understand that it is because she was too sick.

Please pray with us for Cécile and that her soul may rest in peace. The priest who helped her in her last moments said she is in paradise. This is of great comfort to us. Cécile asked me to tell her dear Ruth this, "A branch has been broken so you may be closer to God." This she said...I am not sure you understand her meaning but I promised her to tell you those words.

I loved my dear sister and will miss her forever,

Lulu

"We miss her too," Maggie whispered.

Grams reached into her purse and pulled out the necklace Clinton had given Ruth. "I think my mother would have wanted you to have this, Maggie. The letters also. It's your turn to keep the legacy of Cécile and Ruth alive, my dear."

Maggie's hands shook while she fastened the precious keepsake around her neck. The chain extended long enough to rest the antique medallion against her heart. "She will never be forgotten, Grams. Never."

Maggie had placed a special order with a Parisian florist for their visit to Cécile's grave, requesting that a blossom of edelweiss be included in the arrangement. They picked it up on the way to the cemetery. She feared finding Cécile's resting place at the Gentilly Cemetery could prove difficult, but Lulu's map guided them without error.

Grams lay the bouquet on Cécile's grave. With head bowed, she whispered, "I bring you kisses from Roots. Your life will not be forgotten, dear, sweet Cécile."

Goosebumps chased over Maggie. Standing next to Cécile's final resting place evoked more emotion than Maggie had expected. She had grown incredibly close to this young woman who had died a hundred years ago. Her story had been such a part of her great-grandmother's life, and would always be part of hers.

A sense of calmness overtook Maggie. She rested in it, embraced it. She would allow no bitter root to grow within her. She would only allow love to grow, and with it, forgiveness. Of others. Of herself.

"Maggie?"

Her hand flew instinctively to her belly, and her heart beat wildly, as fast as Clinton's homing pigeons' winging home.

"Grams." Maggie's words came out breathlessly. "Did you tell Cole to meet us here?"

"I'm a romantic, my dear." Her grandmother hugged her close. "Recall how Cécile wrote that Ruth's heart 'was so big' that she could hear it in Paris? Well, yours is that big too, dear. Cole heard it from America. Go. Forgive. Love."

Maggie turned and faced the man who had called her name.

The man she had always loved yet thought she could never love again.

The man who would take her home.

AUTHOR NOTES

Creative liberties were taken with Cécile's letters to Ruth in order to maintain thematic unity and to intertwine in a cohesive way the stories of Maggie, Cécile, and Ruth. Dates have been changed and the contents of some letters merged. The correspondence between Ruth and Cécile extended from 1919 to Cécile's death on January 3, 1923. The story has been highly fictionalized, including the details of Jesse's tragic death and Ruth's trek dressed as Jesse to Colorado to convince her pa to tell the truth about the day Jesse died.

If you are interested in reading more of Cécile's letters, enjoying her artwork, and seeing more photographs of her, visit the Storyology Design and Publication blog, linked to from the website storyologydesign.com. Some pictures are included in this book of Cécile, Ruth, Lulu, Cécile's cat Bidart, and some of Cécile's sketches.

In addition to letters from Cécile, Ruth received letters from Cécile's brother Lulu and Cécile's cousin Francis. Francis's tragic death while serving in the military was a significant loss for Cécile and foreshadows her own death at an equally young age. Cécile's mother comforts her and provides her with insights to help her in her grief, which Cécile in turn passes on to Ruth. You can read Lulu's and Francis's letters and view their pictures on the Storyology website.

One of Cécile's letters was quite delayed in its arrival to Ruth. Background research revealed that a plane carrying the airmail from France crashed. Yet the letter was recovered and eventually delivered to Ruth. You can read archived newspaper coverage about the crash on the Storyology website.

SIGNIFICANT HISTORICAL DATES

June 28, 1919: Official end of World War I with the signing of the Treaty of Versailles.

In her first letter to Ruth, Cécile adds a note that she is posting the letter on the day of peace. She writes, *I put my letter in the letterbox the day of the peace.*" She talks about seeing American soldiers and war leaders, *"There are many American soldiers in Paris. Near my house bombs are dropped in a house which have been demolished, many persons have been killed . . . Have you seen the President Wilson? I have seen him, with his wife, his daughter, and the General Pershing.* In a subsequent letter, she describes how the Louvre was lit up on the day of peace and sends Ruth a postcard of the event: *I send you a view of a great shop of Paris, the "Louvre" lighted up for the day of peace, no, the night of peace. Do you see the entrance of the Metro, that is an underground railway, the tube of London, and the metro and Nord-sud of Paris that is what I will use when I begin work.*

July 14, 1919: Bastille Day.

Cécile writes about the first celebration of Bastille Day after the Treaty of Versailles ended World War I. She writes, *Monday was a fine day, the 14 July. First, Joffre and Foch have passed under the arc de triomphe, then the American troops with their flags, the sailors and Pershing; English soldiers, Belgians, Italians, etc. . . . and last French troops composed by several men of each regiment. Four millions of persons have seen the soldiers pass. We call this day Bastille Day and it was the first since the end of the war.*

PEOPLE AND TERMS ASSOCIATED WITH WORLD WAR I

Ferdinand Foch: Commander of Allied Forces at the end of World War I.

Joseph Joffre: Commander in chief of French armies on the western front.

John J. Pershing: Commanded the American Expeditionary Force in Europe during World War I.

Woodrow Wilson: President of the United States, led America through World War I, helped negotiate the Treaty of Versailles.

Boches: Pejorative term used by the French for German soldiers.

Sammies: Nickname for American soldiers in World War I, presumably referring to "Uncle Sam."

Berthas: Heavy German artillery. The nickname "Big Bertha" was often used.

Gothas: Heavy German strategic bombers.
Cécile describes living through the bombings of Paris and draws Ruth a map showing where bombs fell near her home:

> *During the war many bombs drop from the sky. The little marks are bombs of Gothas and cannons Berthas. The nearest bomb dropped from our home is on the Italy place.*
>
> *Sometime, during war, I would look to the sky and instead of cloud I would see zeppelins dropping bombs on Paris. Zeppelins look like a cloud that makes a great shadow.*
>
> *Nighttime was afraid, too, at 2 am all the siren in the city sounded and we go to the cellar, as was an air-raid of the Boches.*

For the first time I hear exploding shells and barrage fire. So loud!
The next day Big Bertha fired shells, "blockbusters" from the forest
outside Paris, eighty miles away! Everyone looked up in the clouds
for the Gotha.

Soon we could know the schedule of Bertha. Every fifteen min-
utes for many days. So Maman and Lulu could leave home to get
our food. They would wait for the sound of the big gun and would
hurry home ahead of Bertha.

The most bad day was day our neighbors home was demolished,
I mark it on map closest to Italie place. They all die. We were glad
to be not harmed and our home not bombed.

The Boches drop many bombs near the rail to try to take it out.
You can also see I draw the fortifications that circle the city of Paris.
Sometime we go to school but our numbers were not great.

PLACES OF INTEREST IN THE STORY

arrondissement: Paris is divided into twenty districts known as arrondissements. Cécile's address of 18, bis Avenue d 'Italie is located in the 13th arrondissement of Paris.

Bligny Health House: Opened in October 1903 as a tuberculosis sanatorium, located twenty-two miles southwest of Paris. The American Red Cross completed building it at the invitation of the Sanitary Service of the French Army. It has been transformed into a modern private hospital. Cécile stayed as a patient here.

Cragmor Sanatorium: Opened on June 20, 1905, as a tuberculosis sanatorium in Colorado Springs, Colorado, catering to wealthy patients. It is now part of the University of Colorado at Colorado Springs. Before moving to Oakland, California, Ruth lived in Colorado Springs near this sanatorium. You can learn more about this sanatorium in the book *Asylum of the Gilded Pill: The Story of Cragmor Sanatorium* by Douglas R. McKay.

De Bois Robert: Small village located in the Normandy region of France. Cécile vacationed here with a family for whom she served as a nanny.

Dieppe Casino: A casino located on the beach in Dieppe, France, where the Dieppe Raid of August 19, 1942, known as Operation Jubilee, occurred. This is considered one of the worst single disasters to befall the Allied armies during the Second World War. Cécile enjoyed dancing at the casino and going to the beach here, never knowing that the casino would be destroyed during a future war, which would leave dead soldiers strewn across the beach she once enjoyed.

Gentilly Cemetery: Located in a largely residential section of the thirteenth arrondissement at the southern edge of historic Paris at 5 Rue Sainte-Hélène. This is where Cécile is buried.

Longueville: Located in the Île-de-France region in north central France. Cécile stayed there with a family for whom she served as a nanny.

Penmarch: Situated in the Brittany region in northwestern France, twenty-seven kilometers from Quimper. Cécile's family is from Quimper, and they visited Penmarch. She writes of its dangerous waves.

Quimper: Cécile's birthplace. Located in the cultural heart of Brittany and known for its cathedral and its annual festival celebrating Breton culture.

Tea Rooms: Beginning in 1910 and flourishing throughout the 1920s, independent tea rooms were opened in the United States in response to the proliferation of cars and the roadway system. While hotel and department store tea rooms were managed by men, the independent tea rooms were owned and managed by women, often opened as an extension of their homes. These tea rooms provided motorists with places to enjoy refreshments as they drove between cities. They provided women with the opportunity to be business owners in the restaurant industry. To learn more about the fascinating history of tea rooms, read Jan Whitaker's *Tea at the Blue Lantern Inn, A Social History of the Tea Room Craze in America.*

BOOK CLUB DISCUSSION

1. The book opens with Maggie's emotional trauma over the failed reconciliation with her husband, who has been unfaithful to her, and over her pregnancy resulting from that attempted reconciliation. What advice would you put into a letter to her to help her deal with her anger, hurt, and fear?

2. Grams seems to have a "sixth sense" when it comes to her granddaughter Maggie. Do you have that kind of intuition about another person, or does someone have that kind of intuition about you?

3. Grams treats the one-hundred-year-old letters from Cécile as priceless treasures. Do you have any possessions in your family whose histories have inspired strong emotional connections? Who is the keeper of your family's legacy? Do you save special mementoes with the thought that they will be handed down to future generations? Why or why not? Did this story inspire you to do so if you have not?

4. Cécile, Ruth, and Maggie all experience loss in their lives. Cécile experiences loss through war, Ruth experiences the loss of her brother, and Maggie experiences the loss of trust in her husband. How does

loss affect each one in regard to the way she continues to live her life? What, if any, personality strengths and weaknesses do the three share?

5. In the early 1900s, tuberculosis, also called consumption or the white plague, remained a leading cause of death in the United States and many European countries, including France. Those suffering from the disease went to sanatoriums, where they would seek a cure through prescribed regimens of sunlight and fresh air. In Colorado Springs, which is one of the settings in the novel, Cragmor served from 1905 to the Depression as a sanatorium for tuberculosis patients. Cécile describes her stay at the Bligny Fontenay Health House, where she underwent treatment for consumption. How do you think Ruth's familiarity with Cragmor, located near her family's farm, gives her insight into the seriousness of Cécile's illness? Did you expect Cécile to succumb to her illness? How did the death of such a vivacious young woman affect you?

6. Herkimer plays an important role in Ruth's life. His name calls to mind the Herkimer Diamonds mined in Herkimer County, New York. They are the most powerful of all quartz crystals. Some believe that Herkimer Diamonds have healing qualities. The belief is that holding them can help to alleviate physical and spiritual pain. How does Herkimer serve this purpose for Ruth? How does his death help her come to grips with her brother's death?

7. Cécile and her family are close. Her brother Lulu writes to Ruth with a message from Cécile: *"A branch has been broken so you may be closer to God." This she said...I am not sure you understand her meaning but I promised her to tell you those words.* Why does Ruth understand the meaning of the message? What does Maggie learn from Ruth and Cécile about being as strong as a tree?

8. Maggie allows herself to forgive those who have hurt her. What has learning about Ruth's and Cécile's lives and experiences taught her about forgiveness?

9. Grams wanted to visit Cécile's Paris and retrace her steps to pay homage to her for her mother as well as for herself. Have you ever taken a similar trip for someone dear to you? If not, does this novel inspire you to plan such a trip?

10. The world has changed so much since the time of Ruth and Cécile's story, yet in many ways it remains the same. Do you agree or disagree?

RUTH

CÉCILE

CÉCILE, BLIGNY HEALTH HOUSE
IN BACKGROUND

CÉCILE'S BELOVED CAT BIDART

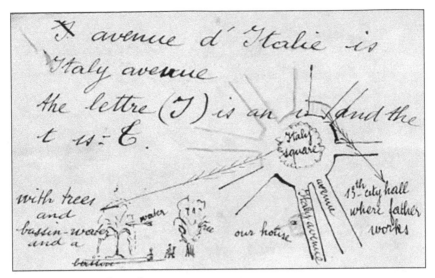

CÉCILE'S MAP OF HER ARRONDISSEMENT

CÉCILE'S MAP OF WHERE

BOMBS FELL

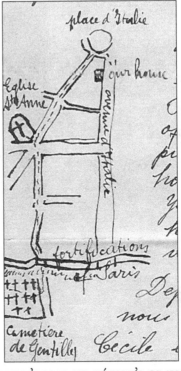

LULU'S MAP TO CÉCILE'S GRAVE

CÉCILE

CÉCILE DRESSED AS
CHARLIE CHAPLIN

LULU

CÉCILE WITH HER BROTHER LULU

COSTUMES WORN BY CÉCILE AND HER FRIENDS ON
ST. CATHERINE'S DAY AT BLIGNY HEALTH HOUSE

CÉCILE'S SKETCH OF
QUIMPER GIRL

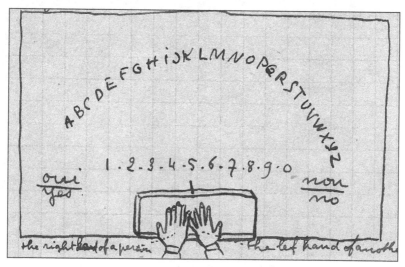

CÉCILE'S SKETCH OF A "WEEJEE" BOARD

ABOUT THE AUTHORS

JAN AGNELLO comes from several generations of hobbiest antiquers. Her love of stories behind the antiques inspired her in 2013 to form Storyology Design, now Storyology Design and Publication. The necklaces Jan crafts from antique coin purses have generated a loyal customer following and garnered attention from the Atlanta Journal Constitution, jewelry network executives, and TV and film costume designers. Her love of books, romance, history, and unique jewelry design led her to collaborate with author Anne Armistead to offer a series of historical novels, each paired with heirloom quality jewelry named for the female protagonist. The first in the series, **WITH KISSES FROM CÉCILE,** is a story of love and redemption drawn from Jan's family history. It is paired with **THE CÉCILE JEWELRY COLLECTION.** Visit storyologydesign.com to learn more about Jan and Storyology.

ANNE ARMISTEAD is a writer of historical romance. She earned her English literature degree from the University of Georgia and her MFA in creative writing from Spalding University. Her background includes project management with AT&T and teaching English at the middle, high, and college levels. She is a member of the Romance Writers of America and the Georgia Writers of Romance. **WITH KISSES FROM CÉCILE** is her second romance, following the publication of **DANGEROUS CONJURINGS** (Soul Mate Publishing, April 2018). Anne writes for and serves as an editor for Storyology Design and Publication. Visit annearmisteadauthor.com to learn more about Anne and her novels.

CPSIA information can be obtained
at www.ICGtesting.com
Printed in the USA
FSHW010852131020
74673FS